You Are the Love of My Life

Center Point
Large Print

**This Large Print Book carries the
Seal of Approval of N.A.V.H.**

You Are the
Love of My Life

Susan Richards Shreve

CENTER POINT LARGE PRINT
THORNDIKE, MAINE

This Center Point Large Print edition
is published in the year 2012 by arrangement with
W. W. Norton & Co., Inc.

The text of this Large Print edition is unabridged.
In other aspects, this book may vary
from the original edition.
Printed in the United States of America
on permanent paper.
Set in 16-point Times New Roman type.

ISBN: 978-1-61173-589-5

Library of Congress Cataloging-in-Publication Data

Shreve, Susan Richards.
  You are the love of my life / Susan Richards Shreve.
  pages ; cm.
  ISBN 978-1-61173-589-5 (library binding : alk. paper)
  1. Family secrets—Fiction. 2. Domestic fiction. 3. Large type books.
    I. Title.
PS3569.H74Y57 2012b
813′.54—dc23
                                                            2012027946

for
Elodie   Julian   Eliza   Padget   Aden
Henry   Isaak   Noah   Theo

You Are the Love of My Life

June 11, 1951:
Washington, D.C.

A Sunday, just after noon, cool, drizzly, the smell of cut grass sweetening the air. Lucy Baldwin's mother turned left onto Witchita Avenue, driving too fast, her tires screeching around a curve. She pulled to a quick stop behind her husband's old blue Chevrolet which was parked in front of the house the Baldwins had purchased as an investment property leasing mainly to groups—graduate students, young unmarried men, junior government employees.

Her father had left their house on Capitol Hill early that morning in his work boots to fix up the house—painting, planting annuals, mowing the lawn, trimming the bushes, the odds and ends that needed doing for new tenants who would be arriving the following day.

"I'll be home by six for dinner with the Sargents," was the last thing he'd said before he left.

Her parents had been fighting for weeks.

"Will you remind your father that we have dinner with the Sargents tonight?" her mother asked, leaving the car's engine running.

"He knows," Lucy said.

"He forgets."

Lucy got out the passenger door, walking in front of the car, across the grass, and up the many steps to the porch. The front door was unlocked and she went into the hall, which was small, the walls freshly painted lime green, pale lime mixed with white. She knew colors and could spend hours before she went to sleep at night examining the subtle changes in the palettes her father had picked up at the paint store.

"Daddy?" she called, wandering through the dining room, into the kitchen smelling of pine and Lysol, all the windows open. She went out to the back porch and down the steps to the garden. No one there but the grass had been cut, the lawn mower resting against a dying elm tree at the far end of the lawn, and annuals, mostly white impatiens, were lined up in flats on the back porch ready to plant.

Upstairs the three small bedrooms were flooded with light, a ladder in the middle of the largest one with a gallon of yellow paint marked SUNSHINE YELLOW, a brush lying on top of the open can so her father must have been in the process of painting, although the walls were still white and smudged with handprints.

"Are you here?" she called again, stopping at the top of the stairs to listen, but there was no answer.

And Lucy might have left then, hurried down

the steps and out the front door, telling her mother that it was evident her father had been there but he wasn't at the house any longer although he might return because the annuals had not been planted and a paint can was open on the ladder in one of the bedrooms.

But when she reached the hall, she noticed for the first time that her father's work boots, the white socks sticking out the top, were side by side in front of a door slightly ajar as if to stop passage into what Lucy thought at first must be a bathroom going off the hall, but checking, she discovered it was the door to the basement, unlit and smelling of dank.

She moved the boots and opened the door wide so there was light enough to locate the switch at the top of the stairs.

When Lucy was young, she used to traipse very slowly around the house holding her father's hand and wearing one work boot which smelled vaguely of sweat and fertilizer while he wore the other, and his boot on her small foot was so heavy she could barely lift it off the floor.

The basement stairs were wood, half painted gray, the paint still wet, a paint can opened at the bottom as if he were planning to wait for one side to dry before he painted the other. She walked carefully down the narrow unpainted half of each step to the bottom.

Slowly her eyes adjusted and traveled to the far

11

corner of the cinder block room, the light spreading from a small window illuminated the wall between an old oil furnace and the hot water heater, and she could see the swinging shadow of her father's long, slender bare feet.

Winter 1973

One

THE AFTERNOON IN February when Lucy Painter was moving from New York City to the house in Washington where her father had died threatened violent storms.

Lucy stood on the sidewalk outside the apartment on Sullivan Street looking between the buildings at a slate gray, agitated sky, a raw damp to the air.

"Snow," she said to no one in particular.

"Snowman!" Felix said.

He was standing on the sidewalk next to his mother holding the large yellow chicken Reuben had given him as a going-away present.

"If it's snowing in Washington, we'll make a snowman when we get there," Lucy said, lifting him into the truck she had leased for the journey.

Reuben was sitting on the back of the U-Haul eating a turkey sandwich while Mickey, the boy he had hired to help with the move, carried the small items down the steps of the four-story walk-up.

"Bite?" Reuben asked, patting a seat beside him on the back of the truck.

Lucy pulled the orange wool cap he had given her for Christmas low on her brow.

"I'm not hungry," she said.

15

But he pinched off an edge of the sandwich anyway, careful to get plenty of turkey in the bite, and popped it in her mouth.

"I'll call as soon as I get to the office in the morning," he said. "And every night before I leave from work."

Not Reuben's first promise nor the only mention of his plan for keeping in touch after thirteen years of living within blocks of each other, together several times a week whenever he could make it work.

"And that's that?" Lucy asked.

"Of course that's not that, Lucy," he said. "We have a permanent arrangement."

She climbed up on the back of the truck beside him.

"Somehow the *permanent* part always slips my mind."

He dropped his hand on top of hers, pressing his body closer, and she knew that what he wanted from her now was silence and her company sitting next to him, the heat of their breaths warming the winter air.

"Can we talk before I leave?" she asked.

"We always talk, Lucy," he said, his eyes half closed. "We've said everything we have to say to each other."

What Lucy wanted was an argument, a chance to fling collected grievances at one another, to set them at serious odds—whatever conflagration that might erupt to alter the sensible path she had chosen, which was to leave New York.

But Reuben Frank wasn't going to budge. He would be even-tempered and sweet, quietly determined to avoid a scene until the moment she hopped in the driver's seat and with the children headed south towards Washington, D.C.

"Your choice to move, remember?" Reuben said.

"It wasn't exactly a choice," she said.

She watched as the boy, Mickey, brought the work table she'd had since college down the steps, concentrating on the details of what she needed to do in the hours ahead—the boxes and suitcases and odds and ends she was tossing in the trash, toys for Felix in the car, books for Maggie—her list of *things to do* so she wouldn't be moved to weep every time she caught a glimpse of Reuben's shock of red hair falling across his forehead.

"Here comes Maggie," Reuben was saying as Maggie rounded the corner, her arm around Rebecca Malone—a tendency he had under pressure to register the obvious.

"Rebecca wants to know why we have to move to Washington," Maggie said, coming up to the truck.

"Because of money," Lucy said as she had said to Maggie many times. "In Washington I own the house and it's less expensive to live there than in New York."

She reached over, brushing her mittened hands across the girls' cheeks, easy with children, half a child herself as Reuben would say.

"That's not exactly true about why you're moving," Reuben said, the words falling into his scarf so the girls wouldn't hear him.

"What would you have me say?" Lucy asked. "The truth?"

"I'm just a little surprised that you're so . . ."

"Upset?"

"Angry."

Maggie was leaning over the large bin of refuse in front of the apartment.

"I suppose you threw out my whole childhood."

She pulled a Raggedy Ann from the trash, shook her, picked dust motes out of the red yarn hair.

"You told me Raggedy Ann could be tossed because she's covered in cat throw-up," Lucy said.

"I said she was covered in cat throw-up, not that she could be tossed." Maggie dropped the soiled doll back in the bin and leaned against Reuben's legs. "So you'll come see us?"

"You know I will," Reuben said.

"A lot?"

"We'll see," he said. "I'll come as often as I possibly can."

"And maybe we can go to the beach this summer?"

"Maybe we *can* go to the beach," Reuben replied, which Lucy noted was a lie. How could he possibly get away from his real life long enough to take Maggie to the beach. And what would he plan to tell Elaine?

"What does *a lot* mean?" Lucy asked after the girls had headed down the street.

"I don't know what it means," Reuben said, agitated the way he got when pressures bore down on him as they had when he first met Lucy and again and again in the years they'd been together, more or less together, depending on the point of view. "This is a trial, Lucy, and of course I want to see you as much as possible."

"Just don't say, 'We'll see.'"

She could feel his furtive glance, sense the familiar fear mounting in him as he scouted an escape route the way he always seemed to do when she wanted more than he was capable of giving.

That was the nature of their lives together. His terms.

Lucy pulled her cap down lower on her eyes so the wool brushed her lashes.

"I won't say *'We'll see,'*" Reuben said. "And I won't lie to you."

"Oh Reuben," Lucy said. "You have *only* lied to me."

She didn't mean that, didn't mean to make a scene on the day of her departure, not in front of

19

Felix, who was sitting beside her while the truck was loaded. Not in front of Reuben especially, who had counted on her free spirit and independence, her willingness to live sufficient unto herself, which was all that had ever been possible between them.

But she couldn't help it. She wanted Reuben to ache for her the way she did for him.

He had opened the *New York Times* to the front page, retreating to the newspaper to avoid a discussion of his personal life with Lucy.

"Have you been reading about Watergate?" he asked, crossing his legs, leaning against the side of the truck.

She shook her head.

"Every day on the front page. Did you see that Gordon Liddy and James McCord were caught up in this shindig?"

"I don't read the newspaper when there's bad news and there's always bad news."

She seldom read the papers at all and never the national pages. The news of her father's death had been reported in the national section—on the front page of the *New York Times* and the *Washington Post* and the *Evening Star*, all over the country according to her mother. Sometimes she read the features, personal stories in the Metro section and occasionally the arts. But never the *real* news that had marked for Lucy the end of one childhood and the beginning of another.

"Well, all of them are lying to us, certainly Nixon," Reuben said. "Lying again as happened with Viet Nam, and how much else don't we know about the truth? There's a regular culture of lies infesting our lives."

Felix had scrambled off the truck, dropping the yellow chicken in Lucy's lap, trotting over to play in the square of garden next to Lucy's building with his friend Ernie.

"If I spend any time thinking about lies, it has to do with you and me," Lucy said, wrapping her arms around her legs, resting her chin on her knees.

Reuben folded the paper and put it down, uttering a sigh of defeat.

"Have you thought again about telling the children what happened?" he asked.

"With you?" Lucy slipped off the back of the truck.

"With *you*."

"I won't tell the children *anything* if that's what you're asking."

"Not asking," he said. "Wondering."

He leaned over, his lips against her temple.

"You know, Lucy, you're really kind of an original." There was weariness in his voice, or irritation or sadness. "Otherwise you'd join the Movement and wear that red and black *Women on Top* T-shirt and leave me for good."

"Maybe I will," she said. "Not the T-shirt but maybe I will leave you for good."

• • •

MICKEY WAS LOADING up the U-Haul with boxes and lamps wrapped in blankets, the couch Lucy had taken from the curb after graduation, left there by students at Brown or friends of hers at the Rhode Island School of Design.

"Our furniture is junk, Mama," Maggie had said the day before as they were packing up, Reuben dropping by with tacos for dinner. "Maybe we should leave it here."

"But it's *our* junk."

"It's secondhand. Other people I know have firsthand furniture. Even Rebecca has firsthand furniture and her mother is poor as a church mouse."

"Your mother's an artist, Maggie," Reuben had said. "She doesn't worry about furniture."

"She writes children's books. That's not exactly an artist."

"I'm her editor, bumblebee," he said, grabbing Maggie's hand, twirling her into his arms. "Lucy Painter is an artist and *your* perfect mother."

Everyone in the neighborhood knew who Lucy Painter was when she walked through the streets of the West Village shopping for dinner or books or off to the playground with Felix or P.S. 117 with Maggie. She was small and girlish with a mop of black curls, in short flowered skirts she made herself like the one on the back of her book jackets, striped tights, a long scarf wrapped

22

around her neck hanging to her knees. Especially the children loved her.

"That's Lucy Painter," they'd call out to their friends or their mothers. And Maggie, walking with Lucy, would whisper, "How embarrassing!"

But she loved her famous mother, loved the way she looked with her bright cheeks and big boots, her tiny hands like the hands of a child.

AT THE TIME OF Samuel Baldwin's death, Lucy's father had been a special assistant to President Truman appointed in September 1945, following the bombings of Hiroshima and Nagasaki—a gentle, principled man of value to the White House for his wise and measured opinions. After the article about his death on the front page of the *Washington Post* with the news of what had really happened, after the Friday service at St. Vincent's on Capitol Hill which Lucy did not attend—"Not under the circumstances," her mother had told her—Lucy and her mother left by plane for Santa Fe.

Her mother's idea to disappear into a strange landscape—to take up residence in a town just east of Santa Fe above the Rio Grande.

In Santa Fe, her mother changed their name from Baldwin to Painter, fearful that someone might trace *Samuel Baldwin* back to them.

"But Baldwin is our name," Lucy said. "It isn't true to make up a new one."

"It is better, a story of who we are," her mother had said. "And besides, it is a good name for us. Baldwin is too Anglo-Saxon for a Frenchwoman, and Painter is a name with the sound of song."

Caroleen Peinture, she called herself.

The dry, brown, craggy-moonscape geography of New Mexico peppered with dots of intense color became a visual expression of Lucy's state of mind.

Lucy was twelve when her father died, and for the next six years until she left New Mexico for the Rhode Island School of Design, she waited. The mind's-eye picture she had of herself was of a girl sitting on the flat brown rock in the backyard of their cottage outside of Santa Fe.

"What are you waiting for?" her mother had asked.

"I'm waiting to go back to Washington," Lucy said. "The place where I grew up."

"You can go back, of course, but I wouldn't recommend it," her mother said in her crisp, matter-of-fact manner. "426 A Street, S.E., just beyond East Capitol. I have no interest in ever seeing the house again."

"Never?" Lucy had asked.

Never was her mother's chosen refrain. *Never tell anyone your real name, Lucia, or where you were born or who your father was,* she would say. *He's dead. That's all a person needs to know.*

Never go home.

· · ·

SOMETIMES LUCY IMAGINED the inside of the house on Capitol Hill, room to room. She'd follow the narrow corridor, the bathroom with its claw-foot tub, next to her bedroom with a bay window where she sat on a seat between the bays overlooking A Street. In winter, the mated cardinals arguing on the leafless dogwood branches, the nervous sparrows on the telephone wires. In spring, the robins, fat with foraging. And lying on the back porch of the Santa Fe cottage where they lived, she'd watch the broad-tailed hummingbird, its shiny green feathers and white throat speckled iridescent bronze, its long beak plunged into the nectar center of a yellow hibiscus, the stem winding around the posts on the back porch. There were yellow hibiscus in a pot in the garden of the house on A Street too but Lucy didn't mention that coincidence to her mother, wondering occasionally what went through her mother's head. Did she ever think about her husband and her marriage? She never spoke of him.

After Lucy left for college, her mother returned to the city of Arles where she had grown up and where her sister, the aunt whom Lucy had never met, still lived.

At RISD, out of the shadow of her mother's shame and disappointment, Lucy invented a public self to live among strangers. A demeanor

25

of mystery and whimsy, the promise of intimacy, but she was skittish if anyone came too close.

"Untouchable," she was called by the other students. She became a subject of conversation.

LUCY MET REUBEN Frank when she was nineteen.

She had gone to New York City at her art professor's recommendation to show her portfolio of strange, supernatural animals painted in the brilliant colors of the desert to publishers of children's books. She was sitting on a bench in the lobby of 555 Fifth Avenue where George Barnes Books, Inc., was located, gathering the courage to take the elevator to the seventh floor, when Reuben, carrying a bag with his lunch, the *New York Times* under his arm, rushed through the revolving doors into the lobby and saw her.

Her shoes were what struck him first, her feet curled under a short orange flowered skirt, her shoes, red ballet slippers with satin ribbons, resting toe to toe under the bench.

"Hello," he said. "Can I help you?"

"I am looking for Mr. Reuben Frank of George Barnes Books," she said. "I have an appointment with him."

"You do?" Reuben asked.

"More or less," she said.

She had found the name *Reuben Frank* in a book listing New York editors and publishers but had not called in advance to arrange an appointment, had not even thought to call. She simply expected that Mr. Frank would be happy to look at her work because her professor at RISD had told her she was an artist of unusual talent.

"At least I hope I'll be able to meet with him when I get upstairs," she said. "I've brought my pictures."

"Luckily you've run into the right person," he said, watching as she wriggled her feet into the ballet slippers. "I can arrange that meeting instantly."

In the elevator, Lucy leaned down to tie the satin ribbons around her ankles, her hair parting to expose a curve in the shape of a half-moon at the nape of her neck.

"That did it," he told her later. Just the sight of her small neck had moved him.

On the seventh floor, the elevator doors opened and he led the way down the corridor, past the cubicles of editors, past the design room, the front desk with a young girl on the telephone, and into his office with its large window overlooking Fifth Avenue.

"So," he said clearing off his desk, "I'm ready to see your work."

There were six paintings, only six she realized when she saw that they all fit on the top of the desk looking more strange than she remembered—the color maybe too bright, the animals unnaturally thin and pointy.

"So what do you think?" she asked quickly.

"I don't *think* about illustrations," he replied, raising the venetian blinds behind his desk, picking up one of Lucy's drawings. He held it at an angle in light that spread across the room from the south-facing window.

"You don't think they're too queer to put in a book for children, do you?" she asked, sensing Reuben's hesitation.

He was leaning over his desk examining a hedgehog-like creature with brilliant yellow eyes.

"I think I love them," Reuben said, reassembling the portfolio, setting it on the edge of his desk. "I can't tell you why exactly. I simply know what I love and what I don't."

Lucy put her feet up flat against the side of his desk, flushed, her heart pounding.

"So now what will happen?" she asked.

"Now I'm going to be your editor."

"You are? And that's that?"

"More or less. You'll go back to school and imagine a story for these creatures of yours and then we'll do a book together."

"Not together," she said quickly. "I do every-thing alone. Always completely alone."

"We'll try it," Reuben said. "If it doesn't work between us, it doesn't work."

He was falling in love. With Lucy. With the wild imaginative figures she had brought to him. With the possibility of flight.

He was thirty-five and married and childless.

"THIS IS VERY lucky, isn't it?" Lucy said as they walked back down the corridor to the elevator.

"Certainly lucky for me," he said. "These wonderful original illustrations."

He reached over, running his finger lightly down the bridge of her nose.

"Goodbye, my new surprise," he said as the elevator doors opened.

"Hello, my new editor," Lucy said, stepping through the doors, her head down, looking at her red ballet slippers as the doors closed.

For hours in the next months, she would lie on her back in the tiny single room of her group house at RISD imagining Reuben, his hand on her belly, his breath in her hair. There was no stopping the rush of feeling, no instinctive fear or hesitation in loving Reuben. He would leave his wife. They would marry as he had said would happen in their long conversations from his office. As he hoped would happen. *Not a good fit with Elaine,* he told her. It was as if the whole of her life since her father's death had led to this particular man, gentle like her father had been, certain of himself. Her editor who could be counted on for everything.

• • •

AFTER SHE GRADUATED from Rhode Island School of Design, after her mother was killed in an automobile accident outside of Paris, Lucy moved to the West Village, fifteen easy blocks from Reuben Frank. The geography was Reuben's idea. Lucy was pregnant.

Lying on her stomach in the apartment where she lived alone on Sullivan Street, Lucy spent hours on the phone with Reuben cloistered in his office.

"Not that things won't work out between us," he said to her. "I didn't know what it meant to fall in love, not with other girlfriends, not with my wife. I want to be with you always," he said. "I can't just yet imagine that conversation with Elaine. But I will."

He wanted her to be sure about the baby.

"I am sure," she said. "Whatever happens, I want the baby."

Of that she was certain. She wanted this baby for herself, is how she thought of it. She had no family except Reuben, and if things didn't work out with him, if, in the end, he couldn't leave Elaine, she would still have the child.

At least, that was what she believed was possible in the magical way she had learned to construct a private world of parallel realities.

MAGGIE WAS BORN when Lucy was twenty-two, the year her first book *Belly Over the Banana*

30

Field was published about Belly, a too-small boy with a too-big belly dropped from the sky into a field of bananas, a book for which she won the Livingston for the best illustrated children's book of 1962.

On the title page of *Belly*, just under her name, Lucy had drawn a tiny broad-tailed hummingbird.

"What little thing is this?" Reuben had asked when he got the final proof.

"A hummingbird," she said.

A sign, she'd thought. She would draw a hummingbird on the title page of every book and mothers and fathers who bought her books, children leaning into their parents listening to them read a Lucy Painter story would think of Lucy and the hummingbird as one.

She told Reuben about the days spent lying on the back porch in Santa Fe watching the hummingbird arrive at the hibiscus. So swift and small. Nothing in the still air, no sound of whirring wings and suddenly the hummingbird.

The first night they were together, she drew a broad-tailed hummingbird on the palm of Reuben's hand.

"Indelible ink," she said.

THE YEAR THAT Maggie was born was the happiest one of Lucy's life—*so far,* she told herself. She was a young mother with a baby girl, a successful book, and a love affair.

"Soon," Reuben had promised her about the eventual demise of his marriage. "Just you and me and Maggie."

IN MARCH OF 1963, two months after Maggie's first birthday, Reuben's daughter Nell was born.

"This is a total surprise," he said when he told her that Elaine was pregnant. "I don't know what to say."

Lucy's first reaction was fright.

"What will become of us?" she asked.

"We will continue our lives somehow," he said, holding his head in his hands. He was tentative for the first time since they had been together and Lucy drew back, not wanting to alarm him.

Months later, sitting across from Reuben at Belinda's coffeehouse on the corner of Sullivan and Sixth, Elaine still in the hospital with baby Nell, Lucy asked about their future again.

"I love you, Lucy," he said. "This is extraordinary what we have together."

She wanted to ask him what *"this"* meant now that Nell had arrived, now that Reuben had the conundrum of a daughter with his wife and a daughter with his girlfriend.

"I don't know how but we will work this out," he said.

She wanted to believe him.

It was still possible to persuade herself that someday Reuben *would* leave Elaine just as she sometimes imagined that one afternoon, she'd walk into a coffee shop and there her father would be sitting alone in a booth with a cup of coffee and a cigarette reading the morning newspaper.

MICKEY CLIMBED IN the back of the truck with the two lamps from the living room, a poster announcing the publication of one of her books, and under his arm, a stuffed Dalmatian missing its tail.

"Done," Mickey said. "The apartment's empty."

Reuben slid off the back of the truck.

"So you can get on the road early, " he said.

"There are still boxes in storage in the basement," Lucy said.

Reuben pulled up the collar of his jacket. The wind had picked up.

"Books and things I haven't looked at since they were packed up in the house where I was born."

"I don't think I've ever been in the storage room," he said. "I'll go get them."

"I'm coming too," Lucy said, leading the way down the narrow, winding stair, flipping on a light in the storage area where wire cages lined the walls in a room smelling of mold and the dank reminder of residential rats.

"These are books," Lucy said, unlocking the combination to her storage room. "And the boxes marked *Lucy, 1951* are from the house on Capitol Hill where I used to live."

That morning before Reuben had arrived with the U-Haul truck, Lucy thought of opening the box with her father's things to show Reuben the story from the *Washington Post* about his death. The story itself with the news she had already told him. He was the only person she had ever told about her life.

The books were packed in boxes of ten, author's copies from George Barnes Books— *Fervid P. Drainpipe Lost in the Chinese Museum of Art* was stamped on the side of one of the boxes and there were several boxes of *Belly Over the Banana Field* and two of *Loop de Lupe and the Spider Monkey from Dordogne.*

Reuben lifted one of the old boxes, clouds of dust rising in the air collecting just above his head.

"Have you ever even opened these, Lucy?" he asked, clearing his throat of dust. "The cardboard is actually disintegrating."

"Once at RISD I opened one box and taped it back up," she said. "I didn't want to look at my childhood then."

"You're going to have to repack them when you get to Washington."

He struggled up the staircase, leaving Lucy to carry the smaller boxes which had followed her since they were packed, traveling from

Washington, D.C., to Santa Fe to Providence, Rhode Island, to New York City, now back to Washington.

"I hope you won't be too lonely, Lucy," he said. "Sometimes you keep too much to yourself."

"I'll be fine," she said, but Reuben knew her too well.

She longed for company, for friends drinking tea in her kitchen, sitting in the window talking as dusk came on while the children played just within hearing. She wanted to be close in the way that she felt to the strange little characters she wrote about in her books, to lie in bed after the children had gone to sleep, alone as she often was, and shuffle through the playing cards of people she could call in the morning or ask to come when Maggie had the flu. A best friend. Someone she could tell about her mother and father. About Reuben.

But always there was with Lucy a conditioned reserve.

The closest she had come to the friendships she imagined beyond the casual gathering of telephone lists from Maggie's school for bake sales and class trips and potluck suppers was walking through the Village with her children smiling at the people who knew her from her books.

In Washington and without Reuben, she would change that.

DARKNESS WAS COMING on early—not the ordinary slow-curtain fall of a winter day's end but quickly, a storm-chased afternoon.

They finished packing up the U-Haul and locked the back door. It was almost four in the afternoon and already dark, the storm threatening but no report of snow on the weather station. Lucy lifted Felix into the cab and Maggie climbed up behind him.

"Do you want to check the apartment to see that everything's okay for the next tenant?" Reuben asked.

"I suppose I should."

"We'll be right back, guys," Reuben said, asking Mickey to stay with the children until they returned.

The apartment was empty. Lucy's breath caught in her throat. She wanted to leave quickly, to hurry down the stairs and out the door into the weather, to tell Reuben goodbye without lingering over what remained between them.

"I'll check around," he said, leaving her in the living room, opening the closet doors, the kitchen cabinets, the tiny cupboard in the front hall where Lucy had kept the children's toys. He was standing at the toy cabinet when she turned around, and headed towards the door.

"Not yet."

He put his hand on the small of her back and pulled her towards him.

"Your smell isn't here any longer, is it?" he said. "It smells of cigarette smoke."

"You're the one who smokes," she said.

He took her hand, a veil of dust between them, his hands dry.

"Don't say anything," she said. "Not a word."

"I was just going to say it's dusty in here."

"It was always dusty."

"I never noticed."

He kissed her sweetly, softly, pressing her body against him.

But she turned, pushed his arms away, and headed down the steps and out the front door to the truck.

FINALLY IT WAS beginning to snow.

"Don't forget to take the tunnel out of town," Reuben called, standing beside the truck as it pulled away from the curb.

Lucy could hear him from the open window but she didn't check the rearview mirror for one more look. The traffic was heavy in the city and the trip was going to be long. Already, Felix had asked to stop to pee.

Two

WHEN THE HOUSE on Witchita Avenue became available after Thanksgiving 1972, the real estate agent called to ask if Lucy wished to sell it. It was possible she could get sixty to sixty-five thousand for the house. Maggie was ten, Felix was two, and Lucy's hope for more of Reuben Frank's time had slipped away.

Not that she had ever expected Reuben to be as he would call it "yours forever." They were always together, was how Lucy thought of it.

But when the call came about the house, she didn't even think.

No, don't sell. I'm taking possession.

She *had* to take action. And so the house.

They spent the first night in Washington in a hotel on Connecticut Avenue north of Dupont Circle, arriving late, after midnight. The roads, particularly the New Jersey Turnpike, were slippery with the kind of wet snow that sticks just enough to cause a problem. The wind whipped snow against the windshield. Lucy had never driven a U-Haul before so she drove slowly in the right-hand lane.

The children slept, Felix happily curled into Lucy's ribs, Maggie's head against the window.

Maggie was surprisingly silent, her feet on the dashboard, looking out the window into the snowy darkness. She was worried about the move, Lucy guessed. They had lived in the same apartment where she was born. She had gone to the same school with the same friends, the same pattern to her days—a mother with a career that allowed her to work at home and "Uncle" Reuben, a regular drop-by at her apartment. The eccentricities of their lives had been what Maggie thought of as normal.

She had never asked about her father until she started nursery school.

When Lucy picked her up after the first day, Maggie was thoughtful refusing her mother's hand. She didn't want to stop for ice cream at the shop on Houston.

"I don't like school so much," she said as they walked up the steps to the apartment.

"How come?" Lucy asked.

"Everybody in my class has a father except Rosie and her father is dead," she said. "Is *my* father dead?"

Lucy should have been prepared. She should have had a story ready for this moment instead of scrambling to invent something sufficient.

"He is not dead," she said, taking milk out of the fridge. "But he's not *here*."

"Then where is he?"

Lucy took a box of animal crackers out of the cupboard and sat down across from Maggie, who was coloring a photograph on the front page of the *New York Times*.

"I don't know exactly where he is but I can tell you the story of how he got to be your father."

Maggie put the crayon down.

"So tell me the story."

"It's a fairy tale. My favorite kind of story," she said.

There was a very lonely girl, Lucy began. *Her father had died and her mother had died and so she lived with her old calico cat in the middle of a wood.* Maggie slipped off the chair and into Lucy's lap. *One night when the very lonely girl was sleeping, there came a knock on her door and the old calico cat meowed and the very lonely girl woke up and answered the door hoping it would be company which she seldom had. And it was company. To her happy surprise when she opened her door, there was a handsome man on the back of a huge black horse. He told her he had gotten lost in the wood and asked her could she help him find the way out. And so she put on her brown tweed jacket and her yellow hat and walked with her old calico cat limping behind her until they came to a large open field, the sky bright with stars and a cookie slice of moon.*

The handsome man was so delighted to be out of the wood that he promised to give the very lonely girl whatever in the world she wanted to have.

"I would like to have a baby girl since I live by

myself in the wood except for my old calico cat."

"No problem," he said. "I'll see that you get one immediately."

And he did.

He gave the very lonely girl a beautiful baby girl to be with her always so she would no longer be lonely, Lucy said. *And that little girl was you.*

"Then the handsome man left on his horse?" Maggie asked.

"He had to leave."

"Did he ever come back?" she asked.

"That's all of the story I know so far."

"I SHOULD HAVE told Maggie the truth?" Lucy said when Reuben stopped by that evening with ice cream and wine.

"The truth. God no, Lucy," Reuben said. "That would be devastating for all of us."

"Someday we'll have to tell her the truth. You know that."

"Until I met you, I had low expectations and now . . . now," he hesitated. "I am . . ." He put his head in his hands. "I don't know. In love with you."

"So we go on like this day to day?"

"Day to day for the moment. Someday we will tell her the truth and our lives will have to change."

Which was the unspoken arrangement Lucy made with Reuben. She felt a kind of power in it.

41

• • •

HER MOTHER HAD told her that after her father died, a matter of weeks later, Lucy went blind. Shadows floating past her were all she saw.

The doctors in Santa Fe could find nothing wrong. *Psychosomatic,* they said when she insisted she couldn't see anything but these shadows. And there was every evidence that she could not.

"Of course," her mother had said, ". . . given what has happened to our lives."

The blindness lasted less than a month, but during those weeks, Lucy could go nowhere without her mother's help. She would sit in a dining room chair, her feet curled over the rungs, and rest her head on her stacked fists, staring into space.

"Would you like to go out to the garden?" her mother would ask, "or to a restaurant or to walk around the streets of Santa Fe?," speaking to Lucy only in French after her father died, as if the English language had never existed between them, except on social occasions when others were around.

"You loved to draw so I got paints and colored pencils and good art paper and put it on the dining room table. You'd run your fingers over the paper saying it felt like crisp cotton," her mother said. "And finally you began to draw."

"So I *could* see?" Lucy had asked.

42

"I suppose you could."

Lucy had a misty memory of blindness that might only have come from her mother's telling. She remembered little at all of the year after her father died except the astonishing colors of the desert. The blindness must have come first before she *saw* the colors and she wondered did the radiance of the colors startle her to sight.

She looked over at Maggie in the darkness lit by the lights from the passing cars, her expression inscrutable.

When Maggie was born, Lucy fell in love.

All through her pregnancy she had been frozen by the limitations of her affair with Reuben. Then Maggie came and Lucy could feel her body give way. She would stand over Maggie's crib while she slept, watching and watching in case this miracle might stop breathing or disappear until in time she began to trust that Maggie was permanent and would not be taken from her.

AFTER MIDNIGHT, LUCY had driven off the Beltway onto New York Avenue, and Maggie, half sleeping, sat up in her seat and stretched.

"Are we there?"

"We're almost at the hotel."

She yawned, reaching into the bag of treats Lucy had packed, taking out a package of peanut butter crackers.

"I was thinking . . ." Maggie hesitated.

"Wondering whether you're ever going to tell me about my father."

"What made you think that now?" Lucy asked, her stomach tightening.

"Because I'm going to a new school on Monday in a new city and I don't have a father to tell people about."

"Well . . ." Lucy was unprepared for the singular clarity of Maggie's request.

"What do you think I should say?" Maggie asked.

"I think you should say that he lives in New York."

"And does he live in New York?"

"He does."

Lucy pulled up to a stoplight, the traffic heavy in spite of the late hour, stalling for time. She was inclined to turn on the radio, to check the weather, anything that would give her time to construct a response.

"Then you *know* who he is?" Maggie asked.

Lucy's hands tightened on the steering wheel, heat rising in her throat.

Was Maggie suggesting that there could be more than *one* possibility for a father? Was she thinking that her mother was unable to identify the only possible man who could have been her father?

"Of course I know who your father is."

Through the years, she had lied about things

44

out of what felt like necessity, but the truth was important to Lucy. A kind of morality she'd constructed of private rules by which to abide as if she were her own society.

Reuben Frank was the only man with whom she had ever slept, the only one she knew. She had been faithful to one man because she loved him. She wanted her daughter to know that.

"Why won't you tell me?" Maggie asked, her tone more curious than accusatory.

"I will," Lucy said. "But just not yet."

"Can you at least tell me something?" Maggie asked. "Just things about his life—what he looks like and where he lives and has he ever seen me?"

"I can tell you he's married to someone else."

Maggie fell silent. She pulled up the collar of her coat so it covered her chin and lips, up to her nose, her head sunk like a turtle's into the collar.

This news was not what Maggie wanted to hear.

Glancing at her in the light from the streetlamp, Lucy wondered whether she should have said *nothing,* whether a little information about her father was more than Maggie really wished to know.

By the time she had parked the U-Haul, registered at the hotel, taken the elevator to their room, carrying Felix and their overnight bag, she was too exhausted to undress, falling asleep fully

45

clothed in her parka and wool hat and levis between Maggie, wide awake and silent, and Felix.

Lucy had not seen the house at 3706 Witchita Avenue since she was twelve and she didn't want to see it until it had been transformed into a house she'd *never* seen before. She chose the paint colors long-distance, deep orange, sienna, golden yellow, fuchsia, lavender, reminiscent of the desert flowers in Santa Fe. She had the old floors refinished in pale natural pine, installed new appliances, a new furnace, new hot water heater, and the attic, accessible through the closet door in her bedroom, opened to a studio she'd designed with skylights and dry wall and painted floors. The basement had been sprayed bone white, the cement floor spattered bright blue.

She wanted the old house to feel uninhabited as if it had never been lived in before Lucy Painter and her family arrived.

SHE WOKE IN darkness, the hotel curtains drawn, no sense of time, the children sleeping on either side of her.

For a very long time she had believed Reuben even after it should have been clear he was not going to leave Elaine.

He would tell Lucy she was his secret treasure, his passion, his one great love.

46

"With you, I am whole," Reuben would say on the weekends his wife was in Connecticut with Nell and her parents, on the occasional mornings before Felix was born or evenings when Elaine was working late in her midtown office where she was a literary agent.

Lucy would slip out of her clothes, her cheeks flushed, her long hair covering his groin as she knelt beside him.

"I belong to you," she'd say to him.

Which was true. Reuben Frank *owned* her secrets.

Ownership is how she thought of it, as if his name were on the title to her house. She *couldn't* leave him. He was the only person who knew her life.

MAGGIE HAD BEEN eight when Felix was born. Lucy's intemperate choice to have another child. An accident, she said to Reuben.

"There are no accidents," he said, but he didn't chastise her. He didn't even resist or insist that Lucy find a way to interrupt the pregnancy. He simply was what he had always been with her—accommodating, detached, and noncompliant.

Lucy had persuaded herself that a boy would capture Reuben. He and Elaine would never have another child. Too much for *Elaine,* he'd told her, too expensive in New York.

So there would be no boy except this one, this tiny bundle of pink flesh and black curly hair, his only son.

But the baby Felix with his full lips and deep brown eyes did not become the magnet that Lucy had hoped he would be. As Nell got older, Elaine became demanding. She no longer went away to the country on weekends, pushing instead for a social life in the city with literary people, expanding her business. She made plans for Nell—ballet lessons and ice skating, French classes, Saturdays at the museums. She wanted Reuben to be an "equal partner"—his description or hers, Lucy was never sure.

But she did know that somehow, sometime she had to bring herself to leave Reuben—the weekends of occasional leftovers stashed in the back of the fridge, furtive calls from restaurants in the city while he was out to dinner with Elaine and one of her clients, bunches of flowers and kisses, their bodies locked together by a stopwatch.

THE HOUSE WAS a faded yellow shingle situated high over the street, small with a wide front porch, twenty-seven steps down to the sidewalk and surrounded by a brick wall which had been built to control erosion. Built at the turn of the century, it was probably the original farmhouse owning the surrounding land, before a developer arrived and Witchita Hills became a facsimile of the Middle West on the northern border of Washington where the District of Columbia crosses into Maryland. A subdivision really, a replication in spirit of the easy trust presumed of midwestern towns. Or so its residents, all transplants from other places, liked to assume, believing that in Witchita Hills, they had chosen the authenticity of middle-class life with proximity to power. A senator and his family lived on Des Moines Street next door to the head of the Washington bureau for the *New York Times*, the widow of a Supreme Court justice lived on Columbus Street and on Witchita Avenue, a young lawyer, Miles Robinson, who would be appointed in May to the office of special prosecutor investigating the Watergate scandal, which so threatened Nixon's presidency that he would eventually be forced to resign.

SHE CLIMBED INTO the cab of the U-Haul and turned on the ignition.

"Ready to roll?"

"Nothing else to do," Maggie said.

"Is it a big house?" Felix asked.

"Bigger than Sullivan Street," Lucy said. "Big enough for us."

"Does it have a swimming pool?"

"What do *you* think, Felix?"

Felix giggled.

"I think yes."

"It's yellow and messy," Maggie said. "I saw the pictures."

"Me too," Felix said. "I saw the pictures first."

"It's all cleaned up now," Lucy said, handing Maggie the directions.

North on Connecticut Avenue almost to the District line. When you get to EMILY'S second-hand books on your right and Café Moxie on your left, turn LEFT at Witchita and head up the hill to 3706 on the left. There is no sign indicating Witchita Hills.

Driving north on Connecticut Avenue, past the shops in Chevy Chase, D.C., Witchita Hills sat on an actual hill, a cluster of houses gathered close together on small plots of land. A sub-division really with individual houses, more accidental in design than planned, and in the last year of Richard Nixon's presidency with Water-gate the most conspicuous of Washington's monuments, Witchita Hills was self-consciously democratic and middle-class, a look of studied poverty about the place suggesting, or so it was assumed among the residents, a new intellectual freedom with responsibility born of the sixties.

A kind of abandon in the way families kept their houses—unlocked doors, clutter in the yards, porches with toys and strollers, baseball bats and bicycles, the winter remains of bright and messy gardens where tomatoes and green

50

beans and zucchini scrambled for space in garden plots often in the front yard.

It had glitter in the way a place can take on its own aura for no particular reason. Which in this case had to do with *community*—a *real* place with *real* people was the word out on Witchita Hills. There was a post-sixties smugness about it—citizens with genuine social conscience in a time of national secrecy, openhearted citizens without judgments, an expectation that the families who lived there had a new moral superiority. *One for All and All for One* was the painted sign at the entrance to the community center on St. Louis Road.

IN THE GRAY fog of an early morning, Lucy strained to see the signs on the shops. The cab of the U-Haul was airless. She turned off the heat.

She had been feeling what she used to describe to Reuben as an out-of-body strangeness which came over her in waves and by surprise. Her mind would go blurry, her heart race with a rising fear of losing hold. She could imagine her own death as if it were in the present tense. It was like descriptions she had read of amnesia, as if she were shelved in the wrong aisle. Who was she and who were these children and where did they all belong?

It wasn't the first time this had happened since she'd made the decision to leave New York.

Long before when she was young, she had learned to depend on her imagination to rescue her from the long days as an only child in a very quiet house.

"Do you know the name of my new school?" Maggie was asking, but Lucy was concentrating on an idea that had come to her weeks ago when she saw the name *sloth* in an article in the Metro section of the newspaper about the Brooklyn Zoo. A three-toed sloth had been found dead hanging, as sloths do, by his tail from the branch of a tree. How odd it was and reassuring that the tail remained stiff enough to hold him swinging from the branch as if he were not really dead, only the appearance of it. *Vermillion the Three-Toed Sloth*, she would call the story. But in her story, the young male sloth would *not* die.

Vermillion might have as his most salient quality, besides slowness, an obsession with Violet, who would be a swift, kenetic sort of creature, maybe a small bird, a cerulean bluebird, with the capacity to fly high above the trees, even above the tree line. She found herself wondering what obsession had to do with love and did Vermillion love Violet?

She had never thought of Reuben as an obsession but perhaps he was. Maybe that was *all* he was.

And if that were true, *forgetting* Reuben ought to be possible if she could find a substitute to hold his place, something substantial to fill her anxious mind until Reuben faded away.

"Mama," Felix was saying, "you aren't telling Maggie the name of her school."

"Lafayette," Lucy said quickly, "Lafayette Elementary. And next year you'll go to junior high nearby."

"Unlikely," Maggie said, putting her feet on the dashboard, turning up the heat. "Unlikely I'll be living here next year."

The day was becoming darker, the traffic headed downtown had headlights on and Lucy couldn't see any of the signs on the buildings until Maggie said, "Café Moxie," pointing to a long green building on the left with red letters lit up, *Café Moxie* in loopy script, a martini glass at either end.

Lucy put on her turn signal.

There was only one way in and out of Witchita Hills and that was Witchita Avenue, easy to miss, to pass right by continuing north on Connecticut since there was no sign announcing the existence of a small utopia at the far northern end of the District of Columbia.

"Is this place really called Witchita Hills?" Maggie asked.

"It is," Lucy said.

"It sounds like the name of a cult."

As Lucy drove up Witchita Avenue, she noticed the lights were on in most of the houses and in the fog they shimmered, bleeding across the horizon. She saw her house at once, the yellow on the shingles more faded than it had seemed in photographs, the house higher from the street.

She was just turning the steering wheel to the left to park behind the movers' truck the real estate agent had promised would be there to help her unload, when she noticed across the street on the right, a cluster of people standing together, witnessing her arrival.

"So here we are," she said, a sudden sinking of spirit.

"We have friends already waiting for us," Felix said. "They are our friends, right, Mama?"

"I hope they will be," Lucy said, putting the truck in park, pulling up the brake.

"Mama," Maggie said combing her curly red hair quickly with her fingers, "take off that awful orange hat."

Three

THE WOMEN GATHERED in front of the Mallorys' house—bundled in coats and scarves, their mittened hands wrapped around mugs of cappuccino Zee Mallory had made from her new machine—were expecting Lucy Painter's arrival.

Her old farmhouse was the third on the left as the hill rose to the end of the avenue where Robin and Miles Robinson lived. From Lucy's front porch, she would be able to hear the traffic on Connecticut Avenue, but only in the winter with the trees bare would it be possible to see it. Lane and Will Sewall lived across the street in a Sears Roebuck bungalow painted mustard yellow with brown trim, a 1970 Plexiglas addition to the living room. Two houses up from Lane and Will, the Mallorys, Adam and Zelda, called Zee, lived in the largest house in the neighborhood, five bedrooms, a big backyard that dipped into the woods, a wraparound front porch with white wicker furniture and dead spider plants left over from summer hanging from hooks above the railings. Next door to Lucy, August Russ, a young widower, lived alone in a bright blue house, similar to Lucy's, copied from it years after the neighborhood began to grow into its name. Across from August, Josie Lerner, divorced with a young son, Rufus, kept a respectable, conventional home, no toys on the front porch, bicycles in the garage, shades on the windows, a red door repainted every year to a glossy sheen, the grass kept watered in the hot Washington summers, the leaves raked and used for mulch in the fall. At the top of the hill, Robin and Miles Robinson lived in a house they had renovated, taking pains gutting the late twenties arts and craft cottage so it looked less like a mushroom, more similar, as Miles would say, to "en plein air."

Among the families on Witchita Avenue, Zee Mallory was the emotional center of daily life. People loved her, counted on her for their social lives, their sadnesses and troubles, spilled out their secrets without reciprocation. Zee never spoke about her own problems, although there was talk in the neighborhood that she had lost a child years before the twins were born.

THE REAL ESTATE agent for Lucy's house had kept the neighbors up to date.

"Did I say she was single? Completely single." Zee Mallory had just come from her house with warm donuts. "She has two children, a boy who's three and Maggie."

"Another girl for your happiness," Lane Sewall said to Zee, who had a softness for girls.

"Divorced?" Robin Robinson asked.

"No husband," Zee said. "She never had a husband."

"Good news," Josie said. "A thinking woman."

The headlights went off and Lucy dropped down to the street, walking around the truck. Stopping at a car parked in front of her house, she leaned in the window.

"She's talking to Wendy, the real estate agent who's been taking care of the place," Zee said.

"Can you tell what she looks like?" Lane asked.

"Small," Josie Lerner said, dressed for work,

56

the only one among them who worked downtown, although the others were professional women, working part-time or full-time or in graduate school, women with expectations for themselves.

"I've seen her picture on the books," Zee said. "You know her books—*Belly Over the Banana Field* and *Fervid P.* something or another and a couple of others I can't remember."

"She has black hair and dimples and sleepy eyes. Pretty. Look at the book jackets," Josie said.

"Her books *are* weird," Lane said.

"Those squat little trolly characters with square bodies and hands and heads in colors like orange and persimmon and electric lime green." Josie shook her head. "You're not kidding, they're weird."

"Luke and Daniel didn't love her books, but they're boys."

Zee was disinclined to pass judgment on others. She liked to think of herself as open-minded and curious out of an interest in people for their own sake. *Not competitive,* was what she wanted to believe about herself. But it pleased her to hear the judgments of others. It made her feel better, always struggling to see herself as *good,* the way she had been as a child in rural Michigan when she *was* good before circumstances got in the way.

"Sara liked *Belly*," Robin said quietly. "It was actually her favorite book when she was little."

"Girls may have more patience for arty books. That's what I've noticed," Zee Mallory said, a quick study, a minor expert on many subjects, responsive to every question whether she knew the answer or not.

The Mallorys had come to Washington when Adam took a job with the Justice Department just after the assassination of President Kennedy, and Zee had worked off and on since then as a research assistant for an investigative reporter at the *New York Times*.

"The perfect job for you," Adam had said.

And it was. Ever since she could remember, Zee Mallory had needed to *know*.

"You're going to be the death of us," her mother had told her when she was young— always asking questions of everyone in town, the shopkeepers, the Sunday school teachers, and Mr. Barton, who was of particular interest to Zee after he ran over the Brooks' little boy with his tractor. "A child doesn't need to know the answers to other people's lives, Zelda."

Zee used to think that *knowing* was her way out of Revere, Michigan. She'd read the newspaper delivered in the morning, the tiny notes of national news on the front page of the local paper, the births and deaths and accidents and marriages. She'd listen to the radio when the news came on and to other people's lives rolled out in conversations she overheard at the drugstore or market or the public library, gathering bits of personal information, discovering the hidden stories in the lives of citizens of Revere who had reasons to conceal them. Sheila Carney's illegal abortion, her aunt Brenda's affair with the pharmacist, Billy Reilly's trouble with the law.

Knowing would be her wings away from the lives her parents had led, and her grandparents and aunts and uncles, very much like death without the drama of dying.

But Revere and what she had missed by growing up in a provincial midwestern town, stayed with her in all the places she had lived since she left for college. In a place like Washington, D.C., or Philadelphia or San Francisco where she and Adam had lived, she might be found out as a Revere girl. And then what? She had to be vigilant. Even marrying Adam Mallory from a family of means and class in suburban Detroit didn't suffice.

So she became an investigator to "cover the bases," as Adam would say. Secrets were her business.

"What *factual* do you know about her?" Josie asked.

"She's thirty-three and an illustrator of children's books and god knows she must be self-sufficient since she's done it all alone," Zee said. "But that isn't a *fact,* Josie."

"Those kids came from somewhere," Josie said.

"She's moving here alone," Zee said. "That's all I know except the stories about the house."

The house had a reputation. A little run-down, the garden a jungle of weeds, rats occasionally reported in the basement especially during the spring rains, tenants changing almost every year, foreigners to the neighborhood. Rumors that a murder had taken place in the front bedroom, that a member of the FBI had rented the house for liaisons, greeting visitors at the door dressed up in women's clothes, high heels, and wigs. Nothing substantiated.

They gathered at dawn to watch Lucy's arrival.

Zee Mallory greeted any stranger as a new opportunity for conquest. Although she didn't think of herself in such military terms, considering her gestures of friendship open and genuine and uncomplicated. But she was canny enough to know that her way of arbitrating for her own emotional safety was to lay claim to friends as if they could not do without her.

"*Now* I remember Lucy Painter's photograph on the jacket of *Loop de Loup*, about the French monkey," Josie said. "Why did the stupid monkey have to be French?"

"What did she look like in the picture?" Robin asked.

"Pretty." Josie shrugged.

"I hope she isn't so pretty that August Russ takes an interest in her," Robin said.

"He's not going to take an interest in her, Robby." Zee pulled her scarf over her head as the wind picked up. "August's completely involved in writing a book about American culture and right now he's working on a chapter on that awful series with the Loud family living out their real lives on TV."

"*An American Family*," Josie said. "I never miss the program."

"Well, August told me how the Loud family fit perfectly in the introduction to his book."

"He talks to you?" Josie asked. "I didn't think he talked."

"You *know* he talks. He and I have long conversations about his work."

"Is that actually true, Zee?" Josie asked.

She shrugged.

"More or less," she said. "He's not exactly verbose, but yes, it's true."

It actually wasn't true. Zee had never had a *personal* conversation with August Russ, although she had spent hours in imaginary conversations with him as she went about her frantic life—her children and her troubled husband, school committees and telephone calls and her job and her friends, all of her friends who counted on her for this and that, who needed her to be the operating center of their lives.

Josie was right. August didn't talk about himself to anyone, not even to Zee, to whom everyone in the neighborhood spilled their secrets.

MAGGIE HAD CLIMBED out of the U-Haul carrying Felix and started up the steps to the yellow house, a backpack on one shoulder, no coat.

"Adorable," Lane said. "She looks to be Maeve's age."

"Should we go over and introduce ourselves?" Josie asked.

"Bring a coffee?" Robin asked.

"No, no, no," Zee said. "Let them get settled first and tonight we'll go over to the house with a rosemary plant or tulips or a cake. I'll bake an angel food."

The young mothers in Witchita Hills assembled from time to time, mainly on the Mallorys' front porch at dusk in summer, dark in winter.

They were women from other places, living in a city which had, particularly since the riots of April 1968, following the death of Martin Luther King, aspects of danger they had never anticipated when they left their insulated childhood homes in the middle of the country where change was slow to come.

"We have to stick together," Zee said, sitting among her friends on the railing of her porch the night of Dr. King's death. "We're a team now."

They would watch over one another's children the way grandmothers had done in their own youths, the way the aunts and uncles had done for one another. They would be family.

IT WAS BEGINNING to snow, a dusty dry snow gathering on their coats as the women dispersed, calling goodbye in voices loud enough for Lucy Painter, standing on her new front porch, to recognize the sounds of their friendship in the air.

"See you later," Zee called, running up the front steps, tearing off her scarf as she went.

So much to do and nearly nine already.

She opened the front door, rushing in the house just missing Onion, the tabby cat, who was lying in wait for a quick escape into the street. She kicked aside the twins' skates left in the middle of the hall, a cereal bowl of half-eaten Cheerios, the milk sticky on the floor, stepped over Blue, her old golden retriever, standing at the entrance to the kitchen considering, she assumed, whether to pee on the rug.

Adam was in his boxers, his bare chest raw with reminders of his tour in Viet Nam, late for work, always a little late for work but smart enough so far to get away with it, to get away with drinking mainly beer but too much of it every night.

He was buttering toast.

When she passed him to put the milk in the refrigerator, he smelled of cheap perfume.

"Greetings, Zelda. All the best," he said. "How does the high-pressured life of an at-home research assistant strike you this a.m.?"

She rinsed the dishes and put them in the dishwasher, grabbed Blue by the collar and walked outside with him, still in her coat, her cheeks numb to the cold.

"Are you planning to close the door?" Adam asked.

She watched him move through the kitchen, struggling up the back stairs. He was particularly slow this morning.

Mornings were the worst.

No one in the neighborhood needed to know about Adam in the morning. There were enough potlucks and dinner parties and dance contests and barbecues for everyone to know that Adam Mallory drank too much but he could be a warm and affectionate drunk, turning evenings at the Mallorys' piano into occasions that everyone remembered with his seductive bass voice.

Who would want to know about Zee's long nights in the queen-size bed, Adam belching and snoring, Zee on the far side, wide awake in the darkness imagining herself dancing with August Russ.

Someday she would do that. Some summer

evening, Adam out of town on one litigation or another, the boys at camp, she'd invite August to dinner, light the candles, chicken in thyme and white wine, chocolate mousse. She'd turn on Frank Sinatra in the living room.

August had moved in 1969 to the house next door to the one where Lucy would live, denied tenure in American Studies at the University of Pennsylvania. That much everyone knew. For reasons never made clear, certainly not by August, something had happened at the university, something *courageous,* as the women imagined it in their conversations over coffee or children.

Zee Mallory was only able to find confirmation that he had been denied tenure by his own department and chose not to contest the decision.

"There were no reasons given," Zee had said. "But I'd guess it was a matter of principle and August took a stand."

"Of course, that's exactly what he'd do," Lane said.

And Zee's guess became fact among the women.

His wife, Anna, already ill with breast cancer when they moved to Washington to be near her parents, died two years later at home.

It was after Anna died that the women took on August in earnest.

The young mothers, children of the fifties, women of the early seventies on the brink of a different tomorrow, liked to think they were half in love with August.

A crush, a soft flirtation, nothing of consequence.

At night, they sometimes lay next to their own husbands whom they had married, believing these men, silent victims of the war whether they had fought in Viet Nam or not, would escort them through the years without diminishing like their fathers had their mothers. Successful men—already diminished, occasionally replaced in the fantasies of their wives by an out-of-work college professor, a childless widower just past his fortieth birthday.

Upstairs, Adam was making too much noise, stomping his shoes on the hardwood floor, groaning as if he were ill, shouting *Where is my striped blue tie and my goddamn new boxers?* He had bad dreams and a cruel streak and a habit of falling into bed at night fully dressed.

Zee picked up the telephone. Lane would be at home. Not Robin, who was teaching photography at the Corcoran, or Josie, who would skip her lunch hour to make up for coming in late that morning, or Victoria, who was at work with her patients by the time they gathered for coffee. But Lane, in her third year at Catholic University studying for a Ph.D., had taken a medical leave of absence for the semester to "reconsider her goals," and mostly she was reconsidering at home.

These women were the core, Zee's dearest friends, her charges, her *chicks,* as she called them. Midwesterners all of them, even the larger circle in the neighborhood, and like mid-westerners who have moved east, they felt just off-kilter, wary of missteps, of personal failures as if they might be seen even to one another for who they really were. Not quite up to standard issue in the East, was how Zee thought of them all.

Zee was not self-assured but she had confidence. Small, thin with enough bottom and breasts, and thick golden blond hair worn shoulder length and mussed, as if she'd just jumped out of bed, to engage the interest of men and women.

SHE HUNG HER coat on the banister and ran upstairs, still in her nightgown since coffee had been early that morning to coincide with Lucy Painter's arrival. Adam was sitting on the edge of the bed making an effort to tie his shoe.

She grabbed her clothes out of the closet and went into the bathroom to change. Lately she didn't want to undress with Adam in the room. Not a matter of modesty, of which she had very little, but of disappointment. Slipping on a short knit skirt, footless black tights, a T-shirt long-sleeved without a bra, seldom a bra, she dressed in darkness. She grabbed the necklaces she

67

always wore, taken from her mother's costume jewelry shop in Revere, kept in a dish beside the sink, silver links and fake stones on chains, amber and amethyst and turquoise, the jewelry making little crackles when she moved. Sentimental, these necklaces, running up her neck like the collar of an Egyptian princess, a nod to the women of Revere for whom costume jewelry was the real thing.

When she came out of the bathroom, Adam was ready to leave.

A Friday morning in February. They had not made love since before Thanksgiving. The Sunday after Thanksgiving week to be exact. Her parents had been in the house for the holidays.

"We had a call when you were in the bathroom."

"From Lane?"

"From Vermont."

Zee's body tightened.

"They were just checking in to see if we're still around," Adam said. "No need to call back."

"If that's a backhanded way of asking will I go to Vermont with you," she said, aware her body was trembling, "I told you the last time you went that I can't bring myself to go."

"Got it. Don't worry. No problem!" Adam said, and pounded down the back steps and out the kitchen door to the driveway.

Zee stood in the window of their bedroom and

68

watched Adam get in the car, turn on the engine, back into the street. Was he looking? she wondered. Did he check if a child was behind the car? A dog?

She dialed Lane.

Lucy Painter possessed her imagination. What little Zee had learned about Lucy was her reputation for a solitary, independent life, and that from the real estate agent who could not exactly be depended on for character analysis. Or was it Maggie who had captured Zee's interest with her curly red hair, defiant, marching up the front steps of her new house holding her little brother in her arms.

She felt a familiar tension in her body, a focus, and by the time Lane answered the phone, a plan was forming.

"I have an idea," she said.

"For a neighborhood party tonight?" Lane asked.

"Later in the spring, but for now I'm thinking of asking Robin to take some photographs of Lucy's house and we'll give one to her as a Welcome to Witchita surprise tonight. That is, if Robin has time to do them before tonight."

"How sweet, Zee," Lane said. "I think it's a lovely idea."

"I'd hoped you would," Zee said, aware that it wasn't a lovely idea at all but a quiet way of insinuating herself into Lucy and Maggie's life.

Zee pulled the spread tight on the bed where Adam had been sitting, hurried downstairs, slipped into her coat, wrapped her scarf around her neck, and headed to the car for a meeting at school about the twins and then to the Library of Congress to research in the wake of Watergate what she could of President Nixon's Quaker childhood for an article she was writing.

But first she would cross the street and introduce herself to Lucy Painter.

Four

LUCY STOOD ON the front porch assembling herself as she was in the habit of doing when she gathered her paints and pencils and sketch pads to begin a new picture, hoping, as she spread out her tools, that the shadowy image surfacing in her mind's eye would resolve itself when she began to draw.

The first thing she did after arriving on Witchita Avenue, even before she walked around the house to see how the colors she had chosen looked, was to check if the telephone she'd ordered had been installed in the kitchen.

It was eight-thirty. Reuben would be walking Nell to school now, stopping afterwards by Sally's Café for a bagel and coffee where most days she and Felix would meet him after dropping Maggie off at her school and they'd stand outside the shop as long as they could until his train, Reuben with Felix on his shoulders holding Felix's legs with one hand and Lucy's hand with the other—his fingers like breath on her palm. They seldom talked then. Reuben waited until the last minute, they kissed and he hurried down the steps to the uptown subway.

"I'll call as soon as I get to the office," he said, the same every time he left her.

She would need another telephone in her bedroom, one in the studio. The telephone, as she saw it, would take on a life of its own.

She walked through the house room by room, the first and second floors, the studio renovated for light according to sketches she had made—a large front window facing the street, skylights in the eaves, the light bright because the house was situated high, though soft-shadowed on this cloudy February morning.

Standing in the living room, she felt a sudden rush of happiness.

Her house now, as if she were seeing it for the first time.

Only the long mossy brick steps were familiar, which she had descended on boneless legs that early afternoon of June 11, 1951, her arms around her father's work boots which for some inexplicable reason she had picked up, walking down the steps with great care so she wouldn't trip or faint or die on the way back to the car

71

where her mother was waiting impatiently in the front seat.

Qu'est-ce qui s'este passé? her mother had asked in her gravelly cigarette voice, gripping the steering wheel, as she did, even in repose.

But her mother must have already guessed what was the matter.

WHEN ZEE MALLORY flew into Lucy's house without knocking, Lucy was in the kitchen wiping out the cabinets, listening to Maggie babbling to Felix. Zee rushed into the room, bright-cheeked, bursting with excitement as if there were something specific to delight her in the arrival of this new family.

"Your door was open," she said, coming into the kitchen. "So I came to meet you and to see the house."

"Of course," Lucy said, unnerved.

"Such extraordinary colors," Zee went on, zipping through the house, running up the steps ahead of Lucy. "Which bedroom is yours?" Even before Lucy had a chance to point out her bedroom, Zee was saying, "Oh my god, I love the tawny brick color, so incredibly rich and vibrant. My whole house is white, white, white because I can never choose which color to use out of all those spectacular colors at the paint store. You'll have to help me."

Lucy found herself hurrying down the steps

after Zee had completed her tour and stopped in the hall to ruffle Felix's hair, to lay her hand on Maggie's cheek.

Lucy felt a twinge of fear or was it jealousy or hurt tightening the muscles in her shoulders.

"Be good," Zee said to Maggie as she headed to the front door. "Not too good."

Lucy slipped her arm around Maggie, who was standing beside her in a baseball cap with the bill pulled down over her eyes.

"Later, Lucy," Zee called. "The movers are on the way upstairs with your bed."

She watched Zee leave through the glass front door, take the long steps two at a time, a splash of pink from her wool scarf blowing behind her as she jumped the last three steps to the pavement.

The old twig bed Lucy had salvaged came through the front door and passed her in the hall as the movers struggled to carry it up the stairs.

"The big bedroom," she said to the movers. "The orange room at the top of the stairs."

She pushed her hands down in the deep pockets of her jeans.

"Be careful of the paint," she added.

"I hate that bed," Maggie said, racing upstairs after the movers heading to her new room.

Lucy's bed. The bed she had rescued before she even met Reuben.

Battered and hastily put together, a bed from a stage set of *Sleeping Beauty* performed at Provincetown Players years before when she was at RISD. She should have tossed it.

The movers finished unloading and Lucy paid them, paid them extra to return the truck she had rented, and took the children to Café Moxie.

"I love that woman, Zee, don't you, Mama?" Maggie asked while they waited for blueberry pancakes.

Maggie's spirits seemed to have soared since Zee Mallory planted herself in their lives.

"I've only just met her," Lucy said. "But she seems nice."

She didn't like Zee Mallory. Not her compliments, nor insinuations as if she had already decided to appropriate their lives.

And something else which had to do with Maggie.

"Maybe you'll get to be friends since you don't have friends in Washington, D.C.," Maggie said.

"Not yet," Lucy said. "But I will."

"She says she's going to give us a big party, didn't she, Felix? And she said there's a girl my age right across the street called Maeve but there's no child in her group exactly the right age for Felix. She promised to find one for him, pronto because she knows everybody."

"What group?"

"She calls it *her group*."

74

"I don't like groups," Lucy said, the words fell quietly to her lap.

"Zee,zee,zee,zee,zee," Felix said happily, slathering butter on his pancakes. "Zee is for zebra."

"Zee is for Zelda, she told me," Maggie said. "Zee/Zelda, she sometimes calls herself."

Something familiar and sweet in Maggie, a reminder of the months before she took out against Lucy, *the way daughters will do,* Reuben had said to her. *I'm sure it will happen with Nell.*

They got groceries and cleaning supplies at the Safeway, $150, a budget now that Lucy was on her own, the fate of children's books up and down, her last picture book a flop, no surprise subsidies from Reuben as there had been in the years he dropped by regularly with tacos or Chinese, a bottle of wine, staying for a few hours or the night or even a weekend. She'd refused support although he had offered.

"The children are my responsibility," she'd said.

"ZEE'S COMING OVER tonight with some of the neighbors to welcome us to Witchita Hills," Maggie said as they unloaded the bags of groceries in the kitchen.

"So fun!" Felix said.

"Not so fun for me," Lucy said, putting the milk

in the fridge. "I'm not ready to be welcomed here. I only left New York last night."

"They're just being nice, Mama. Don't be ungrateful."

"I am a little ungrateful," Lucy said.

But it wasn't a question of gratitude although she did feel diminished by the kindness of others.

She didn't want the neighborhood to see her house until it was entirely done.

The look of things mattered to Lucy. In New York City, she'd arranged the living room at angles, slate gray covers on the chairs and sofa, bright Indian cloth pillows she had made herself, rag rugs from Vermont, her favorite among her own illustrations hanging on the walls, also filled with photographs of people she knew, her children, Reuben, the mothers and fathers of strangers, photographs she'd picked up in the secondhand stores where she shopped, a woman who looked as if she could have been Lucy's grandmother as a young girl but was identified on the back of the photograph as Dorothea, Butte, Alabama. 1906. She had even bought an old spinning wheel and laced it with yarn to create the illusion of a family with a long history.

This belonged to my grandmother, she'd say even to her own children.

"I need help since people are coming to meet us tonight," she said to Maggie, sprawled out on the floor playing with Felix.

"I'll help," Maggie said.

"Me too." Felix pushed his dump truck into the corner of the hall.

From room to room, they opened up boxes, put away clothes and dishes and pots and pans, moved the couch, the kitchen table, Felix's bed so it wasn't under the window in case of lightning. They stood together examining the living room, Maggie leaning into her mother the way she used to do only months ago when they'd been one another's shadow.

"What about curtains?" Maggie asked.

"We never had curtains in New York," Lucy replied, surprised that Maggie should even have noticed.

"Our apartment was high," Maggie said. "No one could see us."

"Except from Sullivan Street."

"No one looked up from Sullivan Street."

Something about curtains was making Maggie irritable.

Lucy sat on the couch with her legs crossed, perspiration trickling down her face.

"It's so hot in here," she said, sidestepping the conversation, wiping her face with the sleeve of her shirt. "I need to learn about the furnace."

"I feel naked with no curtains." Maggie plopped down on the couch beside Lucy.

It was as if open windows had hit a nerve but Lucy didn't know what nerve.

Ashamed of me? was the thought that passed quickly through Lucy's mind like cold air on the back of her neck. *Of us?*

"Curtains block the light," she said.

"I like the dark."

"Then we'll get curtains for your room."

"And for the living room?" Maggie asked, crossing her legs, folding her arms across her chest. "It doesn't look like it did in New York. Do you think it will seem like *us* after we live here for a while?"

"I hope so," Lucy said.

"Maybe we should buy a new couch," Maggie said.

"Maybe we will," Lucy said.

"And white curtains with ruffles like Rebecca's apartment had."

In the kitchen, Lucy hung the favorites of her own illustrations—the picture of Belly sailing earthward and one of Fervid—a flashy red mole, his paws covering his eyes, sleeping next to a Chinese war god from her book *Fervid P. Drainpipe Lost in the Chinese Museum of Art.*

One Christmas, Ruben had given her an original illustration from *Pierre* by Maurice Sendak and one of Caleb, the dog, from *Caleb & Kate* by William Steig that Lucy particularly loved and had kept in her bedroom in New York.

She and Maggie worked side by side filling the bookcases, the chests of drawers, the closets, making the beds, hanging photographs and Maggie's artwork from school, Felix's scribbles, finding a place for the few treasures she had kept from her life, an unframed photograph of her father in law school, one of her mother in a long white summer dress, her hair full around her small, elegant face holding Lucy, maybe six months old, who sat upright and serious in her lap like a nineteenth-century portrait of a child. *Caroline Framboise Baldwin and her Daughter, Lucia,* her mother had written on the back as if she expected to die without a trace except this record of her life as a mother.

FELIX SAT ON the twig bed playing with his firehouse Playmobil, mumbling a narrative under his breath, a low buzz except for an occasional outburst. FIRE. SOMEBODY BURNING TO DEATH, he'd shout.

And then the fire engines—CLANG, CLANG, CLANG. Crash. SPLAT!

It was nearly four in the afternoon—Felix had fallen asleep among his plastic firemen, Maggie was in her bedroom choosing what to wear for the neighbors. The disappearing sun blanketed the living room with a wide gray band across the new floor.

Lucy unpacked her favorite picture of Reuben leaning against the Brooklyn Bridge, the skyline of Manhattan in the background. He was dark and thin, with an angular face, in jeans, a dress shirt with the sleeves rolled up, his arms stretched out resting on the railing, his feet crossed at the ankle.

She hung the photograph just inside the front door.

Perhaps they would be curious about her—a single mother. No man evident in her life. Especially the women would want to know more.

"Reuben Frank," she would say in her absent-minded way, as if they should know of him, someone mildly famous, and guess he was significant to her.

"Uncle Reuben," Maggie would say, and when they asked "Uncle?" Lucy would shrug.

She was refined in the keeping of silence.

THE LAST TENANT of 3706 Witchita had left a full-length mirror on the back of the closet door. Maggie stood in front of it, examining the outfit which she had chosen for the party. In New York, Maggie had worn turtlenecks, usually black, boys' jeans, lace-up boondocker boots. For Washington, she chose a flowered skirt her mother had made, mid-calf with tights and clogs. In her mother's makeup bag which Lucy seldom used, she found loose powder and tried to powder off the freckles sprinkled across her nose and cheeks.

Zelda was glamorous, unlike the other mothers Maggie had known, including her own who wore clothes she made herself or full skirts she bought in the children's department. No makeup, a mass of unruly black curls, bare feet except in winter when she wore striped tights and heavy boots.

Maggie was growing intolerant of Lucy's eccentricities.

She put away the powder, checked her face in the full-length mirror, and turned off the light in her bedroom so she could see outside.

It was dark and the streetlights formed a string of circles up the street. In one a group of women and children were gathered carrying presents.

"For us," Maggie said to Felix, who had come into her bedroom and was leaning against her legs.

There were no men in the group. No fathers.

She had never spoken of her father among her friends in the Village. She had never felt the need to bring the subject up. Her family was in place. She had a little brother, an Uncle Reuben, and many friends, including the dry cleaner and the pharmacist and the policeman who took care of their neighborhood—everyone in the Village, even strangers, especially strangers, felt like friends.

"Uncle Reuben is not my uncle by blood," she told her friends. "He's my uncle by choice."

HER FATHER *COULD* if he wished to materialize in Maggie's life but he was married to somebody

81

else. *Married.* Such a possibility had never entered Maggie's mind, just as his physical appearance had never taken shape.

He was above imagining, a figure who might one day float into her orbit and lay claim to his daughter.

And why, she wondered, zipping up her flowered skirt, slipping into her clogs, if he was married to someone, wasn't it her mother he had chosen?

She took hold of Felix's hand and hurried downstairs as the neighbors spilled into the hall.

Lucy was standing in the kitchen next to the sink with the flowers she'd picked up at Safeway, a mixed bunch of long-stemmed tulips wilting in her arms.

She had forgotten to put them in water.

Zee carried an iced angel food cake with pink letters, *Welcome to Witchita.* Her twin sons dragged their feet behind her. She hurried to the kitchen, setting the cake on the counter, a way she had of walking on her toes, as if she had been blown forward and couldn't stop moving.

"We've bought champagne," she said to Lucy, gesturing to the women following her into the kitchen in their black coats dusted with powdery snow, bright-colored scarves wrapped around their necks, carrying wineglasses. "Lane Sewall," she said, introducing them one by one. "And Robin Robinson and Josie Lerner. And Maeve and Teddy and Sara and Rufus. Victoria, who's a sort of happiness therapist, couldn't come."

Lane Sewall glided into the room, reedy and tall, pale with a cap of wheat-colored hair, just off pretty, a bottle of champagne stuffed into the deep pocket of her coat.

"Here," Zee said, taking the flowers from Lucy.

"I have a vase," Lucy said, her voice thin as if the wind had been knocked out of her by the neighbors whipping through her kitchen, Zee putting things in place as if Lucy were incompetent in her own house.

"Never mind, Mama," Maggie said in a stage whisper. "The glass works fine for a vase."

Lane had wandered over to the illustration of Pierre.

"Sendak?" she asked, talking with Josie.

"Josie and the beanstalk," Zee called Josie, who was more wafer-thin than slender and awkward, with olive skin and long flyaway hair which she wore straight.

"It looks like Sendak," Josie said. "Real?" she asked Lucy, who was leaning against the sink, a slow-creeping anxiety rising in her throat.

"Where can we put the presents?" A wiry blond boy, maybe seven or eight, stuck out his hand holding a red book.

"I'm Rufus," the boy said, handing the book to Maggie.

"I'm Daniel," the taller twin said, "and that's Luke." And "I'm Maeve, and this is my little brother Teddy." And "I'm Sara."

And then they were silent, standing quietly, staring at nothing across the room, not even talking to each other.

Nothing like the chatty New York children Lucy knew in the Village. She wondered if their silence had to do with her or her house or her children and whether she would grow to like them better than she did now, these perfectly attractive children. She wanted them to go home.

"Welcome to Witchita," Zee said, popping the cork on the bottle of champagne.

"We're smug about Witchita Hills," Robin Robinson said, a small woman, Lucy's height with a fleshy figure, thick hair in a ponytail, a self-conscious nervousness about her, fiddling with her hair, the scarf around her neck.

Pressed against her chest, her arms wrapped around it, she held a folder.

"Not smug, Robby. We're simply deliriously happy here," Zee said. "And you'll be happy too, Lucy."

"We hope you will," Lane said. "It's a very close group."

"This is the hour we meet for Chablis after dinner whenever we can," Zee began. "Just before the children's baths. But tonight we brought champagne for you."

She poured Lucy a glass.

"And presents."

"Just little things to cheer you up," Robin said. "It's always lonely at first when you move to a new place."

"It's lonely for you, Robby. Not for everyone," Zee said.

"So the house is yours or rented?" Josie asked, always after the particulars, scooping icing onto her finger and licking it.

"Mine," Lucy said.

"It's been rented out ever since we moved here five years ago," Josie said. "Mainly to creeps."

"Creeps and government workers," Zee said.

"The house has belonged to me for a long time and I've been renting it out," Lucy said, and then because it didn't seem sufficient explanation, "It belonged to my parents who are dead and I'm an only child."

"How awful for you but lucky for us that you're here now," Zee said.

"When the last tenants moved out in December I thought we'd try it in Washington because New York is . . ." She shrugged as if they already knew why she had moved.

"Because New York is so expensive and crowded," Zee finished her sentence for her. "No wonder you wanted to move. And the crime with children. It must be awful."

"I suppose," Lucy said. "And also it's . . ."

But she didn't seem able to form her thoughts or finish her sentences, and why, she wondered later, did she feel the pressure to begin to say something she had no intention of finishing?

"My grandmother was French," Maggie began out of the blue as if expecting currency from such a confession. "Only she's dead."

"French, how very interesting," Lane said, and Maggie nodded.

"I was the only person with a French grandmother at my old school in New York City," Maggie said.

"Excellent, Maggie, a small triumph," Zee said. "I don't think you'll find a single French grandmother at Lafayette Elementary." She put her arm around Maggie. "Now open your presents, you guys."

The prize—the "pièce de résistance," as Zee called it, was wrapped in tissue paper and yellow ribbon with a card: *From the studio of Robin Robinson.*

"From all of us to you," Zee said. "We hope you'll love it here."

Something about the package itself, the crinkly tissue wrapping of it, the wide grosgrain bow, sent a shiver down Lucy's spine.

"Open it, Mama," Maggie said, nervously sensing her mother's hesitation. "People want you to open it."

"Of course," Lucy said with a soft unnatural

laugh, a smothered giggle, realizing she must have been standing there blankly with *some* kind of expression on her face, maybe bewilderment, or fear or humiliation—some neuron shooting *watch out* in her brain.

"I will, of course I will," Lucy said, taking the package from Robin, setting it on the table, undoing the ribbon.

"How lovely . . ." she said with a kind of desperation—*lovely* a word she never used, her mother's word, the only English word her mother had thought more beautiful in English than in French.

She unfolded the tissue, careful not to rip it, to delay what she already *knew* instinctively by the ceremony of the evening, would upset her.

And it did.

A black-and-white 8½-by-11 photograph of the house taken that morning just after they had arrived in Witchita Hills lay in the tissue-paper bed.

"Robin is one of the best photographers in the city," Zee was saying.

"She is," Josie added. "With credentials from the Corcoran."

"We wanted you to have a Robin Robinson like the rest of us do," Lane added.

"Thank you," Lucy said when the room got quiet. "Thank you all very much."

Or *did* she thank them, she wondered later,

reading to Felix before he went to sleep. She must have said something although she couldn't exactly remember what happened next as they stood around the kitchen drinking champagne, eating the *Welcome* cake.

"Why don't you like the photograph, Mama?" Maggie asked after everyone had left.

"I do like it," Lucy said. "It's excellent."

"No you don't," Maggie said. "I can tell."

Lucy wrapped the remaining *Welcome* cake in Saran and put it in the fridge, sank into a chair, and pulled Felix into her lap for body warmth.

"It makes me feel exposed," Lucy said quietly.

Maggie was leaning against the sink, her arms tight across her chest.

"They're going to think you don't like *them,*" she said.

"I suppose they will."

Lucy had not intended to fall asleep with Felix. She lay down beside him, thinking of Reuben, the weight of him across her body, his face above her face, lips on her lips, his long legs against her legs, the way she fell asleep the nights Reuben was there.

I don't sleep with Elaine, he had told her. *Hardly ever. She is not that woman.*

What woman is she not? Lucy had asked.

She is not the woman with whom I sleep, he said. *You are that woman.*

She had decided that Felix would sleep in her

88

bed for the time being because he needed her, because she wanted him there and later when he had adjusted to his life in a new place he'd sleep in his own small bed in the room she had painted tangerine.

"Mama!"

Maggie's voice woke her up and she jumped out of bed in alarm.

"There's a man downstairs in the kitchen," Maggie said, standing over her bed.

"What man?"

"I don't know what man. I was putting away my clothes and I heard a noise and I actually thought it might be a cat who got into the house but it's a man."

"I was sure I locked the doors when the neighbors left," Lucy said, heading to the stairs.

"He's standing in the middle of the kitchen like he lives here," Maggie said.

THE LIGHTS WERE still on and Lucy tiptoed down the front stairs, stopping at the landing to peer around the wall so she could see the kitchen.

The man in jeans and a sweater, ripped at the elbow, the sleeves pushed up, was looking at the photograph Lucy had left on the kitchen table as if it were perfectly normal to walk into a house without knocking and look around.

"Did I startle you?" he asked.

"Of course you startled me," Lucy said.

He lifted his hands in a gesture of surrender—
large hands for a small man and broad as if he
worked out of doors.

"I walked in because the door was unlocked
and I'd seen you in the kitchen with the
neighbors." He pointed to the blue house to the
left of Lucy's. "I'm August Russ next door," he
said. "I've been anxious to talk to you about this
house."

"In the middle of the night?"

"I'm so sorry. Is it the middle of the night?" he
asked, and answering himself, "Almost midnight.
I guess it is. Sometimes I simply don't think."

He was boyish, his hair disheveled, his eyes
behind the thick lenses of wire-rimmed glasses
deep blue in the overhead light.

"I'm interested in your house."

"Why?" she asked. "It's just an ordinary house."

"I have an interest in its history," he said,
starting to sit down, but she waved him up.

"I don't know the history of this house, if that's
what you're hoping to find out," she said.

She was standing next to the kitchen table, still
dressed. Her glasses must have dropped to the
floor when she fell asleep.

"I'm a cultural historian," he said. "My field is
actually American culture and society." His
voice was deep and warm. "I'm a professor.
More or less a failed professor, and a widower,"
he added.

90

A little crazy, this strange man, Lucy thought. But there was something appealing about him— thick curly hair he wore long below the ears, strong cheekbones. Not a large man but compact, athletic, an element of surprise in his eyes.

Even before he took his leave, he was blossoming in Lucy's imagination.

His hand was on the doorknob and he was backing out of the house.

"I'm so sorry to intrude," he said with a wave. "But I'm glad to meet you. Very glad to meet you. See you anon."

And he was gone.

Five

ZEE STOOD IN her bedroom window overlooking the street watching Lucy Painter leave her house in a red parka, the collar up, the child, Felix, in her arms.

It was snowing, the damp, lacy flakes that fill the landscape, blanketing the black streets, the tops of cars, the branches of trees and bushes, a weighty, silent snow.

This was Zee's favorite kind of weather, rare in Washington but familiar from her Michigan childhood when she'd sit in the window seat of the old kitchen, a wood fire blazing in the stove, and watch the snow take over her field of vision.

The small farm just beyond the town limits of

Revere—with its run of chickens and pigs, two milking cows, no heat besides the two wood-stoves, no indoor plumbing until she left for college—could be erased in winter as she sat in the window waiting.

Across the street, next door to Lucy, August Russ was picking up the newspaper, under-dressed as usual, bare feet, Bermuda shorts, a button-down shirt with the tails hanging out.

She wondered if he drank himself to sleep at night, if he slept in his clothes, if he cooked for himself or sat in sorrow at the dining room table eating chips from a bag. She must remember to double her order with the vegetable co-op and take a bushel of beans and squash and apples and pears to him on co-op Tuesdays.

"Good morning, sunshine." Adam came in the door fully dressed, unusual for a Saturday. "The boys are watching cartoons and I've been under the impression that cartoons are off your list of allowables for children along with sugar and guns."

Zee heard him but didn't turn away from the window.

August must have called out to Lucy since she had walked to the end of her front porch and leaned out to speak to him. And then he went inside, leaving the door open, coming back in L.L.Bean boots and the hooded sweatshirt with the University of Pennsylvania logo which he often wore. He closed the door and headed down the steps, crossing his front yard to Lucy's.

"Cartoons are fine on weekends," she said.

"And guns?" Adam asked. "Guns are a good idea too, my treasure, my chosen one, my bride. Good thing I went to Nam on behalf of our great country and learned to use one."

He flopped down on the bed, and when Zee turned around, he was looking at the ceiling, his arms across his chest, tears running down his cheeks.

This was new, the fury of his bitterness. The tears. She could not find it in her heart to respond.

Weeks earlier, on January 27, they had been at the kitchen table eating dinner when the news of the Paris Peace Accords on Viet Nam came over the radio nightly news announcing the end of the war, providing for complete American withdrawal of troops and a truce.

Zee had just served macaroni and cheese, especially creamy, and she would not forget the menu that night since as the news was broadcast, Adam threw his plate against the window overlooking the backyard, splattering macaroni everywhere, breaking the window although the storms were left intact.

"Bull's-eye," he said, getting up from the table. "I'm an excellent marksman, boys."

He walked out the back door and slammed it.

The boys were stunned to silence.

"It's very upsetting for your father that he went to Viet Nam as an American to fight for us against the Communists and we lost the war," Zee said.

"You told us he was a hero," Luke said.

"He *was* a hero," Zee said. "He was given a prize for what he did called a Purple Heart."

"If he was a hero, why did we lose the war?" Daniel asked.

"It was not your father's fault," she said.

The rest of the story was too complicated to explain to the boys. She didn't understand it herself. She only understood that the war had changed her life and Adam's in a way that seemed permanent.

"I've been meaning to ask you, Zelda." Adam's voice was thin. "Did you get back to the people in Vermont?"

"You told me it wasn't necessary."

"It wasn't necessary to call back but . . ." He rubbed his shirtsleeve across his face. "I think you should tell them you won't be coming to Vermont in the near future."

Almost a year since she had been there with Adam, and he'd been twice without her. She wondered would she ever have the strength to go again.

She would not have replied to Adam's request in any case but the phone next to her side of the bed rang and it was Robin calling about the photographs.

"I shouldn't have taken those pictures until I knew her better, well enough at least to have a sense of who she is," Robin said. "I think she felt I was intruding and hated the photograph."

"My fault, Robby," Zee said, always willing to take the blame for things, disarming in her acquiescence. "Don't worry."

She hung up the phone and grabbed her clothes off the chaise heading to the bathroom.

"Have you gotten fat, lovey?" Adam called as Zee shut the door, planning to hurry across the street where August was talking to Lucy Painter.

"I don't know what you mean?"

"There must be some reason you don't want me to see you without clothes."

"There is," she said flatly.

She put on a V-necked long-sleeved black T so her breasts looked full enough but not large, no cleavage, hooked the necklaces, and opened a pot of rouge which she seldom wore but in the mirror her face had taken on the sallow look of illness. Too much winter.

She wanted to look pretty and she did.

By the time she ran downstairs, jumped over Blue, tearing his purple elephant to bits, Lucy and August were sitting on the brick wall in front of Lucy's house, Felix mounding the snow on the sidewalk into a small snowman.

Zee grabbed a coffee from the pot Adam had made and put on her coat.

"I'll be right back," she called to the children. "I'm heading across the street."

FELIX WOKE UP at dawn before Lucy was awake and was looking out the window when she opened her eyes.

"Snow," he said. "All over the place."

She felt the silence settling around the neighborhood, dusting on the windows, the clarity that comes of waking to the silence of a soft white morning. She dressed quickly, helped Felix into his overalls, checked Maggie, who was still asleep, and went downstairs.

August was on his front porch picking up the newspaper when she and Felix went outside to make a snowman.

"Busy?" he called.

"I'm going to be making a snowman with Felix," she said, pulling on her mittens and the orange cap Reuben had given her. "This is Felix."

Felix pulled his hood down over his eyes.

"I'll come over and help," August said. "Just a second."

And he rushed in the front door, returning almost immediately in boots and a sweatshirt, the morning paper under his arm.

"I'm sorry about last night," he said, settling on

96

the top step, his arms wrapped around his chest. "Cold, isn't it? Cigarette?"

She had gone to the first landing between her front porch and the long set of stairs to the sidewalk and was helping Felix roll a snowball into a bigger one for the belly of his snowman.

"No cigarette," she said. "But tell me does everybody in this neighborhood feel free to go into each other's houses? Is that how it happens here?"

"This is an overly friendly neighborhood but I usually don't walk into people's houses, invited or not. I'm a recluse."

Lucy gave him a querying look.

"I work at home."

The snow body was done and Felix was rolling up loose soil as well as snow for the head.

"He's getting dirty," Felix said, stomping his boot on the snow in a temper. "I want him white."

"Felix is a perfectionist," Lucy said, brushing off the soil. "I'll get a carrot for his nose and grapes for his eyes and my old red scarf and maybe you have a man's hat and pipe," she said to August.

"I might." He headed back to his house, returning with a man's hat.

"No pipe," he said, "but I have a cigarette."

He set the hat, an old-fashioned brimmed felt hat like one Lucy's father used to wear, on the snowman's head, stuck a cigarette in the place where the snowman's mouth would go, and tore off two small branches for Felix to stick arms on the round ball of his belly.

"This is great," he said. "I haven't done this since I was a kid and I don't have kids of my own. My wife is dead."

He pulled up the collar of his coat and lit a cigarette, blowing the smoke into a long cylinder that hung in the cold air.

"My wife—her name was Anna—died two years ago, early in the morning of August 30th. I had been up all night with her," he rushed on. "She wasn't the love of my life but the neighbors don't know that. They don't need to know that."

"Of course," Lucy said, on her knees in the snow beside Felix, thinking *What an odd, sweet man* as she helped smooth the snowman's body, brushing off the leaves that had collected, poking the carrot into his snow face, grapes for eyes.

"Done, Felix," she said. "A perfect snowman."

She kissed him on his cold nose.

It was almost eight, the sun striping the snow with glitter, the day warming. Upstairs in the house, Maggie had opened the window.

"Mom!"

"We're making a snowman," Lucy said. "Come on out."

"I can't!" Maggie said, and shut the window with a crash.

"Girls!" Lucy said, bemused. "That was Maggie."

August was sitting on the step while Felix began a second snowman.

"It's going to warm up later today," he said. "Will Felix be upset if it melts?"

"He'll be upset."

Lucy stood away from the house looking up where Maggie had been but the light of the morning sun was on the window glass and she couldn't see through.

"Zee tells me that you write."

"Children's books."

"I've never met a children's book writer," August said.

"*Write* isn't exactly the word for what I do. My books are for young children before they have language."

His beard was blond, Lucy noticed, glancing at the side of August's face, at his strong bones. A new, scruffy beard and she thought to ask him why with such fine bones he wanted to grow a beard. But that was just the wandering of her mind for *something* more to say, at a loss for words as she had a tendency to be.

"Language is the most important part of my life," he said, stretching his legs out in front of him, his bare calves resting against the snowy steps.

Lucy pulled a pouting Felix onto her lap, wrapping her arms around him.

"You're a professor."

"I was. Now I write books, which is why I'm interested in your house."

He stood and started up the steps to the house.

"Are you going in now?" he asked. "It's getting cold."

She looked up at him, standing on the steps, his bare legs red with cold, his hood up. He ground out his cigarette on the bottom of the step.

"I'm not," she said. "We're making another snowman, right, Felix?"

"No," Felix said. "NO more snowmen."

"A snow girl, then," Lucy said. "It doesn't snow every day, Felix, so we need to make one while we can."

August had leaned towards her, clouds of his warm breath between them.

"This is your house, isn't it?"

"I inherited it."

Her mother's name was probably on the deed. Caroline Framboise or Caroline Baldwin. Easy to look up at the Bureau of Records and Deeds, and if he really had an interest in her house, he could find that record too, so she must go downtown and register the house in her own name.

"I was given the house in the will of an old friend of my family's," she said, thinking how one lie leads to another and another and how many she had told and would tell in the future.

100

Lucy got up from the step, took off her mittens and shook them.

"I can't seem to help myself," August said, coming back down the steps, standing next to her. "I'm passionate about information."

In the clarity of morning light Lucy noticed that the soft crepey beige skin just under his one eye was quivering and then his one eye closed, and conscious that she was looking, he turned his head away from her.

He had a tic. That pleased her. So he must be apprehensive too, cautious with people. Something so small as a tic, but revealing. Lucy thought better of him already.

"I'm sorry," he said. "I'm so sorry. Obsessional, my mother used to tell me growing up. I get on a subject . . ." his voice trailed off.

Across the street, Zee Mallory was walking down her front steps with a cup of coffee, heading in their direction.

"I'm doing research for a book called *Biography of the Outsider* which isn't really a biography but ten stories of distinguished people—outsiders, all of them," he said. "So I'm always locked up in my house researching with too many books around me and too few people. I live entirely to myself."

"An academic book?" Lucy asked.

"More general than academic," he said.

Lucy brushed the snow off her coat.

Did he want her to ask why he was no longer a teacher or would he have told her if he'd wanted her to know. She wasn't particularly curious about secrets. Reuben had said that about her, finding it surprising, especially in a woman. Perhaps that was because she had her own secrets. Or perhaps her mind was too full of children and Reuben and the imaginary creatures who peopled her books. All her head could hold.

"I'm going in to fix breakfast," she said, taking Felix's hand. "We'll be back to make the snow girl later."

"I'm looking for a reader," he said.

But Zee was coming up the front steps.

"Hi, guys," Zee called. "Such a gorgeous day!"

"It is." Lucy opened the front door and walked with Felix through the hall into the dining room, glancing out the window as she passed.

August was seated on the top step and Zee, one boot resting on the step where he was sitting, her hand on her hip, her head thrown slightly back, was laughing.

She caught Lucy's eye and waved.

MAGGIE WAS SITTING on the edge of the kitchen table in jeans and Lucy's best blouse that Reuben had given her, long-sleeved, billowy at the wrist, and she always wore it for dress.

Some nights when he came to her apartment

after the children were sleeping, he'd lock the bedroom door, shut off the light so the room turned luminous with filtered streetlights. He'd slip the blouse off her shoulders, his lips soft against her temple, her eyes, her lips. And then, as if to the rhythm of a soundless song, he'd undress her, sliding the blouse over her hips, unbuttoning her trousers.

"I borrowed your blouse," Maggie said.

Lucy opened the fridge, her back to Maggie.

"Last night when that man came in the house, I called Uncle Reuben but his wife answered the phone and said he was already in bed. I don't even know her name."

"Her name is Elaine," Lucy said, taking out eggs.

"How come we don't know her?" Maggie put her feet up on the chair.

"Reuben is my friend and editor. I've never met his wife."

"Not even for dinner?"

"Reuben and I are not that kind of friends."

"Then I guess Uncle Reuben's not going to be much use to us now that we live in Washington, is he?"

"Not if we're in danger of strangers in our kitchen," Lucy said, trying to be light, "but I doubt we'll be in that kind of danger, darling, and we weren't last night." She cracked the eggs into a bowl. "Bacon?"

"I want bacon," Felix said.

"Bacon has too much fat," Maggie said. "And carcinogens."

"The man you saw last night lives next door and his name is August," Lucy said. "He's interested in our house."

"Well, he's a creep to walk right in it without knocking." Maggie picked up Robin Robinson's photograph from the kitchen table, setting it on the counter against the wall. "You know about carcinogens?"

"I do."

"And they're okay for Felix to eat?"

Lucy shrugged, scrambling the eggs, putting two pieces of wheat bread in the toaster and pouring orange juice, taking the bacon back to the fridge.

"No carcinogens for you today, Felix," she said. "Too bad."

"You want to know what Elaine said?" Maggie asked.

"I don't ever call Uncle Reuben at home."

"I got his number from information," Maggie said. "I told Elaine that I was your daughter and we had an emergency and she said she was sorry to hear about it but Reuben didn't take professional calls at home and she hung up before I even had a chance to say this *wasn't* a professional call."

Nine o'clock, a Saturday morning. Occasionally

Reuben worked in the office on Saturday. Maybe August, still on the front porch with Zee Mallory, would let her use his phone. She didn't want to call Reuben in front of the children and the phones upstairs had not yet been installed.

"I'll be right back," she said to Maggie, and thought to add, *Please take off my favorite blouse and put it back in my closet.* Which she knew she should have said but didn't.

"Don't bother with August. Use my phone," Zee said. "No problem at all. The front door's open. It's always open. Just don't let Onion, the cat, out."

The sun was moving overhead, the snow had stopped, and cars were sliding along the street. She crossed carefully in order not to fall.

"You know," Zee said, coming up behind Lucy, "I'm sure August has a phone but none of us has ever been inside his house as far as I know. He has a trunkload of secrets. That's what we all think. You probably already know he was denied tenure at the University of Pennsylvania."

"He told me he was a failed professor," Lucy said.

"Or a hero. There's that possibility too," Zee said, opening the front door, calling upstairs to the boys—*Luke, Daniel, I'm back*—she headed into the kitchen, Lucy following behind.

"Zelda," someone, a male, shouted from upstairs, "the goddamn cat got out."

"Oh dear," Zee said. "Phone's in the kitchen. Take your time."

She rushed past Lucy and out the front door.

THE PHONE IN Reuben's office rang once and he answered.

"I thought you might be there," Lucy said when Reuben picked up.

"Lucy!"

He took a deep breath, an exasperated breath that signaled irritation.

"You know what happened last night?" he asked.

"Maggie called information for your number. A stranger was in our kitchen in the middle of the night."

"I am in New York, Lucy. There's nothing I could have done about a stranger in your kitchen," Reuben said.

He was still talking when Lucy replaced the receiver and walked through the Mallorys' kitchen and out the front door just as Zee, holding a fat yellow tabby with his back claws exposed, was coming in the door.

"The call was long-distance," Lucy said, "but short."

"Never mind," Zee said. "Come over anytime and bring Maggie. Use the phone. Have a cup of coffee. The door is always open."

Six

THE DAYS, EVEN the dark days of late February and the beginning of March, were almost agreeable to Lucy. August Russ would arrive at the back door with his manuscript around nine, shortly after Maggie left by the front door for school to meet Maeve at the Sewalls' house and walk arm in arm with her down Witchita Avenue.

Maggie was given to long periods of staring out the kitchen window at nothing in particular, or lying on her bed on her back, her legs against the wall looking at the ceiling, occasionally short with Lucy. Some days, she didn't talk at all except to Felix.

"Are you missing New York?" Lucy asked.

Maggie shook her head. "I love Witchita Hills," she said. "I love everything here but this house and the people in it except Felix."

Normal behavior, Reuben had said to Lucy. *She's just the age for trouble with her mother.*

Mornings after Maggie left for school, August would sit at the kitchen table while Lucy made Felix's breakfast and washed up the dishes, started the laundry for the day, dropped Felix off at play school, and then she'd sit down across from him sketching in pencil ideas for *Vermillion the Three-Toed Sloth* while he *talked* his book out loud to her.

"I thought you meant you needed a *reader-ship*," Lucy had said to him the first morning.

"A listenership is more like it. I need to talk out what I'm thinking."

The particular morning of the fifteenth of March, August was in especially high spirits—Lucy remembered the date later because that early morning Adam Mallory had slammed his car into the empty passenger side of Miles Robinson's new Toyota station wagon as Miles was on his way back home from the market with milk.

She didn't hear the crash but August arrived late that morning to tell her.

"The Ides of March have come," he called in his rolling baritone as he came in the back door. *"Ay . . . but not gone.* Did you hear the crash?"

"I didn't. I must have been doing the laundry. Who crashed?"

She poured August a cup of coffee.

"Adam Mallory. He blamed it on President Nixon and the news that Nixon is reinstating the death penalty. Adam was so furious that he failed to check his rear-vision mirror coming out of his driveway this morning and shot back in reverse straight into the passenger side of Miles Robinson's car."

"Sorry, man," Adam had said to Miles according to August, *"but the goddamn president of the United States is a criminal and should be hanged in a public forum."*

108

Miles had shrugged.

"No problem with that except to remind you that the body-work bill for the Toyota will be delivered to your address." And Miles headed up the hill with the milk.

After August arrived, Zee Mallory rushed over, knocking on the front door with her tiny fists. She apologized to Lucy for the commotion after the crash, retelling the scene again and again to the neighbors.

"Adam just takes the news too seriously," Zee said, reporting the incident in detail. "I worry sometimes, especially now—these damaged vets out of Viet Nam and we've lost the war there and Adam's such a darling man."

And then she headed down the steps and across the yard to August's house to deliver the same news.

"Zee?" Lucy called.

She looked up.

"August is here having coffee. Would you like to come in?"

"Oh no," Zee said too quickly. "Never mind. Not at all. I'm in a rush. Tell August hi."

And she dashed across the street, hopped into the driver's seat of her van as if she had suddenly forgotten an appointment.

IT WAS WARM for March, not warm enough for the shorts which August was wearing with sandals and his University of Pennsylvania sweatshirt, standing with the manuscript spread out on the kitchen table when Lucy came back.

"That was Zee."

"I heard her voice." He was leaning over the manuscript with a pencil making some notes. "Are you becoming friends?"

"Why do you ask?"

"I saw Zee walking with Maggie to school today before the accident when I picked up the paper on my porch."

"Maggie always walks with Maeve," Lucy said, wondering was Maeve sick this morning and should she call Lane.

"Maeve wasn't with her."

She slid into the chair opposite him, her mind spinning.

She would ask Maggie about that when she came home from school, ask her *why* had she walked to school *with Zee* and *where was Maeve*. It was nothing really, she told herself, nothing to be concerned about. Nevertheless.

The picture in her mind's eye was Zee Mallory, a little taller than Maggie but small, reaching down to take her daughter's hand, Lucy's only daughter and why would Zee have an interest in someone else's child. Was this jealousy sneaking in, Lucy wondered, something she had never known before. Not even with Elaine.

Holding hands had been her favorite thing with

Maggie, just walking down the streets of the Village holding her soft or mittened hand like a treasure resting in her palm.

She couldn't bear the thought of Maggie's hand in Zee's.

"Were they holding hands?" Lucy asked August in spite of herself.

"I was too far away to see." He lifted his head. "You don't like her, do you?"

"I don't trust her," Lucy said.

"Oh that," August said. "Trust."

The word hung in the air between them, a life of its own.

Lucy opened her sketch pad. She would draw Vermillion with his detaching heart, she thought. Poor complicated Vermillion, so slow and witless. He loved too much. He dreamed that he could swallow Violet, the cerulean blue bird—*cerulean,* Lucy liked the sound of it—swallow her whole so she would never leave him.

Vermillion's little boomerang heart flew out of the top of his head, wings flapping, into the sky, she wrote at the bottom of the page.

She was always glad to see August, relieved morning after morning, that he was there in her house with his pages, his rumpled hair and wire-rimmed half glasses perched on his nose so he could see her over the top of them.

"I've been thinking about the hypothalamus," he was saying, examining the pages of his

manuscript. "Did you know about the ther-
mometer in our brains—a tiny, sensitive gland
called the hypothalamus that sounds an alarm
when something *dangerous* crosses our path."

"I didn't know that."

Lucy was sketching Vermillion and his
detached heart whipping above his sloth head
hoping to obliterate the image of Zee and Maggie
walking down Witchita Avenue maybe holding
hands.

"When I started this book—well I actually
started it while I was still at Penn before I came
up for tenure and was denied—but I've always
been interested in the outsider and how the
outsider is *feared* in spite of the fact that we're
all outsiders in America or once were." He got up
from his chair, pacing as he often did when he
was talking. "I've been thinking how *difference*
creates a sense of shame and shame leads to
deceit. Am I making sense?"

Lucy was listening at a remove, pleased by the
sound of his voice, by the way the top of his head
looked when he was reading his manuscript so
only the mass of golden brown ruffled hair was
visible and his large hands holding the paper. But
it never occurred to her that August Russ, a
scholar of American culture with a certain turn of
mind, had anything in particular to *say* to Lucy.

"The outsider in American culture. That's the
basis for my thesis."

Something personal had slipped into August's conversation that Lucy couldn't identify. Did he expect more from her than simply listening, which she had been doing morning after morning. Was there a request in his demeanor that she mistook for simple conversation. She was suddenly restless.

"What are you saying to me?" she asked.

"I was talking about the hypothalamus," he said.

"I mean what else?" she said.

Her stomach tightened the way it sometimes did with Reuben. The kitchen turned claustrophobic with expectation. She got up and turned on the water for tea.

"Do you think we're friends?" she asked, her back to the stove. "Becoming friends?"

She wasn't sure what was going on with her, whether the restlessness she felt, adolescent, awkward in its discomfort, was an attraction between them. Or had nothing to do with August. She had no initiation in the rites of love affairs. Reuben was the only man she had ever desired.

What silent message might she be sending to August Russ these mornings together, herself uncertain. Was it simply that she wanted Reuben to know she was desirable to someone else, or was it possible that August *did* desire her. Or was this restlessness simply a translation of lingering hope and her own longing.

113

"We're certainly becoming friends," he said, shuffling through his papers.

When the telephone rang in the kitchen, Lucy picked up quickly, thinking it was Reuben calling. A Thursday after ten, already he was late getting to the office.

But the principal of Lafayette Elementary was on the line to say that Maggie's permission slip to go to the Smithsonian Museum of Natural History had not been signed by her parent, rather by Mrs. Mallory, and was that agreeable to Lucy.

"Otherwise Maggie will not be allowed to go on the field trip."

"How did that happen?" Lucy asked.

"I don't know how it happened, Ms. Painter. I only know that the permission slip was unsigned and Maggie said you had forgotten and Zee Mallory, who was with Maggie, signed it for you."

Lucy's knees gave and she leaned against the wall.

"I didn't actually *see* the permission slip," Lucy said, hoping she wasn't reflecting poorly on Maggie, but she hadn't seen it that she remembered. Or had she? Had it been left on the kitchen table for her to sign and in the confusion of a new house and Reuben and the general anxiety reflected in her twice-misplaced keys and wallet and even her winter coat left at the library in the middle of a storm, she had forgotten as well to sign the permission slip.

"The buses are loading now. All I need from you is an okay that Mrs. Mallory's signature is sufficient permission. This is protocol, Ms. Painter."

"I understand."

"I know you're new to the D.C. public schools but permission slips are very important," she said. "It might be a good idea for you to check Maggie's book bag every evening until you've established a routine."

"I'll look into that," Lucy said coolly.

She hung up the phone and put her head against the back door, tears thick in her throat.

"What happened?"

"Nothing," she said.

"Something happened, Lucy. You're white as a ghost."

"Zee Mallory signed Maggie's permission slip to go to the Smithsonian."

August shook his head.

"But nothing awful happened, right?"

"Something awful did happen," Lucy said, slipping into her coat to pick up Felix. "Zee Mallory is appropriating my daughter."

BY THE TIME Lucy got home from play school with a sleeping Felix, August had made bacon, lettuce, and tomato sandwiches on wheat toast.

115

"Hot chocolate?" he asked.

"I love hot chocolate."

She carried Felix upstairs, putting him down in his own bed.

"I just wanted to finish our conversation," he said. "So I made lunch."

"Your conversation!" Lucy sat down to lunch. "Sometimes it's a miracle we understand each other."

"You and me?"

"All people, *even* you and me."

"I don't particularly want to be understood."

"Maybe I don't either."

But she was pleased that August felt at home in her house, that he cooked for her, serving sandwiches on plates with a napkin and hot chocolate with marshmallows melting in the heated milk.

"I like it that you're here," she said, "just doing normal things that people do who live together. And then you go home."

He laughed.

"You've never lived with someone?" he asked.

"My children but they're my children."

"What about their father?" He reached behind him and got a paring knife out of the drawer to cut up a pear.

"I never lived with him."

"Does he, the father, matter to you?" he asked. "I was thinking recently that I loved my wife—I believe I loved my wife but she didn't matter as much . . ." He hesitated. "I suppose as much as she should have."

"He matters," Lucy said, disarmed by August's curious honesty. "More than he should."

"Well these mornings here at your house are perfect for me," he said. "I come, you listen, sort of listen but enough to make me happy, and then I go home."

"And what's for you at home?"

"Myself, of course," he said, looking at her, his blue eyes grave under the heavy-lens glasses. "I am for me at home."

"That's enough for you?"

"Plenty."

His face softened. She imagined his lips on hers. He would lean across, any moment now, he would lean across and kiss her.

And he did lean across the table, stretched his arms, his hands touching hers but with a purpose that did not include romance.

"We are in a lost time. You know that."

"You mean *now?*"

"Now. 1973. Exactly." He tipped back in his chair, his arms folded across his chest. "So much changed in the sixties, the war, the rights of women, civil rights, the vote, protest against the war. On and on. I was getting my Ph.D. in Chicago and you were in college but that time was upheaval with a purpose. Now we've drawn back into our shells, wondering what have we done and what do we believe? And is there any purpose to our lives?"

"I don't think in generalities," Lucy said. "I think about Vermillion, my three-toed sloth, but not sloths. Not sloths as a group."

He smiled at her.

"You are a funny girl, you know," he said. "I suppose I *do* think in generalities, but if I were to give *shame,* for example, a specific story so you'd understand what I mean by it, I'd talk about myself. That's the starting point always, isn't it?"

"What story would you tell?" Lucy asked.

He laughed. "I said *if* I were to tell you a story . . . but I'm not. Among other things . . ." he started, and got up then, put his plate in the sink, finished the rest of his hot chocolate. "I seem to have left the introduction to the book on my desk at home," he said. "I'll be back."

"What other things?" she asked as he was leaving.

"Other things?"

"You said *among other things.*"

"Oh, yes, I did," he said. "Two minutes. Don't go away."

ZEE MALLORY WAS on the porch of her house with the electrician when August came out of the front door of Lucy's house and crossed the lawn

118

to his own. She wondered was it possible August visited Lucy more frequently and used the back door, and the fact that he visited at all was somehow crushing that morning after Adam's accident.

She paid the electrician, closed the door, and called Lane, who would be home and mildly depressed, as she tended to be by nature and always around noon.

Coffee and donuts were still on the kitchen counter untouched. No one in her group had come for coffee that morning.

"Laney!" Zee said when she heard Lane's weary voice. "I'm loaded with donuts and coffee and nobody showed up today. Do you think it was because of Adam?"

"I think . . ." Lane hesitated. "I think I'll come over and have one donut, no more."

They sat on Zee's front porch, in jeans and boots and sweaters, their arms around their knees.

"Nobody knew exactly what to say about the accident," Lane said. "Adam's so funny and warm when we have our parties that his temper surprised me."

"He's a litigator."

"I know."

"He likes to fight," Zee said.

"I suppose that makes you lucky. I wish Will fought." Lane took a second donut. "Or talked. I dream about August Russ."

"August?" Zee shrugged. "It looks very much as though he's fallen for Lucy."

"For Lucy?"

"I see him there morning after morning at least in the last week and a half—he walks across the yard and must walk right in the door as if she's unlocked it for him."

"I can't imagine him in a relationship."

"But he was married after all and Lucy's available and next door and he's single."

Lane laughed and leaned her shoulder into Zee's.

"Oh, Zee, so are we available!"

"Not me, Laney. I love Adam. Even when he goes through these dark tunnels, I know he'll come out on the other side. It's marriage, right?"

"Marriage?"

"Well . . . that's my general understanding about marriage."

"I was pregnant," Lane said.

"You never told me that."

"With Maeve, and Will was seeing another girl at Northwestern, just beginning to see her since we'd broken up a couple of weeks before. And there I was single and told him about the baby, and being a man of probity, he married me. Or we married. However you want to look at it."

"Oh, Laney, you make it sound so empty."

"It's lonely."

Zee leaned her back against the steps, her hand on Lane Sewall's knee.

"I'm so sorry, Lane."

"Not worth being sorry about and I'm a whiner. You know that." She hugged Zee around the shoulders. "And you're my best friend."

Zee watched Lane walk home, her coat open blowing behind her.

She was pleased with Lane's confessions about her marriage although the pleasure she took in the misfortunes of others disturbed her.

Lane wasn't *her* best friend. No one was. Even when Zee was very young, she had never had such a friend, only the illusion of shared connections, she thought.

As she got up from the steps to go inside, she noticed that August was on his way back to Lucy Painter's.

"Busy day?" she called out.

"Pretty busy," he waved, hurrying up Lucy's front steps.

Zee watched as he went in the house. Then she went back inside and put her coat over the banister and slipped down to the floor where Blue was sleeping, leaning against his fleshy belly, her hand resting on his fur.

LUCY WAS JUST cleaning up after lunch when August returned with a folder which he opened on the kitchen table, rubbing his hands together as if he were preparing to give a lecture, anxiously, she thought later after he had left.

"I don't want you to think that the reason I didn't get tenure at the University of Pennsylvania had anything to do with the quality of this book," he said.

"Oh I don't," Lucy said. "I don't even think about that at all."

"I was asked to leave Penn for personal reasons."

"You don't need to explain," Lucy said. "I'm happy to listen and very interested," she added, worried she might have hurt his feelings.

"Actually," he began, looking over his half glasses across the table at Lucy, "I don't know whether to tell you this but I will because it's on my mind and usually I say what's on my mind, whether or not it's a good idea."

"Of course," she said.

"Remember the first time I came over in the middle of the night?"

"I couldn't forget."

"And I said I had an interest in this house."

"Yes, you walked right in without knocking," she said lightly, hoping to intercept what felt like rising tension in the room.

"Did anyone ever tell you that a man died in the basement of your house?"

"No," she said quickly, her throat constricting. "No, no one has told me that."

"Well he did. A long time ago, in 1951. I didn't know about this house when Anna and I bought our house next door but I already knew about the man who died here. At the time of his death, he had a national reputation as President Truman's most trusted advisor and he happens to be one of the ten biographical sketches in my book."

LATE THAT NIGHT, after Felix and Maggie were sleeping, after Lucy had written and torn up a long letter to Reuben about August's book, fearful the letter would be opened by his personal assistant, she stood in her bedroom window and watched August at the long table in his dining room. He was typing, a glass of wine beside the typewriter, his broad hands flying across the keys.

For hours now, her heart had been beating irregularly. And this was nerves, she told herself, not a heart attack but an impossible wish that in August's research he would never discover that Lucy was the daughter of the man who had died in her basement.

She wondered would August be back as usual the next morning after Maggie left for school and what would he have to say then, what would he ask her and what would she reply.

She would lie certainly. She knew how to do that.

Seven

REUBEN CALLED LATE the night of March 15 to say he had *reason* to come to Washington. He had acquired a scientist for George Barnes Books who lived in Washington and was writing a book on genetic engineering, and after Reuben met with the writer at lunch on Monday, he would be able to slip away, maybe for as long as two days, to spend with Lucy.

"And the kids," he said. "I cannot wait."

It was after midnight when Lucy replaced the receiver on its cradle, which, late as it was, meant Reuben must have left the apartment with Elaine and Nell sleeping and gone to his office just to call.

She couldn't fall back to sleep, tossing and turning so Felix, snuggled beside her, tossed too. Finally she got up, tiptoed downstairs, and made a batch of sugar cookies from the recipe of her French grandmother whom she had never met. She was still up when Felix scrambled out of bed and came downstairs.

"Uncle Reuben is coming to visit us," she told him, giving him a cookie.

"Uncle Reuben, Uncle Reuben. Maggie . . . guess what?"

And he flew upstairs, waking his sister.

"True story?" Maggie asked when she came down still in her pajamas.

"He is. He'll be here on Monday."

"I can't believe it, Mama. I thought we wouldn't get to see him until he took us to the beach."

"I knew he would come," Felix said. "We are his favorites. His very favorites in the world."

Sometimes Lucy felt badly for Nell. Surely Reuben's heart was with Maggie with her thick red hair like his, her brown eyes wide-set but dark like his, her strong mind and fierce spirit. Reuben had even said himself that Nell was *wimpy*. His word *wimpy,* and who wouldn't be with Elaine commanding her young life.

"His favorites in the whole world?" Felix asked.

"In the whole world."

When Zee knocked on the door to invite Lucy to coffee with the other members of the group of friends, Maggie answered the door and told her about Uncle Reuben coming to Washington, pointing out his picture on the Brooklyn Bridge to the left of the front door.

"His name is Reuben Frank," Maggie said.

"Your mother's brother?"

"He's our uncle, but not by blood," she said as she used to tell her friends in the Village. "He's our uncle by choice."

"How lucky to choose the one you want," Zee said, heading into the kitchen where Lucy was making oatmeal. "Fun for you. An old friend from New York City?"

"My editor," Lucy said.

"Very attractive," Zee said. "I just came to ask you to come over for coffee if you can."

"I can't," Lucy said. "Not this morning."

She had no intention of crossing the street to Zee's front porch for that morning. The women in the neighborhood assumed an intimacy, even passing on the street on the way to the post office or the market, as if they *knew* Lucy in ways she didn't know herself. There was something unsettling about their almost religious sense of community.

"Do you hate Zee?" Maggie asked, taking a cookie.

"Of course not."

"That's how you act and all she wants is to be friends. She's that kind of person."

"Friendly," Felix said.

"I'm sure she's friendly," Lucy said, setting the yellow bowls with Cream of Wheat and brown sugar on the table. "And I don't *hate* anyone, Maggie. None of us in this house hates."

She wasn't going to talk about Zee Mallory, not this morning when her heart was trembling with happiness that Reuben was coming to see her.

When Maggie left for school—Lucy checked to make sure that she *was* walking with Maeve, looking out the dining room window as Maggie crossed Witchita Avenue and headed down the street with Maeve Sewall, their arms around each other's shoulders.

"Uncle Reuben will love our new house, Mama," Felix said. "Maybe he can stay until Christmas."

"Christmas is months away, Felix," she said, kissing the top of his head, kissing her own hand, testing the softness of her lips on skin.

Reuben's voice had been pure joy—that's how it played in her ear—*he was coming to see her, he could hardly wait, he could taste her lips, he could feel the heat of her body against him.*

It was the constancy of nights without Reuben that had been difficult. Not that Lucy was accustomed to him in her bed, but he had been with her at least two nights a week for years really, and though he stayed *all* night only occasionally, needing to go home since his excuse to Elaine was that he was working late or seeing an author or having dinner with another editor, it was the nights he stayed that she missed.

"It's Uncle Reuben on the phone," Felix called from the kitchen. "He *is* coming. He says he really is coming."

Lucy took the phone from his hands.

"Reuben?"

"Hello, darling,"

"Hello, Reuben."

"I'm so happy to be seeing you," he said.

"Me too," Lucy said.

"So think about whether we'll get hours together, just us, in the day maybe while the children are in school, maybe late at night. I want to be sure there's enough time with you to last me weeks until the next time and the next and the next."

WHEN LUCY CAME back from taking Felix to play school, August was in the kitchen with coffee and an English muffin in the toaster.

"Good news!" he said.

"For me too."

"I finished the introduction last night. Can I read it to you?"

Lucy took a deep breath.

"What about later?"

Since Reuben called, she had forgotten about her father as a subject in August's book but she didn't want talk this morning, certainly not about the book.

"Later this afternoon?" August asked.

"Maybe tomorrow morning when you come. Now I have too much on my mind."

He picked up a page from the stack of manuscript.

"Just the first page to give you a sense of the range of the book."

"No, August. I can't. My editor is coming."

"Today?"

"Not until Monday but I'm so exhilarated. He never comes to work with me and now he is and I can't settle down."

She opened the fridge and took out a yogurt.

"Want one?" she asked.

"I have the feeling you'd rather be by yourself. I understand that," August said, gathering his papers, flushed, probably embarrassed. "I like to be by myself too, most of the time, all of the time."

"August," Lucy said, "would you like a yogurt?"

"Yes, yes. I would like a yogurt. Strawberry."

She set a carton of strawberry yogurt and a spoon on the table.

"Sit down," she said. "I can't talk to you about your book today but you eat your strawberry yogurt and I'll eat mine. I want you to stay."

Something in the way he was standing, rubbing his hands together, his cheeks bright with color, his pupils dilated as if in darkness, reminded her of a moment she had had with someone else, someone she knew well, in this very kitchen, in the morning light—but the memory flew through her mind just beyond catching.

She reached over and touched his hand.

LUCY AND MAGGIE cleaned all of Saturday and Sunday, scrubbing out the refrigerator while Felix drew pictures of superheroes in his drawing book. They vacuumed and washed the woodwork and cleaned the mirrors and picture frames, opened the windows to air out the house even though it was chilly. They rearranged the living room, creating a circle of furniture around the fireplace, and filled a tub with forsythia and pussy willow next to the couch.

"Let's get a new couch, Mama."

"You think?"

"This is so ugly and old and dirty."

Lucy stood in the living room imagining Reuben's arrival at the front door of this house he had known about since she met him. And there in the living room, the beautiful cantaloupe living room with forsythia in full bloom, was a brand-new couch. Certainly he would think that Lucy was doing well, that her life was full of opportunities and friendship. It might even sadden him to think she was doing so well without him. Fill him with longing for what they could have together. Reuben Frank and this strong, resilient woman who was the mother of his very favorite children in the world.

"We will get a couch," she said.

And they did at Conran's in Georgetown, in a pale yellow soft material with puffy cushions and rolled arms. August and Will Sewall helped them carry it from the VW van into the living room.

"I'll probably be tied up with my editor until Wednesday," Lucy told August Russ. "But after that . . ."

ON MONDAY MORNING, Lucy was up at dawn, showered, dressed in the tight little green blouse that Reuben loved and one of the short skirts she made herself and tights.

She wandered through the house seeing it through Reuben's eyes, the new couch at an angle in the living room, the soft light from the side windows falling randomly across the pale yellow, the cantaloupe walls. In her studio, she pinned her unfinished illustrations for Vermillion on the clothesline between the rafters, a bowl of purple tulips on her drawing table, the windows open just enough to give a sense of air.

Maggie left early for school, sweetly, kissing Lucy goodbye for the first time in days, taking the front steps two at a time. Lucy took Felix to nursery school for the day expecting Reuben would arrive sometime after two, but in any case before Maggie got home from school at three-thirty, so at least they would have an hour together until the children came home. She had made coq au vin for dinner and bought a bottle of good red wine at the liquor store on Connecticut Avenue. She had never spent so much on wine but the wine merchant had promised it was worth it.

The telephone was ringing as she came into the house with groceries, croissants for breakfast, thick sliced bacon. Possibly Reuben had already arrived in Washington on the shuttle.

She caught the phone on the third ring, dropping it first, breathless from hurrying up the long front steps.

But it wasn't Reuben.

It was his chirpy assistant calling to say that Reuben had pneumonia.

"Pneumonia?" Lucy's breath vanished.

"He got sick on Friday and he was worse on Saturday and his wife took him to the emergency room at New York/Cornell Hospital and they diagnosed pneumonia and that's where he is."

In all the years Lucy had known him, Reuben had not been sick, nothing more than a sinus infection. He had never missed work.

"Reuben never gets sick."

"Well, he is now and he hasn't been top form for the last few weeks, at least in the office."

"He said nothing to me about feeling ill."

"Well, Reuben is close to the vest about things. I don't know how well you know him."

"I know him," she said, and she wanted to tell the assistant everything she knew about Reuben. And then to kill her.

"Can you tell me anything else?"

"Only that Elaine called this morning and said that he was in the hospital and could not take phone calls and I should call this new science writer we've signed up to write a book whom he was coming to see in Washington today. And Elaine said that I should call you because he was going to talk to you about your new children's book. That's all I know except that he will reschedule."

"I can't talk to him?'

"Elaine says no calls. He needs complete rest. I'm sure you understand."

I CAN'T CALL? He can't call me? Rueben Frank can't call the mother of his children to tell her he is ill, that he wishes it were she with him and not Elaine. That he loves her beyond all measure. That he will come soon and live with her forever.

Lucy leaned against the wall.

"Thank you," she said.

"No problem," the assistant said.

And then Lucy called the hospital and asked for Reuben's room.

"I can't connect you," the operator said. "Mr. Frank is not receiving calls. I'll connect you to the nurses' station on his floor."

"I am Reuben's sister," Lucy said when a nurse answered. "I'm calling to inquire about him."

"His wife is here if you'd like to speak with her."

"No thank you," Lucy said. "I would not."

"Mr. Frank's condition is critical but stable," the nurse said. "I'll tell him you called. Are you his only sister?"

"I am," Lucy said, and hung up.

His only sister.

She threw on her parka, left the groceries on the kitchen table with the flowers, hurried out the front door, down the steps, climbed into the van and drove. She drove into Maryland along Connecticut Avenue to Knowles and left on Rockville Pike and back into Washington, left on Porter Street to Connecticut, relieved to be in a familiar place, but she needed to drive and wished it were not in the city so she could drive the old VW as fast as it would go, maybe up to 70 miles an hour and she'd open the windows so the cold damp of March blew over her, stripping her of everything she had known, all of her past, until at the end of this long journey she would be emptied out of history, left with only herself, and her children, her darling children.

She drove all the way south on Connecticut Avenue until it became 17th Street and intersected with Constitution Avenue, turning left on Constitution past the Washington Monument, the Museum of American History, the National Gallery of Art—past the Capitol where her father had worked before he died—she had not even brought the children downtown to see the city of Washington, to tell them their grandfather worked at the very center of it where north and south and east and west meet at the Capitol, at the heart of the heart of the known world. She turned right on 1st Street, past the Supreme Court, left on East Capitol, the Library of

Congress to the right, the Folger Shakespeare Library, wandering through the back streets of Capitol Hill to a right on 4th Street, and again on A Street—two blocks to 426 A Street, S.E., a blue clapboard, three stories with a turret.

She had not been back since she was twelve.

Traveling slowly down A, she almost drove by the house and then she saw the bay windows on either side of the front door and remembered the afternoons when she got home from school and kissed her fingers and touched the window on the right and then the one on the left.

"Why do you kiss the windows?" her father had asked.

The scene came back to her intact, a small frame in her mind's eye.

Her father standing at the door in his suit and tie, just her father, his hand out to take her hand.

"I kiss the windows for good luck," she'd said.

"But that's superstition," he'd said. "Do you believe kissing the windows will bring you good luck?"

"I do," she said.

"I'm glad to hear that," he said. "Then I will kiss them too."

Tears spilled down Lucy's cheeks.

Whatever it was that August Russ had written in his book about her father would be wrong, the wrong story. August would misunderstand everything about Samuel Baldwin, was bound to

135

misunderstand. Lucy would go over to August's house sometime when he was at the library or the grocery store and take his stupid book and burn it.

She drove deeper into Capitol Hill collecting the landmarks of this geography for reassurance that she could find her way in and out of that neighborhood again where the houses were unspecifically familiar. But she could get lost unless she were vigilant, and as she drove, just in the process of navigation, the weight of Reuben's absence lifted and she was capable of going home.

It occurred to her more as an intellectual observation than raw fear that Reuben could die, and if he were to die, she wouldn't know about it until, with the rest of his authors, she was notified by the chirpy assistant. He was in fact no more than an editor in her life. She had no claim.

Spring 1973

Eight

APRIL 17 WOULD have been Samuel Baldwin's seventieth birthday and Lucy celebrated it, as she always celebrated her father's birthday since her children were young, at breakfast with Felix and Maggie, clicking wineglasses full of orange juice.

She had been up since dawn slipping out of bed without waking Felix, tiptoeing downstairs barefoot to make cupcakes—cupcakes for breakfast with chocolate icing in honor of her father at seventy. Standing at the counter measuring the sugar and salt and sifting the flour, she tried to imagine how he might have looked at seventy. Not necessarily old but would Samuel Baldwin have been an old man had he lived? She had thought of him as already old when he died at forty-eight, his hair sprinkled with silver, heavy pouches under his gray eyes, a certain weight of years to his bearing that made him seem older than the fathers of her friends.

Outside the kitchen window August Russ was on an extension ladder cleaning out the gutters. Cool and damp, no rain expected, becoming cloudy after noon, according to the weather report, but he was wearing a short-sleeved T-shirt, his jeans rolled up, his back to her.

139

August still came every morning with his book and sat at the kitchen table, worried about the introduction which he couldn't get right. The subject of the man who died had not resurfaced. She had come to trust that he had no reason to assume she was related. Sometime before the book was published, if it was ever published, she would ask to read it and see for herself, or so she told herself and pushed her fears to the back of her mind, where Reuben claimed she stored all troubling matters in her life.

Reuben was still unwell. Pneumonia had *leveled* him, he told her. He'd been run down, concerned about the future, conflicted about his marriage, and susceptible to illness. He hoped to come to Washington in May. He seemed too weary to care about anything, even his work.

"To your grandfather at seventy," Lucy said when the children had sat down for breakfast. "Happy Birthday, my darling father." They clicked orange juice glasses. "My father was my favorite person in the world."

"Our grandfather is dead," Maggie explained to Felix, delighted to take charge of bad news while Felix, indifferent, plunged his spoon into the sugar bowl and licked it.

"Did I ever tell you that I was only twelve when he died?" Lucy asked.

"You tell us that a lot," Maggie said. "And I've told *you* that twelve is old enough." She took the rubber band out of her ponytail, shaking loose her curly hair. "I'm almost twelve."

"Twelve is not old enough to lose your father," Lucy said, knowing even before Maggie had spoken that she'd stepped into a black hole with her daughter again.

"I lost my father before I was even born," Maggie replied smugly.

She lit the candles on the table, ignoring Felix, who was slowly pouring orange juice onto his eggs.

"Every year on his birthday you say *my father was my favorite person in the world,*" Maggie said.

"Because it's true and now my favorite people in the world are you and Felix," Lucy said quietly, wishing to dignify the occasion.

It was the only *true* fact Lucy had told her children about her father and at least in the near future, the only thing she would tell them. They didn't know that the old yellow clapboard farmhouse was the same house in which their grandfather had died. They didn't know who their grandfather had been or how he had died or why. They didn't even know his name, not his real name. Lucy referred to him as Sam Painter.

On the table beside her bed, Lucy kept his photograph in law school, next to the black-and-white photograph of the children with Lucy and

141

Uncle Reuben—a photograph she had insisted on taking against Reuben's "better judgment," in February before they left New York. In the smaller photograph, her father is leaning against a lamppost, wearing sunglasses and a suit, his hair long and wavy, a fedora at an angle, his face in shadow. He could have been any medium-height, slender man in his early thirties, holding a cigarette to his lips.

"What happened to my dead grandfather?" Felix asked.

"He died," Maggie said. "So he was dead."

This seemed to please her as she licked the icing off the top of the cupcakes.

"How come he died?"

"Sometimes that happens to a person when they get older," Lucy said.

Felix was cutting his cupcake in little pieces with a dull knife, eating it very slowly in his organized, determined way.

"Will you die, Mama?"

"A very, very long time from now," Lucy said.

"We all die," Maggie said happily, taking her dishes to the sink, slipping into her jacket, lifting her backpack over her shoulder. "Nothing is forever, Felix."

She kissed the top of Felix's head and headed out, no longer kissing Lucy goodbye when she left for school. Making a point of it.

Lucy was still sitting at the kitchen table with

Felix when there was a knock on the window and August waved.

See you later, he called. Then he moved the extension ladder around to the front of the house, out of sight.

It was almost nine, not a school day for Felix so Lucy picked up his Playmobil and headed to her studio where he would play on the floor while she worked.

The studio was spare—a table made from a door supported by sawhorses, the door stripped of stain and splattered with paint, a high stool, Lucy's drawings in progress hanging on a clothesline which angled from beam to beam under the pitched attic room. She could work for hours standing up.

Lying on her back in these breaks from work, whole scenes from her life in no particular order would float across her horizon, sometimes at a great speed—a red scooter she rode up and down A Street, the torn inside of her father's beloved Chevrolet smelling of gasoline, the tiny German clock on Reuben Frank's desk in Manhattan exactly like the clock on her father's bureau in the house where they had lived in Capitol Hill.

Some mornings when Felix was at play school and after August packed up his book and went home, she wondered if *this* was what it felt like to go crazy.

As she passed the dining room window lugging

Felix upstairs to the studio, she made a mental note that it was getting late and Maggie was still sitting on the front steps waiting for Maeve Sewall to come out of her house.

MAGGIE SAT ON the top step of her house, her arms folded across her chest, watching the Sewall house for a glimpse of Maeve, who was late as usual, always late, forgetting her lunch box or her library book or her social studies project. Most days they arrived at school after the bell, which upset Maggie, who was careful with the impression she made.

She was in a bad humor. Lately she was furious at this and that—impatient, irritable, combative, and for no particular reason except the inescapable fact of hating her mother.

This morning of her grandfather's birthday, she was sickened by her mother's testimonials about a man whom Maggie and Felix had never known, who had died with a secret so terrible that his grandchildren had never been told his real name. She was forced to sit at breakfast while her cheerful mother toasted this stranger, making believe that the orange juice in wineglasses was champagne.

Maggie was tired of the way Lucy pretended everything was fine when it was not.

Pretending is what the Painter family did.

Across the street at the Mallorys' house, the

twins were fighting on the front porch, Daniel slamming Luke with his book bag, Luke falling backwards, crying for his mother, his mother calling down from the upstairs window to "stop fighting." Maggie didn't like the Mallory twins. Certainly not Daniel.

But she loved their mother, Zee, who kissed her fingers and ruffled her frizzy red curls and told her she was the most *interesting* girl Zelda Mallory had ever met.

"You're so delicious," Zee would say with delight.

Across the street, Maggie saw Maeve Sewall come out of her front door and look up at August Russ's house. Her head was tilted back, her hands covering her mouth, and all of a sudden she was screaming.

AT HER DRAWING table working on Vermillion's round black eyes, Lucy heard Maeve's scream and rushed to the wide window of her studio just as August Russ, clinging to the top rung of an old extension ladder, floated by the window.

Lucy watched almost to the last moment.

The way he fell like a dancer, not even struggling, one leg straight out as if to catch his landing. The expression on his beautiful face registering only mild surprise as he passed close enough for her to reach through the glass and touch his olive skin. Nothing in his appearance to suggest alarm. Simply wide-eyed astonishment that in the middle of cleaning gutters, he had found himself in a free fall careening to a reversal of fortune at 8:40 in the morning.

The avenue was sprinkled with children on their way to school. In the corner of her eye, she caught a splash of red, maybe Maggie's hair as she crossed the street where she was meeting Maeve. Not in harm's way, no child as far as Lucy could tell at that glance would be in the line of the ladder's fall.

She held her breath, mesmerized by the elegant drama of August's descent, by the way he turned his head just so, assessing, as if he had time to reconsider. And then just before he landed, the ladder almost parallel to the avenue, she turned away from the window, unable to watch the inevitable conclusion. His body splayed on the asphalt as it would be, under the extension ladder—the fall three stories high, the ladder heavy. Like railroad tracks covering him, is how Lucy saw it, having no trouble imagining the scene.

The children on their way to school had begun to scream. They must have seen the extension ladder as it went down. Maggie must have seen it hitting the street directly in front of the Sewalls' house not far from where she would have been waiting to walk to school with Maeve.

Lucy sank to the floor, resting her head on her knees, barely breathing.

After she discovered that her father had killed himself, after she saw his feet dangling and knew not to look up at this face, she was for a moment completely rigid. And then in a single move turning, she had rushed up the stairs, grabbed his boots in her arms, opened the front door and closed it behind her. Since that afternoon, her body in an emergency went quiet as if she were falling into sleep, her eyes open, fixed on a spot which at that moment was the taupe-colored underskin of her arm.

She could hear the shouts of children but in the distance.

In the corner of the studio, Felix, stretched out on his stomach, was playing war with painted metal soldiers which had belonged to Lucy's father when he was growing up.

"What happened, Mama?" he asked.

"I'll check in just a second," Lucy said, her voice too thin to carry.

"I'm playing Viet Nam," he said.

In the distance, the screech of advancing sirens.

Across the room, Felix had gotten up from war and was padding barefoot across the hardwood floor in the direction of the window overlooking Witchita Avenue.

"Don't climb up to the window, Felix," she

said, but she was satisfied that he was too small to reach the view of the street.

Downstairs, the front door opened and slammed—a crash against the wall, the sound of breaking glass.

Maggie was racing up the steps to the second floor, her sneakers slapping through the bedroom and into the closet where the steps to the third-floor studio were concealed.

Lucy didn't move, didn't lift her head, waiting for Maggie and her accumulating temper to arrive, bracing for it.

"Mama!" She was out of breath. "What are you doing sitting on the floor? Can't you hear the sirens?" Maggie asked.

"I hear them," Felix said quietly.

"Something terrible has happened and *all* the other mothers are helping out."

Lucy's heart was beating in her throat, uneasy with Maggie, even a little afraid of her as she headed ferociously into her last year of child-hood.

"August Russ fell from the top of his house and his ladder fell on top of him and he's lying in the street maybe dead and the ambulances are coming and the fire department and every other mother on this street is there trying to save him."

Lucy grabbed the edge of the table and pulled herself up.

"Dead?" Felix asked.

"Not dead," Lucy said quickly.

"Zee says the children have to go to her house and talk about what happened."

"Not go to school?" Lucy asked.

"We *can't* go to school until we've expressed our feelings," Maggie said. "Zee's calling the principal to tell her that we *witnessed* what happened right in front of our eyes and we *need* to talk about it."

Lucy was speechless.

"Do you want to know the details?" Maggie asked. "Or do you care?"

"Of course," Lucy said.

"On his head he fell and blood is coming out of everywhere and it's *very* awful."

Felix's face buried in her shoulder, not the sort of boy who had an interest in blood.

"So are you coming with me to Zee's house?" Maggie asked. "Or not?"

"It's a school day," Lucy said.

Maggie turned away, slapping down the stairs, out the door calling, *"The Brooklyn Bridge photo with Uncle Reuben crashed,"* slamming the front door so the broken shards of glass made a pinging zinging sound.

Lucy rested her chin on top of Felix's head.

"Are we going to the Mallorys' house with Maggie?" he asked.

Glancing out of the window, Lucy saw Will Sewall, surrounded by a circle of children, was

149

holding an end of the ladder, lifting it off of August's body, gesturing to the children to move out of the way. The Sewalls' unpleasant beagle, normally burrowing in the neighborhood trash, seemed to be licking August's head but Lucy was too far away to see anything except the dog's brown and white tail wagging.

"No, Felix," she said, shifting Felix, who was getting heavy in her arms. "We're not going to the Mallorys' house yet."

Nine

ZEE MALLORY WAS first on the street to see not the fall itself but August under the ladder lying in the avenue two doors down from her house. She was in her bedroom, half dressed, watching her twin sons head down the hill towards school when she saw the ladder just before it crashed to the ground.

And she ran.

Down the steps in her short jean skirt, a pajama shell, barefoot, gaudy necklaces slapping against her chest, jumping the last step where Onion was sleeping, over the Tonka trucks and a paint set strewn across the rug and Blue with his purple elephant in his mouth, out the door, into a chilly spring day.

Kneeling beside August Russ, holding his face in her hands, she whispered:

150

"August, do you hear me. It's Zee. Zelda. It's me."

Blood was spilling everywhere. Zee knew a little about everything, spread wide but thin, nevertheless she knew enough not to move August, to barely touch him until the ambulance arrived.

"Laney," she called to Lane Sewall, who was leaning over the railing of her broad front porch with the lunch boxes that Teddy and Maeve had forgotten. "Take the children to my house. I'll call 911."

Will Sewall had hurried out of the house, zipping up his trousers as he ran, no belt, no shirt, headed towards the children who had gathered around the ladder.

"Should I lift the ladder off him?" Will asked.

"The ladder, yes, but don't touch him," Zee said. "Just sit with him until the ambulance comes. Lane can take the kids to my kitchen so they don't have to see the blood."

Zee stopped by the Lerners' house, Josie already in the car off to work.

"Help Lane out with the kids," Zee said. "They can't just stand there watching August die."

Josie got out of the car.

"Is he unconscious?" Josie asked, unflappable.

But Zee was already heading to her house and the telephone.

She rushed up the steps, through the front door,

over the laundry tossed at the door to the basement, a cereal bowl on the floor of the kitchen, a street hockey stick. She picked up the telephone to dial 911.

Adam was in the kitchen in his boxers.

"Busy morning?" he asked.

Zee turned her back on him.

"North on Connecticut Avenue almost to the District line," she instructed the dispatcher. "Then LEFT at Witchita," she said. "You can't miss it. He's in the middle of the street."

By the time Zee got back to Will Sewall, the children of the neighborhood still bunched together like nesting birds, she could hear sirens in the distance.

"I couldn't get the kids to move," Will said from the ground, sitting next to August.

"Any signs?" she mouthed to Will.

"He's breathing."

"But completely out?"

He nodded.

"Is he going to be all right?" Maggie Painter asked, her freckled cheeks pale, her arms tight across her chest. "He doesn't look so all right."

"We have our fingers crossed," Zee said, running her fingers lightly through Maggie's hair. "You help take care of everyone, Mags. I'm counting on it."

"I will," Maggie said.

"They'll go to my house," Zee said to Will.

152

"And I'll follow the ambulance to the hospital."

"What about school?" Will asked. "Shouldn't they go to school?"

"They need to be together. We have to talk to them," Zee said. "It's too much reality for their little minds to take in without our help."

AT THE PUBLIC telephone, outside the emergency room, Zee waited for someone to answer her home phone that rang and rang. The answering machine could have been disconnected by the boys. Electricity hounds, those boys, always sniffing around the house for something to connect or disconnect, for sparks to fly.

Lane answered the second time she called.

"Everyone's here," she said. "I called the school to tell them what had happened and that we're keeping them here for a while and then the mothers will walk them to school."

"Thanks," Zee said.

An emergency room nurse stopped at the phone and pointed to Zee's feet.

"Shoes are required," the nurse said.

"Of course, of course I'm so sorry. I rushed here with a patient."

She reached into the enormous bag in which she carried a change of clothes, her makeup, a new line of cosmetics she'd found the last time she'd been to New York called *natural for aging girls,* a nightgown, *Endgame* in paperback, a

153

picture of Samuel Beckett she'd torn from the *New York Times* with the intention of sticking it up on her bulletin board where she kept pinups of dead writers and jazz musicians the way she used to do with six-foot posters of James Dean, tampons, some weed in an old ring box, a birthday present for her father wrapped to send, a mini bottle of Merlot and her ballet slippers which she slipped on her feet while the nurse watched.

"So who is at the house?" Zee asked.

"Josie and me and the kids," Lane said. "I was wondering should we ask Lucy Painter?"

"Is Maggie there?"

"She is."

"I've asked her to help since she and Maeve are a little older, but I never know what to do about Lucy. She's so distrustful of us. Your call, Laney."

Lane hesitated.

"Maybe I won't call Lucy."

ZEE PUSHED THROUGH the doors of the emergency room and went to the reception desk to ask about August.

"Trauma is where they've taken him," she said. "But you'll need to leave your name and wait here."

"Zelda Mallory," Zee said.

Her mother's choice Zelda, not a family name

154

like her brothers had been given. But Zelda for F. Scott Fitzgerald's crazy wife.

"Are you a relative?" the receptionist asked.

"Mr. Russ doesn't have relatives in Washington," Zee said. "I'm his friend. His closest friend," she added.

She knew nothing to report except that August's wife was dead, that he had grown up someplace in New York State and she believed his parents were dead. He had been to the Mallorys' house for parties but Zee had never been in his house. No one as far as she knew had been inside his house since Anna had died unless it was Lucy Painter.

She sat down on one of the turquoise plastic chairs in the waiting room, slipped off her shoes, tucked her feet under her so she wouldn't tap,tap,tap them nervously on the linoleum floor as was her tendency, and thought about Lucy.

Not that she didn't like Lucy, Zee told herself, uncomfortable with judgments. She *did* like her. But Lucy was not easily accessed. Something odd about her, at least, in the way she regarded a person with caution, even a neighbor like Zee Mallory or harmless Lane making chili in the Mallorys' kitchen at a potluck supper in Lucy's honor.

"Zelda Mallory?"

A doctor, young, short, plump, and balding, was summoning her to the entrance to the emergency room.

• • •

LUCY WAITED UNTIL the sirens disappeared to a thin thread of sound rising from Connecticut Avenue and then she looked out the studio window. The ladder had been moved to the curb along her side of the avenue. A few people, mainly women, were mingling on the sidewalk just beyond a small ragged circle of darkness— surely blood—where his head had landed.

She dialed Reuben Frank. It was nine and he would be at home, going late into work since he'd been ill. It was safe to call. Elaine would have left already for the office and Nell was at school.

"Reuben?" Her voice was tentative.

"Bad timing," he said in a whisper.

"Bad timing here too," she said, her voice breaking.

"I'll call back soon as I get downtown."

She heard the click of the receiver.

She opened up her paints, turned on the overhead fan to low, just enough to move the air around the room, and pulled up a stool for Felix, spilling out crayons, taking a stack of paper from the shelf under her work table.

"I don't want to make pictures today, Mama," he said. "I want to be Captain Amazing."

"Captain Amazing is on vacation."

"Uncle Reuben said he was going to send me a Captain Amazing costume with a red cape. He wrote me that in his letter."

156

"I know," Lucy said, a flash of anger.

Reuben had promised a Captain Amazing costume weeks ago, said he would package it and send it.

"I'll remind Uncle Reuben when I talk to him today."

She leaned over and began to draw, no thought in mind beyond the frame of August falling slow-motion past her studio window—a general sense of rising panic. She reached for a green pastel and a yellow one trying for vermillion.

It was almost ten, and on the avenue, the women in the neighborhood had probably gathered at Zee's house with the children, including Maggie, who ought to be in school.

She would have liked be the kind of woman who could leave the safety of her house and join the neighbors assembling for coffee and intimate conversation, gathering in the wake of a disaster. To be *normal* with an ordinary childhood and parents about whom nothing remarkable could be said. But she didn't seem to have the necessary mix to merge into a common stream.

After her father's very public disgrace, she removed herself. The mark of shame had worked its way inside her skin.

"Mama?" Felix had stopped drawing and slipped off the stool where he'd been sitting. "What happened to the Magic Train?"

The Magic Train had been Reuben's invention.

157

He would rush in the front door of the apartment on Sullivan Street, less than an hour of free time to spend between the end of the work day and dinner with Elaine and Nell at his own apartment.

"I'm here, guys," he'd call in his booming voice. "The Magic Train brought me back to you."

Felix was putting the crayons back in the jar, the paper for drawing back on the shelf.

"Mama?"

She looked over at him on the floor now, arranging the crayons by colors.

"I don't want you to tell me what happened to August Russ."

MAGGIE RUMMAGED THROUGH Zee's fridge for more juice, putting "Lucy in the Sky with Diamonds" on the boom box. Lane Sewall was calling for silence.

"Children." Her voice was hushed. "Does anyone have any questions about what happened?"

"August Russ was on a ladder cleaning out his gutters and fell backwards all the way down to the street and he was squished under the ladder right in front of me," Maggie said.

"That is not true," Zee's taller twin, Daniel, said. "I happened to see *you* on your front porch so you couldn't have exactly seen *him*."

"*We* were right there," Luke said. "Me and

Daniel just like next to where he fell and Mr. Russ hit so hard we could hear it."

"It was terrible," Sara Robinson said sadly, hanging her small head.

"I was not on my front porch," Maggie said. "I was standing almost beside you, Daniel, but as usual you weren't paying any attention to me standing there so what do you know about where I was."

"There was a lot of blood," Daniel was saying.

"Maybe he was killed," Maeve said.

"He wasn't killed, Maeve," Lane said quickly. "He was injured."

"His eyes were closed tight," Sara said. "I could see."

"Me too," Maeve said. "His skin looked purple."

"Is August Russ dead now?" Maggie asked.

"We don't know how August is yet," Lane said. "We're here to talk about the accident."

"I don't want to talk about it," Sara said. "I want to go to school and do my work."

IT WAS ALMOST ten when Zee's Ford economy van flew up the avenue and turned into the driveway. Zee hopped out, throwing her arms around Lane, who was waiting on the front porch and headed to the kitchen.

"So tell us how he is," Josie said.

"Gotta go to school now, chicks," she said, embracing Josie.

Zee stopped in the middle of the room and held up both hands, waiting until Lane had come back into the kitchen.

"Everyone quiet?" she asked.

The children nodded solemnly.

"August is alive," she said.

As if she were announcing the end of a war, her hands palm out, the fingers spread wide.

"Now, time for school."

The children clapped and cheered, jumped on the kitchen bench, threw their arms around each other, their voices rising to the ceiling. They headed for the front door.

Zee didn't stop them. With Maggie in tow, she went through the hall, passing Lane and Josie. Lane fell in step.

"Zee, if you've got some time," Lane said, "later. I'm home all day."

Zee draped her slender arm over Lane's shoulder.

"Oh, Laney, today couldn't be a worse day for time but soon . . ."

She squeezed Lane's hand.

And she was off, swinging Maggie Painter's hand back and forth, the other children following in higher spirits than the day had promised.

IN NEW YORK City, Maggie had thought of her mother as beautiful and brave. "Brave" was Uncle Reuben's description of Lucy.

"Your mother has the courage of a lioness," he'd said, and Maggie's heart swelled with pride.

No other mother among her friends, even her favorite mothers, could be described as *brave,* only her mother, Lucy Painter, who had no husband, had never had a husband or boyfriend. Only an Uncle Reuben coming in and out of the apartment, maybe twice a week.

But after the Painters moved to Washington, Maggie's image of her mother splintered until there were mornings such as this one after August's terrible fall, when Maggie liked to pretend Zee Mallory, arriving in her life like a lightning bolt, was her real mother, her flesh and blood.

She would sit in her bed at night, a book open on her knees, thinking of Zee, pretending she was at the Mallorys' house, Zee coming up the steps with her jangling necklaces and her bright, breezy smile to kiss her good night.

"Today is my grandfather's birthday," Maggie said as they walked to school. "We always celebrate it even though he's dead."

"That's lovely," Zee said. "It's a wonderful way to keep him alive in your heart."

"He's been dead for a very long time, since my mother was twelve. Isn't that a little weird?"

"But very nice to think of him alive even though he isn't here."

Maggie shrugged.

"We don't know *anything* about him. Felix and I don't even know his real name," she added.

"Your mother knows his name."

"She calls him Sam or *my father*."

"He was not Sam Painter?"

Maggie shook her head.

"Painter is a name my mother made up when she decided to be a painter," Maggie said, the words out of her mouth, flying through the air, too late to protect her mother.

Zee leaned over to kiss the top of Maggie's curly head as they arrived at school.

"Lucy Painter, the painter. That's very charming," she said. "Come over for tea or hot chocolate anytime, Maggie. I miss having a daughter, only these crazy boys."

THE PHONE WAS ringing when Zee ran up the front steps but by the time she got in the house to find the chicken carcass from last night's dinner thrown up by Blue and in the middle of the hall rug, it had stopped ringing. Maybe the hospital, she thought. She grabbed Blue by the collar and let him out in the backyard. The chicken could wait.

She dialed the hospital emergency room. Yes, it had been the hospital calling, the receptionist said, but no emergency. Mr. Russ's condition was stable but would Zelda Mallory be able to locate some family member with whom the attending

162

physicians could communicate. Or was she, Ms. Mallory, the one in charge.

"In charge for now," Zee said, closing the fridge, getting paper towels from under the sink.

She cleaned up the chicken on the hall rug and dragged the rug out on the front porch to air, poured cat food in Onion's empty bowl, let Blue in from the back door, and settled for a moment on the soft white couch in the kitchen, resting her bare feet on Blue's dependable back, unanticipated tears running down her cheeks.

MAGGIE SLID INTO her desk in the front of the classroom—half a row between her desk and Miss Beacon's—and raised her hand asking to be excused.

"You have just arrived," Miss Beacon said, "already almost two hours late."

"I can't help it," Maggie said, standing up, her hand on her desk, feeling faint and woozy. "I'm going to be sick."

She was sick. She could faint on the floor of the girls' room. Surely she was going to throw up.

She had lied to Zee Mallory about her mother.

Lucy had *not* been the one to change their name to Painter. Her grandmother had made that change when they moved to Santa Fe after her grandfather's death.

"I'd rather you not tell anyone that we changed

163

our name," Lucy had said to Maggie. "People take exception to peculiarities like changing your name, which is what some Jews coming to this country did in order to protect themselves from prejudice. Not Uncle Reuben but other Jewish families," she said. "I think of us as *the Painters*. That is our name."

Maggie had asked Reuben about the Jews since he was Jewish and was, in any case, her source of dependable facts.

"The Jews were killed by Hitler for being Jewish," Reuben told her. "Many, many of them died. And some pretended they were not Jewish so they wouldn't be killed."

"Did you change your name?" Maggie asked.

"My name was always Frank," Uncle Reuben said. "But I was living here in America and was not in any danger of dying."

She asked her mother what her name had been before Painter.

Later, I'll tell you, Lucy said. *But not now.*

Not now like so many things.

The door to the girls' room opened with a long squeak and then Miss Beacon's voice, "Maggie? Are you here?"

"I'm here," she said.

"Are you all right?"

Maggie didn't reply.

"The bell's about to ring. Will you be out of the bathroom in time for math?"

"I'll be in math," Maggie said.

But she didn't move. The bell rang. The room filled with chattering girls stopping between classes. Someone pulled on the door to her cubicle.

"I'm in here," she said.

Then the second bell and the girls' room emptied.

She unlocked the door to the cubicle, washed her face in the sink, examined it in the mirror, pale against the scattered freckles. A sense of unease. Maybe she was actually getting sick, Maggie thought. Or worse, maybe something was about to happen, some punishment for exposing Lucy, for betraying her only mother, headed in her direction.

LUCY WAS LEANING over her work table lined with sketches for *Vermillion* which she had imagined would in one way or another be like her other books about the triumph of the outsider, the disenfranchised, the ridiculed, the cast-off, the failure, the shamed.

Her chin was in her hands and she was staring into the middle distance, almost unaware that the phone was ringing.

Lucy Painter and the Freaks had been the header in the Book List review of her last picture book, *Head First Out of the Ferris Wheel and Over the Yellow Sun*, the summer before she left New York.

The Vermillions on her work table took on a variety of representations—a baby sloth in one drawing, an obese, hairless sloth in another, a sloth with a half-closed eye, a missing leg, but the sloth she could not erase from memory was the dead one hanging by his tail at the zoo.

That morning when she woke up, Felix curled in the crook of her arm still sleeping, she had a mind's-eye picture of her sloth, who would be hairy and black with only a little tuft of cotton at the top of his head and that tuft would be vermillion.

Lucy began a book with an image, drawing on sheets of inexpensive paper, one drawing after the other, the drawings gathering in piles on the table until something began to happen like a love affair, a kind of overwhelming attraction and she would *know* to choose one picture over all the rest. That moment of knowing when she fell in love was her favorite part of making books. The story came later. But her mind's image of the sloth at the zoo was too dark a character for a children's book—she would have to find a way to give him life.

Her mind was a card catalogue of images giving rise to memory which she sorted through at will and which, after this morning, would include the image of August Russ floating by her window.

Perhaps August *was* dead.

See you later, he had said, and *later* he had passed her window. Swinging past her as if he were driving the ladder down.

For weeks, months, she had been working on Vermillion and his story had not materialized—still stuck with the article on the dead sloth at the Brooklyn Zoo. Now she felt as if she were coming untethered, as if discovering the story of Vermillion was the ball of string that would hold her in place and with August's fall, it was unraveling.

"Don't you hear the telephone, Mama?" Felix called, barreling down the steep steps to Lucy's bedroom. "I bet it's Uncle Reuben."

"It IS Uncle Reuben," he called from downstairs.

"I can't talk," Lucy said. "Tell him I'm busy."

"But you're not busy," Felix said, his head cresting the stairs on his way back up to the studio. "You're not doing anything at all."

"I'm thinking," Lucy said.

"I'll tell him that you're busy thinking," Felix said.

The front door opened and Lucy heard "Oh no, glass!" from a woman's voice—familiar, someone in the neighborhood, certainly one of the women who considered all doors of the houses in Witchita Hills open to them.

"Lucy?" the woman called. "Are you home?"

Felix went to the top of the steps, peering down

167

waiting for the visitor to come through his mother's bedroom and appear at the bottom of the steps.

"Zee!" he said happily. "We have company, Mommy. It's Zee."

Lucy stiffened.

"Hello, hello, hello, you little munchkin," Zee said. "I can't kiss you because of this."

She held out the crushed picture frame with Reuben on the Brooklyn Bridge.

"I always like a man with a cigarette and this one looks like John Lennon down to the wire-rimmed glasses," she said.

She put the photograph on Lucy's work table.

"It's my Uncle Reuben," Felix said.

"I know. Your sister told me," Zee said, reaching in the pocket of her short skirt, taking out a list. "You know about August?"

"I know he fell. Maggie told me."

"It's touch and go," she said.

"It's terrible."

"You should have seen it."

Zee brushed some glass shards from the bottom of her bare foot, shook her hand into the wastebasket.

"We're going to have round-the-clock vigilance at the hospital so he isn't alone if he D-I-E-S," she spelled it out so Felix couldn't understand. "If you'd like to be a part of this, just call me. We're starting right away, tomorrow afternoon."

"Thank you," Lucy said.

"This must be particularly painful for you since you and August were so close," Zee said. "I'm very sorry."

And she headed down the steps, calling back over her shoulder.

"I love Maggie," she said cheerfully. "I want her for my own daughter."

Ten

WHEN MAGGIE CAME home after school the day of August's accident, Lucy was at the kitchen sink making lasagna. Maggie slid into a chair next to the one where Felix was dipping oatmeal cookies in his milk and dumped her social studies books on the table.

"The ladder's been taken away," she said.

"I noticed that," Lucy replied, lining up the noodles on the bottom of a Pyrex dish.

"And there's *blood* where August fell." She articulated the word for Felix's benefit. "It's in a circle and the circle is black."

Maggie had seen it on the street, darkening the asphalt, when she and Maeve walked home from school after dance class.

A small crowd of women had gathered on the sidewalk. Robin Robinson was there with her camera hanging from a strap around her neck and Lane Sewall and Victoria still in her leotard after teaching the dance class at Lafayette and Mrs. Greene who lived next door to August on the other side, a large woman, older but very strong, her arms folded across her ample belly, her thick silver hair in a long braid, her face the color of butcher paper and crinkled, her black eyes set close to her nose.

"Is August better?" Maggie asked.

"We have no information about August's condition," Mrs. Greene said brusquely. She wasn't a part of the neighborhood women and Maggie was a little afraid of her.

"Zee will know." Lane put her arm around Maeve, pulling her close, nuzzling her face in her daughter's silky hair.

"He's not worse," Victoria said. "That's what Zee told me just a minute ago. No worse, no better. Unchanged is what she said."

"There was a lot of blood," Maeve said.

"The head is like that," Victoria said. "It bleeds and bleeds and bleeds."

Something in the way she repeated *bleed,* the long *e, eeee,* the sound of chalk scraping a blackboard, took shape in Maggie's body.

She bolted, crossing the street to her house, up the long steps, stopping at the top to check the Mallorys' house in case Zee happened to be standing on the front porch.

Lucy had finished assembling the lasagna, set the casserole on the lower rack of the oven, running the back of her hand across her damp forehead.

"Hot," she said. "So how was school?"

"Okay." Maggie rested her chin in her hand, a creeping unease lingering in her stomach.

"Do you remember the name of August's brother?" Lucy asked. "He told us the other day and I have forgotten."

"Gabriel, like the angel," Maggie said. "He works in a shoe store in Albany and August said he's small enough to be a child."

"Now I remember." Lucy broke the last oatmeal cookie in half and gave half to Maggie. "The hospital needs the name of a family member and Zee called to see if I knew."

Lucy had spent the day inside, in the morning in her studio too distracted to work, later wandering aimlessly through the house with Felix at her heels, stopping from time to time to check the place where August had fallen. She watched the ladder as it was carried off the curb by Victoria and her boyfriend, who took it up the steps and around the side of August's house, resting it against the basement wall.

While Felix was napping, she stood in the kitchen unconscious of the time—looking at the ladder as if expecting it to materialize into another story of the day. She called Reuben to let him know how close she had been to catastrophe.

But Reuben was not at work.

"Is he at home?" Lucy had asked his assistant.

"He came in before noon and left, possibly to the doctor's office for a checkup," she said. "Or off on a romp with Elaine."

A romp with Elaine?

Ever since she had moved away from the dailiness of her life with Reuben—the coffee shop in the morning, calls whenever he had a minute, evenings at least twice a week—she wondered had she disappeared from his thoughts. Did nights go by when Lucy didn't cross his mind—propped up next to Elaine in bed reading a manuscript even if they didn't make love. How was she to know whether her imagined life with Reuben had materialized with Elaine now that Lucy had left New York.

Elaine Frank, his wife. She had to remind herself.

Maggie watched her mother making salad, tearing the lettuce, slicing goat cheese, licking off the remaining cheese that clung to her fingers. She seemed suddenly so young with her curly hair in a turquoise scrunchie, a line of green paint from her work on *Vermillion* across her face, her cheeks flushed from the heat of the stove.

"I'm not hungry for salad," Maggie said.

"Me neither," Felix said.

"But you love lasagna, Maggie."

"I feel too sick to eat," she said.

It was possible that Zee would *tell* the women in the neighborhood when they met in the street for coffee in the morning or in the evening before the children went to bed.

Painter is NOT Lucy's real name, she might say. *Maggie tells me that she made it up.*

And the women would wonder what dreadful thing could have happened in Lucy's family that she would *lie* about a name.

The Painters' family story would be passed on one woman to the next until even strangers as far away as Urbana Road or Cleveland Avenue would be talking about them.

Maggie pushed her plate of lasagna away, waiting for Lucy to go upstairs with Felix for his bath.

"You really aren't eating, are you?" Lucy asked on her way out of the kitchen.

Maggie shook her head, listening for the sound of bath water running before she left. Then she opened the front door quietly so it didn't squeak and her mother wouldn't hear her go.

A CALL FROM a doctor at the hospital came while Zee was serving dinner to ask had she had any luck locating August's family.

"You ought to get on the horn to find that brother you mentioned if August is planning to go AWOL on us," Adam called from the TV room where he stood with a beer watching the

173

evening news. "Otherwise you're going to be left in a pretty pickle."

"I *have* called him," Zee said. "Gabriel Russ."

"I THOUGHT WE weren't allowed to talk on the phone at dinner," Daniel said.

"*You* aren't allowed to talk on the phone." Adam had come into the kitchen.

"Shhh," Zee whispered, her finger to her lips.

It was Gabriel Russ.

"Thank god," Zee said, slipping out of her sweater, tucking her feet underneath her. "I'm so glad you called."

She told him the whole story.

"We are a close neighborhood and August is in the middle of our lives," she said after she had explained the situation at the hospital.

She gave him the doctor's number.

"Call me anytime and let me know your plans. I could pick you up at the airport."

"Yes," Gabriel Russ said. "Yes, of course and of course. I will be at the airport. I am at the airport." He giggled and hung up the phone.

Crazy, she thought to herself, and would have said it aloud were Adam not so quick with his growing unkindness.

"That was August's brother," she said.

"So it would appear." Adam leaned backwards in his chair and opened the fridge for another

174

beer. "So his brother's now in charge and you're off the hook?"

"Actually, Adam, at the moment, I am the one in charge."

"No question, Zelda," Adam said, his delivery deadpan. He never raised his voice. "I should have been able to see that in a heartbeat."

Daniel finished dinner, pushed his plate away, and asked to be excused.

"Luke put his spinach in his napkin," he said, getting up from the table. "So he shouldn't have dessert."

"There's no dessert for anyone. Not for Luke and not for the boy who told on Luke," Adam said, getting up. "Someone's at the front door, Zelda."

"Anyway, I don't like dessert," Luke said, blowing out the candles which Zee lit every night to diminish the noise level in the kitchen.

"It's Maggie Painter at the front door," Adam called.

Zee's spirits rose.

"I hate Maggie Painter." Daniel punched Luke on the arm.

"No hitting, Daniel," she said abstractly. "No hitting and no hating."

Maggie stood in the hall in jeans and a long-sleeved white T-shirt with a fuzzy black cat on the front.

"I'm so glad you're here," Zee said, reaching out to hug her. "Come in."

"I came to find out about August," Maggie began. "My mom wants to know."

"Your mom sent you?" Zee asked, picking up Onion, who had a habit of running out the front door and up a tree. "As soon as I get the boys to bed, I'm going to head over to the hospital and then I'll have an answer to August's condition."

"You're going to *what?*" Adam called from the television room.

Zee put her arm around Maggie's shoulder and led her into the kitchen.

"I promised you hot chocolate," she said. "Is it cold enough outside for hot chocolate or would you rather have lemonade?"

"Just lemonade," Maggie said, sitting on the kitchen table.

Luke was still in the kitchen looking in the freezer for ice cream.

He held up a gallon of Bryers vanilla.

"Okay?" he asked.

"Two scoops and make a bowl for your brother and then you guys can have half an hour of television before your baths while I talk to Maggie."

Zee took a chair and sat down, resting her chin in her hands.

"I'm very happy you came to visit," she said.

"TV on a school night, Zelda?" Adam called from the den.

"Just for tonight."

She split an ice cream sandwich and handed a half to Maggie.

"I came over for a reason," Maggie said, looking just past Zee into the dark of the Mallorys' backyard.

"Something serious?"

She nodded.

"When I got home from school today, everyone was standing around looking at the blood where August Russ fell," Maggie began, "and then I went home and I was in the kitchen watching my mother while she was making dinner and I suddenly felt terrible that I told you about my grandfather and how my mother made up her name."

"No big deal," Zee said.

"It's a big deal because I lied to you. My mother wasn't the one who made up our name. My grandmother did that because she liked the name Painter and now she's dead."

"Hmm." Zee drew her legs under her chin, resting her chin on her knees. "That's a funny thing to lie about."

"I don't know why," Maggie said, nervously swinging her legs. "Sometimes I just do things and don't know why I do them."

"Of course," Zee said almost under her breath. "We all do that kind of thing."

"I hope you won't tell *anyone* what I said," Maggie said, pulling her knees. "I mean I know you won't but I feel miserable."

"I understand completely."

"And you won't say anything?"

"Don't worry another minute," Zee said too quickly, knowing she had already told Lane Sewall about the Painters more than an hour ago and was planning to tell Robin and Josie the next morning at coffee.

She hadn't exactly *broken* a trust, Zee thought. She didn't know it was a secret.

Zee was terrible with secrets. Over and over, she promised herself to protect the confidences she had been given. And then she failed. Almost immediately she failed. She couldn't seem to help herself. She wasn't to be trusted.

"Cross my heart and hope to die," Zee added, *wishing* to be loyal in the way Josie was loyal or Robin or even Lane.

"I *do* trust you," Maggie said, a shy, cockeyed smile lifting the corner of her lips, happy to be sitting in Zee Mallory's kitchen in the full light of her attention.

AT THE WINDOW of her bedroom on the front of the house, Lucy was holding Felix in his pajamas, hot from a bath, watching Maggie standing in the glow of the Mallorys' porch light, Zee's arm around her shoulders.

"Did Maggie tell you she was going to the Mallorys' house?" she asked.

Felix shook his head.

178

In the large window just to the left of the Mallorys' door, Adam was standing in front of the television taking off his tie, Daniel or was it Luke doing somersaults on the couch.

The Mallorys had no sense of privacy, Lucy thought. No shades or curtains, no boundaries between their lives and those of others who lived on Witchita Avenue. There was nothing Zee couldn't extract from other people.

Lucy longed for her apartment in New York where everyone on Sullivan Street was a familiar stranger.

Now Maggie's head upturned, talking to Zee, hugging her tiny perfect waist—Lucy hated that, hated it—and Maggie left, waving goodbye, swinging around the tree on the Mallorys' lawn.

Zee got in her van then, which was parked in front of the house, did a U-turn and headed towards Connecticut Avenue and the hospital.

ZEE MALLORY WAS Maggie's third love affair in a series that began when she was seven. First Uncle Reuben, the man she wished to be her father. Uncle Reuben with his curly golden red hair—more red than brown, and bright eyes and dimple in his chin like hers. Then Leo James in fourth grade who wore black-rimmed eyeglasses and straight brown bangs and told her that he loved her. Now Zee/Zelda Mallory, the mother of her dreams.

She opened the front door quietly, took off her shoes and tiptoed barefoot across the hardwood floor to the kitchen.

She opened the freezer, searched through the frozen peas and carrots and Saran-wrapped bread her mother made on Saturdays and sausage and chicken and homemade meatloaf. Reaching into the bottom where the ice cream sandwiches were hidden, she took one from the box, flopped on the couch, her feet on the arms, and thought about Zee.

On the first page of her social studies text, she wrote in pencil *Zelda Mallory*. And then, covering the title page in red ink, she wrote sideways, right side up, upside down—*Zee, Zee, Zee, Zee, Zee, Zee, Zee.*

Lucy went down the steps to the front hall and through the dining room to the kitchen where Maggie, bent over her social studies homework, did not look up.

"Maggie?"

"Mmmm."

"What were you doing at the Mallorys'?" Lucy crossed the room, a sense of Maggie's critical eye as she turned on the burner under the teakettle.

"I was *doing* nothing."

Maggie put a marker in her social studies book, closed it, dropped the book in her book bag so Lucy wouldn't have a chance to see Zee's name written all over in red ink.

"I needed to talk to Zee Mallory."

About what? on the tip of Lucy's tongue but she didn't ask.

"Tea?"

"No thank you."

Lucy poured a cup of tea, turned out the light over the sink, and went upstairs, feeling a weight of sadness and accumulating loss.

ADAM WAS HALF asleep, sitting up when Zee got back from the hospital.

"I met August's brother," she said. "He arrived just as I was leaving."

"What a lucky break for you!"

"What does that mean?"

"Nothing. Just nice he has a brother and the brother's at the hospital now and you can come home and tend to your family."

"I tend to my family," Zee said, slipping out of her jeans and sweater. "The brother's weird. Something is wrong with him."

August's brother, Gabriel, had arrived just as she was leaving the hospital. She gave him the doctor's report the neurologist had given to her. *The first forty-eight hours after a head injury are the most crucial.* He sat next to her, his legs so short they didn't touch the floor. She reached out and touched his arm while she told him what had happened and how she and August were friends, how he had many friends, especially among the

181

women in the neighborhood. She left her hand on his while she was talking, wanting to reassure him that she had no prejudice whether or not he was brain-damaged or demented or whatever word would be used to suggest limitations besides his size.

"Do you think August will die?" he asked, looking straight at her.

"We have our fingers crossed," she told him.

"That he will die?"

"That he will live."

As she left, she kissed him on a rubbly cheek.

"WEIRD?" ADAM ASKED.

"He is very small and has problems other than size."

She took her pajamas off the hook in her closet.

"Isn't it strange that their parents named one child August and the other Gabriel?"

"Why would you say that?"

"I'm just making conversation, Adam."

"Then you should stick to meaningful conversation. Isn't that what you've been asking for from me?" He turned on the light beside his bed. "Which leads me to Maggie Painter. I can see where that's going, Zee. You've been there before."

"What do you mean?" Zee asked, suddenly anxious.

"You know what I mean. All these little girls.

182

It's wrecking things. Between us and inside of you."

Zee slammed the door and headed barefoot down the hall to Adam's office where she sometimes worked and sat down on the couch. It was almost midnight and beginning to rain.

She spread an afghan over her, a pillow behind her back, turned out the light and stared at the ceiling.

The bedroom door opened and Adam, barefooted, padded down the hall, the heavy smell of beer accompanying him into the study as he shut the door and sat down at the end of the couch where Zee had settled.

"Mind?" His hand had fallen almost casually against her stomach.

"Mind what?" Zee replied.

"Mind that I've come in when you're trying to sleep."

"I don't," she said. "I don't sleep is what I mean."

"What if I say I forgive you," he asked. "Does that make a difference?"

"I just wish you'd stop drinking," she said as she had said so many times before.

Eleven

LUCY STRUGGLED OUT of sleep. It was still dark outside, the crescent shadow of a silver moon low in the sky, the only sound coming from a refrigerator that was on the fritz. Something had awakened her, some noise or nightmare that might have had to do with August Russ.

At first she thought she was in the bedroom of her apartment on Sullivan Street with only one window and that view flat up against the brick building next door and overlooking an alley. Had Reuben been there with her and left before dawn? Had she heard a telephone ringing?

She sat up, Felix sleeping beside her, his arms tight around the yellow-haired spider monkey Reuben had given him when he was born. Why holding on so tight to the monkey? she wondered. Shouldn't Felix's baby arms relax in sleep? Or was he too having a silent nightmare?

Even in pale darkness she could see the blue shingle on August's house, the light still on in his second-story bedroom, and she hadn't noticed that when she went to bed.

It *was* August who had awakened her.

The dream, if it had been a dream, more like a painting before her eyes, the image of August next to her, leaning against her, her body absorbing the weight of him. Dusk and in that smoky light, his eyes were startling blue. More purple really than blue, and at a distance the pupils sparkled the color of a cloudy morning.

She wondered had she ever dreamed in color before. Or did she *only* dream in color. She could not remember.

LUCY CLIMBED OUT of bed, opened her closet door, taking out jeans which she wore rolled up and a white smock with the sleeves loose around her wrists, paint on the smock, mostly green and yellow—her hair gathered in a scrunchie high on her head. This morning she didn't shower.

In the bathroom she watched herself in the mirror as she brushed her teeth—a failure to recognize her own reflection which happened to her sometimes, and then she'd stretch out her hands to check if they were the same hands she remembered from the day before.

August was in the hospital unconscious, no clear prognosis, no sense of the extent of his injuries at least for the next forty-eight hours according to Zelda Mallory, the medical expert.

It was almost 6 a.m. and Lucy called the hospital.

"August Russ is my oldest friend," she told the nurse in the trauma unit who answered the phone. "I would like to be able to see him."

There was a long pause. The nurse spoke to someone else and then came back on the phone.

"The doctor says you may see him," she said, "but very briefly and best to come this morning.

FELIX OPENED HIS eyes and stretched, reaching his arms above his head.

"Are we having waffles for breakfast?" he asked.

"Waffles and yummy maple syrup."

Lucy opened the window beside her bed to check the temperature outside.

"Waffles?" she asked when Maggie came down for breakfast.

Maggie didn't reply. She poured orange juice, took a box of raisins from the shelf, a blueberry muffin from the bread box, slipped her book bag over her shoulder, and left through the front door without saying goodbye.

Lucy sat down next to Felix, sweeping her index finger through the maple syrup and across her tongue.

"Was that Uncle Reuben on the phone?" Felix asked.

"He called this morning from the airport."

"TROUBLE," LUCY HAD said when she answered Reuben's call. "Maggie has decided to more or less stop speaking to me."

She repeated what had happened the night before when Maggie had gone to the Mallorys' without asking permission.

"Girls!" Reuben said. "They can be so impossible. Nell has turned into a complete sourpuss."

"Maggie isn't sour," Lucy said. "Just silent with me and . . ." she hesitated. "Contemptuous."

"Maybe it would help to have someone to talk to besides me, Lucy," Reuben said.

"Who would you suggest?"

"Like a shrink. A child psychologist, someone professional." He paused. "I'll pay."

"I talk to *you* because you are the only one who knows my life," Lucy said.

"I was thinking of someone who's objective, which I am not."

"In my family, we take care of problems ourselves, as you know," Lucy said quietly.

There was a thick scratchy sound coming from his throat or phlegm like choking or was it tears. An intake of breath.

"Are you smoking?" she asked. "You *are* smoking and I thought you were recovering from pneumonia."

"I am recovered," he said, and in the distance, she could hear the loudspeaker announcing a flight to Kansas City.

"I've got to dash," he said.

Dash! She replaced the receiver.

FELIX WRAPPED HIS arms around Lucy's neck.

"Is Uncle Reuben coming here to see you and me and Maggie?" he asked.

"Soon," Lucy said, "but not today. This morning he's going to Los Angeles for a meeting about books."

"I wish he lived with us day and night," Felix said.

"That would be nice."

"And maybe we can get a kitten," he said sleepily. "My friend at school just got a yellow kitten with fluff. Maybe Uncle Reuben can bring me one of those when he comes."

ACROSS THE STREET, Maggie had stopped at the Sewalls' house to wait for Maeve, and watching through the window on the front door, Lucy saw the two of them walk up the Mallorys' front steps, across the lawn along the brick path, up to the porch. But only Maggie walked into the house without even waiting for someone to answer the door, disappearing into a pool of sun shimmering off the glass until all Lucy could see was light.

Something bilious rose in her throat, a bitter taste from her own body seeping into her mouth.

If Maggie wanted to change mothers in the middle of her childhood, Lucy wasn't going to be the one to stop her.

• • •

THE TELEPHONE WAS ringing in the kitchen and Felix picked it up, handing it to his mother.

"Hi, Lucy, it's Zee." Her voice was cheery. "Just to tell you I'm bringing dinner to Shock Trauma at the Hospital Center tonight so I hope you can come. Chicken Kiev. You could bring a bottle of Chablis."

In her mind's eye, beyond the light from the morning sun exploding across the Mallorys' front door, Lucy could imagine Maggie at the Mallorys' kitchen table, her face in her fists, the way she always sat in repose, maybe fiddling with her frizzy hair, listening to Zee talk on the telephone to her mother.

SHE SAT DOWN on the couch next to Felix looking at the pictures in *Frog and Toad*. Concentrating on pictures to keep at bay a growing sense of desperation.

Frog and Toad sitting side by side in their predictable arrangement.

It was possible she could find Reuben before he got on the plane if she called the airport to ask that he be summoned over the loudspeaker: *Reuben Frank. Paging Mr. Reuben Frank. Please call home.*

Please come *home.*

After the move to Washington, the panic attacks she had had since she went away to college returned slowly like whispers in the back of a room, sufficient to distract her but nothing like they had been when she was younger, when her father died, when her mother was killed, when Reuben had his daughter, Nell, after Maggie was born.

Nell Frank, she'd scribble on her drawing pad. *Elaine Frank.* She had never seen Elaine but Reuben had a picture in his office, tall and thin and hawkish, with Nell Frank as a toddler standing beside her, holding the cloth leg of a Raggedy Ann.

Maggie Painter, she'd write, over and over until the name itself took the form of her daughter. *This is my daughter with Reuben Frank,* she'd say to herself—imagining his sperm swimming, not in a hurry, bumping against the soft wall of her uterus, into the narrow channel of fallopian tubes, upwards into the center of her being making a baby girl.

The operator at JFK agreed to page Reuben. Although Lucy didn't know the name of the airline, the operator told her that American was the next flight that morning going to Los Angeles direct.

Lucy waited, straddling the arm of the couch, her head against the wall, pattering on to Felix. The operator kept her on hold for the longest time, so long that the tension gradually went out of her. Surely with such a wait, they were locating

Reuben. He would rush to the Information desk, pick up the phone, his deep warm voice through the wires. "Lucy." Comforting the way he said her name. "Are you okay?"

But just as she was certain they had found him, the operator came on to say that the plane had actually left the gate. Not airborne yet but taxiing down the runway in preparation for takeoff.

Lucy turned on the tap, filled a glass with water, drinking it slowly, careful not to choke.

I can't do Vermillion, she would have told him. *My eye for making books has gone.*

She couldn't find the story. The wastebasket was filled with her attempts.

ZEE WOKE UP before the sun, the house quiet, the boys sleeping. She went into the bedroom where Adam was, lying on his back, the covers thrown off, naked, his mouth open.

On the way to the bathroom, she had an urge to slap him. She stopped short, took off her nightgown, put on the slip of a dress she'd worn the night before.

Onion was sleeping on the bottom of the bed with Blue. They stretched, jumped off without waking Adam, and followed Zee downstairs.

On the kitchen counter, she had left her *to do today* list. She let Blue out the kitchen door, fed Onion, put on coffee to brew, and sat down at the table with a pencil.

Lucy Painter, she wrote in her organized way at the top of a new page in her notebook.

Questions to Ask:
1. Name before Painter
2. Father of children?
3. Parents?
4. Who owns the house on Witchita Avenue?

If Lucy Painter's real name had been worth changing, there must have been something in Lucy's life to hide. Zee understood the value of secrets. A person doesn't keep a secret unless there is something worth concealing.

She poured a cup of coffee and leaned against the stove, warming her hands around the mug. With spring in the air, a sweet dampness floated through the open window over the sink, a rising sense of possibilities. Nothing specific that Zee could name except Maggie was on her mind.

In the back of her mind where the darkest of thoughts were corralled, Zee knew that what she wanted was Maggie Painter as her own.

It was too early in the morning to call the hospital for news of August's condition. Too early for her family to get up.

She took a broom out of the closet to sweep up the glass that Adam or one of the boys had broken the night before, always something broken in the house, dishes, glasses, her mother's antique lamp, trucks without their wheels, stuffed animals gone flat, their stuffing in the trash. She was tired of too many careless boys in her house.

And as she bent down to collect the shards of glass in a dustpan, a storm cloud must have passed across the pale sun. Darkness seeped into the kitchen and she absorbed it. This happened to her when she least expected it—a drop in barometric pressure, a storm cloud across the sun. She'd be somewhere, maybe alone or surrounded by people, and it would be as if she'd lost her sight. She'd stop what she was doing, take a deep breath, and go on.

Her mother's repeated chorus: *Whatever happens,* she'd say, *get up, brush off the dirt, and go on!*

It was not in Zee's nature to linger in sadness. She'd crowd the day with things to do, her work, long lists of people to call, presents to buy, lives to help, always edging sorrow out of the room.

She hurried upstairs, grabbed a skirt and sweater, footless tights and flats, changing quickly, took her stash of necklaces, and headed downstairs. She picked up her enormous purse, dropped her *to do* list in the bag, and was on her way to the front door just as Maggie Painter arrived.

"I think I left my copy of *To Kill a Mockingbird*

when I came over last night," Maggie said, a blush of shyness on her cheeks. "It's in the kitchen, on a chair I think."

"My favorite book in the world," Zee said, waving to Maeve on the porch, holding open the door. "If I ever have another baby, I'll call him Atticus."

THE BOOK WAS lying on a chair where Maggie had left it and she put it in her backpack.

"Scout is my favorite name," she said, heading to the front door.

"My favorite girl's name is Miranda," Zee said, speaking quickly and without thought, surprised at her unexpected irritation, her voice sharp in her ear.

"I'll see you later," she called as Maggie went out the front door heading down the steps with Maeve.

She hadn't meant to push Maggie away with her temper, but she was in a hurry and bad-humored. The bickering boys, Adam pounding on the floor above the kitchen in his heavy shoes. She was getting a headache.

She had to finish her notes on Nixon's Quaker childhood by noon and go to the hospital and then the dentist. She had promised Lane she'd go with her to a follow-up doctor's appointment at Sibley Hospital. And be back for the twins when they got out of school at three.

She made a new pot of coffee, wrote a note to her friends who should be arriving as usual and taped it to the glass on the front door.

Girls of my heart. Door's open. I'm off for a dentist appointment and then the hospital. Coffee percolating in the kitchen. Honey donuts in the bread box. Strawberries in the fridge and don't let Onion out the front door. See you at Shock Trauma tonight at 6. Z/Z

And she ran down the front steps, got in the van, closed the car door and in the side-view mirror she saw Lucy Painter pulling away from the curb, Felix in his car seat in the back. She waved out the window.

"See you tonight," she called.

LUCY DROPPED FELIX off at nursery school and drove across the park to the Washington Hospital Center. Nine o'clock when she arrived. The nurse who answered in Shock Trauma said she could see August but visits were limited to five minutes.

"I'll come for you when five minutes is up," she said. "We have restrictions particularly with head injuries."

She followed the nurse down the corridor, into a large room noisy with monitors, the beds separated by curtains, most of which were open.

"He's not conscious," the nurse said, pulling back the curtain. "I'm sure you know that. But

195

you can talk to him. Perhaps he'll hear you. There's evidence that a patient does hear but we never know."

"Thank you," Lucy said. "I will talk to him."

August lay in a triangle of pale blue light, some combination of lights in the ceiling and the monitors. His head was bandaged in gauze, wrapped in a high headdress, his eyes covered.

"To protect his eyes so he isn't bothered by the light," the nurse said, closing the curtain around them.

His arms lay by his side, a sheet pulled up under his armpits, his breathing shallow. He was hooked up everywhere.

She touched his hand.

"Hello, August. It's me, Lucy."

She pulled up a chair beside the bed, kneeling in it so she could speak to him close to his face, leaning over his body.

"I think you can hear me," she said.

She noticed his boyish hands freckled with fawn spots—she had not actually noticed that before, all those mornings he had sat at her kitchen table holding his papers talking to her about his book.

His body was eerily still but the hand over the sheet and by his side was trembling.

"I've been thinking about us. About our friendship," Lucy said, leaning closer, speaking next to his head, his ears uncovered. "I love our friendship because it's so accidental and surprising. I've never met a man like you—kind of like a child taking the world as you find it without judgment. And then sometimes you're my mother fixing me lunch and sitting in my kitchen, looking at my drawings of poor Vermillion. My house feels like home when you're there."

She stood up, pushed the chair back against the wall. She could hear the squeak of rubber soles of the nurse coming down the hall to tell her to leave.

"Nothing since I was a child has felt like home." She kissed his freckled hand.

"Time." The nurse opened the curtain, tapped her on the back.

She had been thinking she would say *I love you* to him but she did not. Maybe he *could* hear her. Maybe he would remember.

"HE BROKE HIS back as well," the nurse said, leading Lucy through the doors of Shock Trauma to the elevator. "But it's the head we're concerned about."

"Of course."

"Someone told you that?"

"They did."

"The first forty-eight hours are critical."

It was 9:10 on the clock by the elevator. Lucy had been in August's room for less than five minutes.

NOON AND DR. Ziegler, the neurologist on August's case, was late. Zee had been waiting in the lobby outside the Trauma unit for an hour.

She had seen Gabriel Russ. He was eating a mint chocolate chip ice cream cone and reading a magazine.

"Are we friends?" he asked, extending the ice cream cone in her direction. "Have a lick. Green is my favorite color."

"We are friends but no ice cream, thank you, Gabriel. How is everything?" she asked.

"Well, well, well but August is bad. That's what the doctor tells me. Critical means bad and August is critical."

"I was afraid of that," Zee said.

"Well don't be afraid because he *is* bad and so there's nothing to be afraid of because we know the truth." He smiled. "My brother, August Russ. Already he is bad, you see?"

"I do. Of course I see."

This seemed to please him and he settled into *Newsweek*, turning the pages.

"I saw Dr. Ziegler," he said, looking up.

"Good. I'm hoping to see him now."

"He has a red mustache with leftover coffee cake on the whiskers. I told him to wash his whiskers. If he washes his face, the coffee cake will disappear, don't you think?"

"I'm sure it will."

"Off his rocker," as her mother would say, and like her mother, anything outside the ordinary could worry Zee that she might be held accountable.

"It's a problem, yes?" Gabriel asked.

"It's a problem."

Gabriel wandered off down the corridor in the direction of Cardiology and Zee watched him as he walked, a little half step on his right foot as if he were slightly lame but instead he seemed to be taking a dance step.

"Ms. Mallory," Dr. Ziegler sat down beside Zee gripping her hand—*gripping* was the word she used later when she told Lane and Josie.

Zee slipped her shoes back on, sliding *People* magazine in which she'd been reading *Death Notices* into her bag, wondering, should August die, would he be included in the death notices in *People* since falling two stories with a ladder had the kind of original ring that *People* was inclined to consider news.

"We have a problem," Dr. Ziegler said.

"With August?"

"Oh he has problems of course. As I'm sure you've been told, it's a matter of waiting to see what happens. But my concern at the moment is his brother."

"Gabriel."

"He's *not* going to be useful to us," Dr. Ziegler said.

"I know. I met him last night."

"Can *you* help?"

"Count on me," Zee said.

"You have my numbers at the hospital and my pager," he said. "And I know how to reach you."

Zee caught sight of Gabriel out of the corner of her eye as she left, ducking into the ladies' room to avoid another conversation. He was carrying a large brown teddy bear and humming a familiar tune, maybe from the Beatles, as he went through the doors into Trauma.

On the way back to the car, her head tumbling off her shoulder with weariness, Zee wondered what might happen to *her* in the event of an accident. Adam would be her *next of kin* and how would he react if a call were to come.

Mr. Mallory, I'm sorry to inform you but your wife . . .

Would he rush to the car, turn on the engine, thinking . . . *my wife* . . . or would he find himself quite unexpectedly relieved. *An accident, what good news!*

Adam didn't love her. That realization had come on slowly like her father's dementia, small losses, here and there, here and there, an argument, a profound sadness, a growing distance. And then the *fact* of the matter.

He might not ever love her again—and she was responsible for that at least in part. The responsibility for the rest was, like land run, erosion.

· · ·

MAGGIE SAW ZEE at school just after the dismissal bell. She was standing with Lane Sewall outside the second grade classroom to pick up the twins just as Maggie was headed to homeroom to gather her books and papers for the end of the day.

"Hi, sunshine," Zee said, giving Maggie a kiss on the top of her head. "I have something for you."

She slipped off a silver chain necklace among the ones she always wore and put it over Maggie's head.

"I'm making a delicious dinner to take to the hospital tonight," she said. "Chicken Kiev. Chocolate mousse in little ramekins. I told your mom and I hope she's coming."

"I don't know if she is." Maggie was breathless, thrilled and embarrassed, fingering the necklace that fell just between her budding breasts. "Probably not."

"Probably not," Lane said, and it wasn't unfriendly the way she said it, rather matter-of-fact, a statement of probability, but Maggie took it as criticism.

A comment about whether Lucy was a willing friend, which she had not shown herself to be, and Maggie was ashamed. It seemed as if her mother were not equal to these women, could not compete in the arena of friendship like they did.

201

"Well if Lucy can't come," Zee was saying, "why don't you stop by my house around five-thirty and come with Lane and Josie and me."

"Maybe I will," Maggie said.

"Ask your mom," Zee said. "Tell her that we hope she'll join us but I know, I really understand, it's hard with Felix and no one to help her out."

No husband, was what Zee meant by no one to help out. No father, no ordinary family life. Something your mother has failed to provide for you.

That was the way Maggie heard *no one to help out.*

Zee was right. There was no one to help out, just Maggie and Felix and Lucy in the house on Witchita Avenue, not even a cat to slink around the house, rubbing its body up against their legs, curled in a living room chair giving off a sound of home.

Maggie pushed the door into her homeroom, taking her seat, opening the top of her desk where her books and the report on Indians were stacked.

If she were to ask Lucy's permission to go to the hospital, her mother would certainly say no. Especially if she were going with Zee.

She would simply *go* without asking. She'd call her mother from the public telephone at school, tell her she was going to the library to work on her Indian report, say she was joining a friend just so Lucy wouldn't be worried thinking of Maggie on Connecticut Avenue at the Chevy Chase Library alone in the early evening.

And then she'd head the back way to Zee's house, going through the Mallorys' yard into the garage.

Five-thirty. Lucy would be in the kitchen making dinner, Felix drawing dinosaurs with magic marker and art paper on the kitchen table.

I'm going to the library with my friend Vivienne, was the story she told Lucy when she called from the public telephone at school. *I may be home a little late.*

When the clock over the Information desk at the Chevy Chase Library got to five, Maggie packed up her things, crossed Connecticut Avenue, and headed up McKinley to Witchita Hills, taking the back way along Columbus, turning left just above the Mallorys' house, through their yard to the back door, where Zee was in her jacket ready to leave.

"Are you coming?" she asked, seeing Maggie. "I'm thrilled."

Zee had brought dinner in a wicker laundry basket, chicken Kiev and white beans, thin sliced tomatoes—she passed out brightly colored pottery plates, cloth napkins and forks, opened a bottle of Chablis. They pulled their plastic-covered chairs into a circle, rested their plates on their knees. Zee and Lane and Robin and Victoria and Maggie. Josie had to work late again.

In the sixth chair, pulled up between Zee and Lane, Gabriel Russ was eating a drumstick.

"I had no idea August, my brother, had so many friends," he said. "He always told me Washington was a lonely town."

"Except Witchita Hills is not lonely," Zee said. "Here we all love August."

"Yes," Gabriel agreed, reaching out his glass for seconds on wine. "He is my favorite brother."

"You have others?" Zee asked, looking around for the team of doctors who were on night rounds.

"I have Cicero and Flat but Cicero lives in Vancouver and we never see each other."

"And Flat?" Lane asked politely.

"Flat lives with my mother who is dead because he's an alcoholic and doesn't have any control. That's what my parents have always said. *Flat has no control,* but I think she wanted him to live with her because she didn't get along with my father who is also dead. Ours is not a very good family. That's what my therapist says. I work in a shoe store with smelly feet. Especially the women in their nylons."

Zee gave Lane a look which passed to Robin, who was not the kind of woman to continue a public humiliation, even one so minor as that one.

"What you might not know about August is that he had a wife named Anna," Gabriel was saying. "And Anna died."

"We do know that," Zee said.

"Of cancer," Gabriel said. "I didn't see her when she had cancer but I came to the funeral in McLean, Virginia. There was a lunch at the country club with Black Forest ham which is my favorite food except for chocolate pudding. Did you go to that lunch?" He addressed his question to Zee.

"I didn't know your brother that well then," Zee said. "So I wasn't at the lunch."

"I didn't know him either except my mother told us he was the smartest in the family except Flat who ruined his smartness by getting drunk." He helped himself to another glass of wine. "Be careful, Gabriel," he told himself in a stage whisper. "August got fired at his job. He wrote me a letter about that and told me how lucky I was to work at a shoe store where I was important to the customers and how I should try very hard not to get fired," Gabriel said. "I do try and it works. I stack the shelves. Once I got in trouble for eating a box of sugarcoated vitamins which I found in the purse of a customer trying on high heels but they just told me not to do it again and I said I wouldn't and I haven't."

Zee leaned over, lowering her voice.

"Do you know *why* August was fired?"

"I do," Gabriel said. "He was fired for sexual intercourse."

Maggie giggled. She couldn't help herself and Gabriel, brushing imaginary lint from his trousers, crinkled his nose and smiled shyly at her.

"I have never had sexual intercourse before that I remember," he said to the group in general, looking very pleased with himself.

"I know the person with whom he had the sexual intercourse," he said, "but I am not allowed to convey that information to anyone outside of our terrible family. That's what my therapist says about us. We have a terrible family."

THE DOORS ACROSS the waiting room leading to the Shock Trauma unit swung open and four doctors in white coats, masks hanging around their necks, their heads in white caps covering their hair, came through, heading first to the assembled women.

"Are you here for August Russ?" one doctor asked.

"We are," Zee said.

"All of you?"

"All of us."

"Sisters?"

"Friends," Lane said.

"And August's brother, Gabriel, whom you've met," Zee added.

"We actually have two other brothers, Flat and

206

Cicero, but I made them up myself. I am August Russ's real brother in the flesh," Gabriel said. "Is he dead?"

IT WAS JUST almost seven, a late April golden light fading to darkness. Maggie had called Lucy to say she was going to the library with her friend Vivienne Browning and would be home for dinner.

In her studio with Felix lying on his back listening to a tape of Roald Dahl's *James and the Giant Peach*, Lucy could smell the pot roast in the oven, a slight burnt smell of leathered meat. Maggie was late.

Lucy didn't know Vivienne's family well but she had met them at a school potluck and she knew they lived on Ohio Lane, just behind the playground. There couldn't be more than one Browning in Witchita Hills and she found the listing in the local phone book under Victor Browning, dialed the number, and he answered after several rings.

"Mr. Browning?" She sat down, her back to Felix, who was drawing dinosaurs in his art book. "This is Lucy Painter and Maggie is my daughter."

"Yes?"

His response suggested that he didn't know Maggie.

"I know your daughter Vivienne. I've met her with my own daughter several times."

Which wasn't exactly true. She'd met Vivienne only once besides the potluck dinner and that was on the playground behind Lafayette with a lot of other children.

"Vivienne and Maggie went to the library this afternoon to do a project for social studies."

There was a pause. Mr. Browning cleared his throat. In the background a baby was crying.

"Vivienne is in the kitchen eating dinner with the rest of us."

"I'm so sorry to bother you," Lucy said, her heart beating hard or was it fast—she couldn't tell. "Perhaps you could ask Vivienne if she knows where Maggie is."

"I'll ask," he said, and Lucy could hear the judgment rumbling in the tenor of his voice.

"Mrs. Painter," Victor Browning was back on the phone, "Vivienne wasn't at the library. She's been at home since school let out."

Lucy took a deep breath, her voice trembling, her body cold as ice water.

"Do you mind asking her about Maggie anyway?"

Lucy could hear Vivienne in the background.

"I don't know," Vivienne said. "I haven't seen her since fifth-period math when we walked to our lockers together."

"What happened to Maggie?" Felix asked, rolling over on his stomach.

"Nothing happened, Felix. Just . . ."

She had to be careful. Felix picked up every scent.

She reached out her hand and Felix followed her downstairs to the second floor and then the first where she looked out the dining room window, across the street to the Mallorys' house. Upstairs, the twins seemed to be fighting, and in the background, in Zee and Adam's bedroom, Adam, shirtless, stood in front of a television.

She looked up their number in the phone book.

"Is your father home?" she asked whichever twin broke away from the fight long enough to answer the phone.

"Somewhere," he said.

"Could you get him?"

She watched Adam cross the bedroom and pick up the phone.

"Maggie's with Zee," he said. "Girls' night out, dining on chicken in Shock Trauma. You shouldn't be missing the fun."

Heat rose in Lucy's throat.

"Zee ought to have asked *me* if Maggie could go with her," Lucy said, her face hot. "I'm her mother."

She was unaccustomed to her own temper, gliding through difficulties without drama, a quality of character *achieved,* not necessarily intuitive. Cast into the world of adults early, she had learned to negotiate with a measure of grace.

"Why Zee?" Adam asked. "Maggie should have asked *you*."

Lucy hung up the phone, took Felix's small hand in her own and went upstairs.

"Where did Maggie go?"

"She went with Zee," Lucy said, running the bathwater. "You'll have your bath and then dinner. You and me."

"I don't want to take a bath until Maggie gets home," Felix said.

"But you will, sugarplum."

Lucy undressed him, added bubble bath, dumped his bath toys into the tub, her eyes smarting.

He was still in the bath, Lucy on the closed toilet seat, watching without seeing him. How long had he been in the water, she wondered, on his stomach, his skin wrinkling, and then, just as she was struggling to pull her attention back to Felix, Maggie called from downstairs.

"I'm back."

Don't criticize, Lucy told herself. *Not now before she has a chance to offer her own defense.*

"Hi," she said as Maggie flew by the bathroom door heading to her room.

"Maggie's here now," Felix said, scrambling out of the bath. "Hi, Maggie."

"Hi, Felix," she called back.

"Can Maggie read me a story?" Felix asked following Lucy into his bedroom.

"I can't, Felix," Maggie said. "I have too much homework."

"Tomorrow?"

"Yup, tomorrow."

She sounded confident and disengaged, somewhere beyond Lucy on the way to grown up, leaving her mother behind.

Lucy sat on the bed reading *Winnie-the-Pooh*, the words swimming, her eyes flying across the page in some kind of nervous dance, unable to focus. The room was hot but she felt a chill running down her spine, across her shoulders, and she shivered all over as if she might quite literally jump out of her skin.

"What's the matter?" Felix asked.

"Nothing," she replied.

"You stop talking. Read the book to me the right way."

"I'll try to read the right way," she said.

She read slowly, letting her voice trail off until Felix seemed almost asleep and she got up to turn out his light.

"I'm not going to sleep now," he said. "I don't need to."

She kissed him good night, turned on the nightlight, and as she started down the hall towards Maggie's room, she heard his bare feet on the hardwood floor and felt his body brush her legs.

"I'm going with you wherever you go," he said.

Maggie was lying on her back, her legs against the bedroom wall, the door wide open.

"Dinner's in the oven," Lucy said.

"I smell it," Maggie said. "It's burned and anyway I've already eaten."

IN HER STUDIO, Lucy leaned over a drawing of Vermillion, trying for just the amount of green to make the sloth *surprising,* a sloth to take seriously.

"Maybe you could tell me a story." Felix climbed on a stool, watching Lucy.

"Maybe."

She was listening for Maggie just in case she decided to cross the street to the Mallorys' house, hop up the steps to the front porch, walk through the front door, join *their* family in the kitchen.

"Do you think Maggie will run away? She told me yesterday she might."

"I don't think she will."

"How do you know?"

"I just know," Lucy said.

"Maggie told me you don't know everything."

"That's true," Lucy said.

She was listening as Maggie came up the steps to the studio, her mop of red curls surfacing at the top of the stairs.

"I was at the hospital in case you were wondering," Maggie said.

"I wasn't actually wondering," Lucy said. "I knew."

"You wouldn't have allowed me to go if I'd asked."

Lucy didn't look up from her work, careful to choose her words.

"Right?" Maggie asked.

She was leaning against the wall, her arms folded across her chest.

"How come you don't ask about August and how he is?"

Lucy put her brush in the green paint, swirled it around and began to paint.

"August is in a coma. Possibly, he'll die. That's what Zee says."

Something burned in Lucy's stomach.

"Don't you want to see him?" Maggie asked.

Lucy hung the green-splattered sloth to dry on a line over the table with clothespins, turned off the overhead light, and picked Felix up.

"I saw him this morning."

"You're lying," Maggie said. "Where did you see him?"

"At the hospital."

"How come you didn't tell me?"

"I am telling you now."

"I don't believe you," Maggie said, going into her bedroom, closing the door halfway.

LUCY PUT FELIX under the covers on her bed, kissed him good night, and headed downstairs to lock the front door and turn off the lights. When

Lucy came upstairs, the door was wide open to Maggie's room and she was in her pajamas, sitting up in bed reading. She had on blue flannels, the collar up, a halo of curly hair, and she looked like she had when she was a little girl. But now when she lifted her head, her face darkened in fury.

How could this have come to be without evident cause, taking Lucy's breath so she had to lean against the wall for support.

"If you are planning to tell me I lied to you today about going to the library with Vivienne," Maggie's voice was preternaturally calm, "I did lie and I'll probably do it again because what we do in this family is tell lies."

Twelve

GRAY AND COLD, it was the second Saturday after August had fallen with his ladder onto the avenue, and Adam Mallory was in the bedroom packing.

Across his side of the queen-size bed, he had spread starched shirts back from the cleaners in boxes, a couple of polo shirts, two pairs of trousers, striped boxers and athletic socks. He stuffed them into a duffel, zipping it shut, and stretched, his arms clasped above his head, his back arched, and Zee, watching from the bathroom door, felt a fleeting rush of desire at the sight of the curve of his back.

She assumed that Adam knew she was watching him pack but he had made no mention of a trip requiring luggage. Nor had he suggested where he might be going or with whom or for how long, although Zee knew.

In the bedroom on the third floor, above them, Gabriel Russ was doing what he called *my calisthenics*—a tiny man jumping rope on a hardwood floor, something which he did every morning since the day he arrived from Albany and moved into the Mallorys' house.

"Here for the long haul," he said when the taxi dropped him with an old-fashioned suitcase almost the size of a steamer trunk.

"Awfully nice to have you," Adam had said, the sarcasm barely perceptible and certainly not to Gabriel.

"Yes, yes," Gabriel replied, hailing the twins to carry his suitcase up the two flights of stairs. "Especially nice to have me."

"One of your very best ideas, Zelda, to invite this engaging gentleman to share our living quarters indefinitely," Adam had said that night, lying in the dark next to Zee curled facing away from him.

"Not indefinitely," she said. "Briefly. I thought he needed a sense of family around him. After all."

"After all, we're a perfect choice," Adam said.

"He's just here until August either comes out of the coma or dies," Zee said.

"I was under the impression that he was *not* going to die," Adam said. "In fact, that impression came from you."

"He might die, is what I said." Zee turned over on her back. "But probably he won't."

August had improved. He was responding to voices, to touch and to light, but he was still semiconscious with regular seizures, several a day. The neurologists had decided that he should be put in a medically induced coma to give his brain a rest. When the seizures ceased as the medical team hoped would happen, then they'd bring him slowly to consciousness. There was no telling what the ultimate outcome of his fall would be but his recovery so far was reason for some optimism.

"Do you mind?" Adam asked, walking past Zee into the bathroom. "If you move away from the door, I'll close it so the sound of my urinating won't offend you."

"Are you going to tell me where you're going today?" she asked, sitting at the end of the bed when he came back out.

He picked up the duffel, lifted the strap over his shoulder, and headed out of the room.

"You know where I'm going."

It was early and the boys were just getting up, heading sleepily downstairs in their pajamas to watch cartoons.

"Cartoons?" Adam asked.

216

"It's Saturday," Luke said.

Zee followed Adam down the stairs.

"Are you going to tell the boys?" she asked.

"Tell them what?"

"Where you're going."

"Certainly I'm going to tell them, Zee."

"But you're not going to tell them *why,* right?"

"Not yet. Not this Saturday at least."

Her stomach was in knots, her throat and shoulders cramped, and the carefully constructed defenses necessary for the high-wire act of her marriage to Adam were fraying. She watched him open the fridge and take out a carton of orange juice, put two pieces of wheat bread in the toaster, pour a cup of coffee. She was losing a sense of who Adam was even more than when he first returned from Viet Nam.

They had made promises to one another and Zee was beginning to think that Adam could betray them.

"How come you've got a suitcase, Dad?" Luke asked, padding barefoot into the kitchen for a banana.

"I'm going to Vermont."

"How come?" Luke asked.

"I have business in Vermont," Adam said.

"How come Mom isn't going like she used to do?"

"Not this time, Lukie. This time it's just me and Route 95 North."

Luke got a second banana for Daniel, and headed back to the television.

Wearily, Zee slipped into a chair. Once a year, occasionally more, they drove to Cavendish together or flew to Burlington, but in the last two years, Adam had gone alone.

"Why are you doing this?" she asked quietly.

"More to the point, Zelda, why aren't you doing this with me?"

She rested her chin on her folded hands and closed her eyes.

"I can't," she said.

Which was true. She was not able to go to Vermont with him. Not strong enough, not sufficiently detached.

"Are you going to show me up?" she asked.

"No," he said, opening the back door. "I'm going because I have to go."

"But you went already in January. I thought that was your trip this year."

"Apparently not," he said, finishing his coffee and heading out the back door.

"Call," she said.

"I'll call when I get there."

From the kitchen window, Zee watched him put the car in gear and back out of the driveway and down Witchita to the entrance to Witchita Hills, then left to the Chevy Chase Circle and out Connecticut Avenue to 495 Baltimore and north to Vermont. Maybe ten hours.

Six or seven hours on Route 95 past Wilmington and New York to Hartford and then straight up Route 81, the length of Vermont to Cavendish. Six o'clock at night, he'd be in Cavendish checking into the Goosedown Lodge, where they had stayed the other times they had driven to Vermont together.

"Forty-five minutes," she said to the twins, slouched side by side in front of the television, Luke's leg slung over Daniel's. "And at nine-thirty baseball practice at the field and then we'll go bowling with Josie and Rufus and then you have Eric's birthday party at Chuck E. Cheese."

Upstairs, she changed the sheets. She wanted to sleep alone on clean sheets.

Maybe she'd cut her hair, short like Twiggy, a boy's cut close to her head.

She lay down on her back on the unmade bed and crossed her legs at the ankles, lying very still looking at the ceiling, her eyes half closed.

Gabriel was on his way downstairs from the third floor.

"Goodbye," he called in the singsong voice he favored. "Goodbye, goodbye, goodbye. I'm off to see the Wizard, the Wonderful Wizard of Oz."

She shut her bedroom door.

He was on the second set of stairs going down to the first floor.

Above the splash and rumble of the washing

machine, she could barely hear Gabriel talking to the twins.

Should she remind him to be careful about Onion getting out the front door? Or should she simply lie there and wait to see what happened? So what if Onion did escape. He'd climb a tree or wander across the avenue on his fuzzy white paws. He could be hit by a car if he happened to walk out on Witchita Avenue at the wrong moment. Stupid cat. And then what? Would such a possibility be worth getting up and dressed to prevent from happening? And would it matter deeply to her if Onion died? Or did she already have responsibility for too many lives and one white-pawed alley cat, almost fifteen years old, who peed on the laundry with increasing frequency, did not make sufficient difference in the scope of things.

A thought floated through her mind. Onion had witnessed her whole life since she'd been a junior in college in Ann Arbor when Zee found her outside the coffee shop, things that no one else knew except Adam and the cat, her sweet old cat had no point of view about Zee, unless it was affection or gratitude.

Eight-thirty by the clock on Adam's side of the bed.

She had never in memory, even as a child in rural Michigan where time moved unchanging through the day like cloud cover, been so still that her body sank into the mattress. She almost slept. The cool air through the open window washed across her face and arms. Something else was seeping into consciousness. In her groin the rumbling of sickness or was it desire.

SATURDAY MORNING, A whole long day, hours and hours of it in front of her. Maggie needed a plan.

She had been up early, disappointed at the dreary rain pelting her windows. Checking her closet, she dressed in pants even though she was in the process of transforming her appearance after Zee's and Zee never wore pants. She wore skirts and little tight tops but Maggie didn't have so many skirts, not the right ones at least. She took a black top with long sleeves and a deep V from the shelf in her mother's closet, a little blush on her cheeks from her mother's top bureau drawer.

This morning her plan had been to ride her bike down Witchita to the other side of Connecticut Avenue where Vivienne lived on Ohio Lane. Maeve Sewall was going to come along with her father's copy of *The Joy of Sex*, which they planned to study in detail sequestered under a large weeping willow tree in Vivienne's backyard. And if it was warm enough, they'd swim in Vivienne's pool.

But today it was going to rain and rain, a long,

221

slow steady rain, Maggie thought, watching Adam Mallory with a duffel bag get into his car and back out of the driveway.

Crazy Gabriel had come out of the Mallorys' house with an umbrella and was standing on the front porch looking one way and then the other as if he imagined the Mallorys' yard was not a yard at all but a busy street. He opened the umbrella, walked down the steps, a little dance move like a skittish squirrel, walking almost on his toes, and turned left towards Connecticut Avenue.

Lane Sewall glided across her front porch in a splashy red robe. She picked up the newspaper, Maeve in pajamas behind her.

Maggie was watching the neighborhood from her bedroom window—Victoria hurrying up the street with a yoga mat, her frizzy hair secured in a ballet dancer's bun, the Sewalls' beagle barking madly at a squirrel in the maple in the front yard. She wondered what Zee was doing. Adam off on a trip, only the twins downstairs watching cartoons.

And then she saw Onion meandering across the street, his tail, clipped at the end so it curled, straight up. Crossing to the south side of Witchita, he disappeared into the yard of the house next door to August belonging to Mrs. Greene.

Maggie hopped up, slipped on her yellow rain slicker, and ran out the front door barefoot.

"Be back in a second," she called to her mother, and headed past August's house to Mrs. Greene's where Onion was sitting on the top step of the porch biting at something between the pads of his paw.

"Onion!" she said, gathering the old compliant cat in her arms and heading to the Mallorys'.

"Upstairs!" Daniel said when Maggie asked where their mother was.

"Onion got out," she said, but neither of the boys sitting on the couch with mangy Blue lying across their laps showed an interest in Onion so Maggie walked up the steps with the cat under her arm, knocked on Zee's bedroom door, and walked in.

Zee was lying on an unmade bed, her head on a pillow, in a short nightgown, her arms above her, her hair a pillowcase of blond, and just the stillness of her was quite beautiful and stirring.

"Onion crossed the street," Maggie said. "I found him on Mrs. Greene's porch."

"Gabriel probably let him out when he left," Zee said. "Poor Onion."

"Crazy Gabriel just headed towards Connecticut Avenue with his umbrella swinging back and forth over his head in the rain so he's sopping wet."

They both laughed and Maggie put her knee on the bed as if she might sit down or might not, might stay or leave. She had never seen Zee

Mallory in a nightgown, in bed, and she seemed fragile and small.

"Adam's gone to Vermont for the weekend, in all this rain," Zee said. "So it's just me and the boys."

"I've made plans to go to Vivienne's house with Maeve and maybe swim and now we can't," Maggie said, balancing against the edge of the mattress.

"Sometimes I love the rain. It reminds me of Michigan where I grew up, day after day, gray, gray, gray," Zee said, patting the side of the bed for Maggie to sit down beside her. "You could put Onion out in the hall and close my door so he doesn't pee on my rug and lie down with me on this sleepy morning if you don't mind a bed with no sheets."

Maggie hesitated, mentally anticipating her movements as if by lying next to Zee or not, or choosing to sit on the end of the bed with her knees drawn up under her chin or even to leave, say *breakfast is ready at home and I haven't eaten,* would be a commitment.

The moment felt strangely reckless.

"I've been meaning to give you some of my necklaces." Zee was sitting now, stretching, her back against the headboard. "I have so many necklaces from my mother's shop in Michigan and you have a lovely neck."

A lovely neck.

Maggie had never thought about her neck

before. No one had even remarked on her looks that she could remember. Only Uncle Reuben, who told her she had an Italian kind of beauty except for the curly red hair which was pure Irish. But never anything about her neck.

She sat down on the end of the bed, a high bed so her feet dangled and didn't touch the floor.

"Do you like silver or gold?"

"Maybe silver," Maggie said.

"They're not real silver, I should tell you, and certainly not real gold," Zee said. "But they jangle and that's the point."

"I love jangle," Maggie said, climbing onto the bed next to Zee, her back pressed against the soft quilted headboard, their bodies touching. Zee's hands, folded lightly on her stomach, were trembling.

"I can't stay long," Maggie said, noticing Zee's shaky hands, nervous about it.

WHAT LUCY HAD in mind for Saturday morning, after Maggie went to Vivienne's house and Felix to play at the Lerners', was to search August's house for the manuscript. She had watched him from her bedroom window working on the dining room table or in his study on the second floor. When he came over in the mornings, he brought the book in a manila file marked BOOK in red magic marker, held together with a rubber band. It should be easy to find.

225

Her plan was to go into the house through the back door which he kept unlocked so the people on Witchita Avenue wouldn't see her, only Mrs. Greene who lived next door to August. She was a woman likely to be clearing out her garden for spring planting even on a rainy day. The kind of woman who made everything from scratch, bread and soups and gardens from seeds. She even changed the oil in her old Chevrolet and once, according to Zee, she had changed a tire lying on her back half under the car.

She keeps to herself, Zee had said, *but she's vigilant and probably knows a lot more about us than we think.*

Lucy didn't ask how long Mrs. Greene had lived in the neighborhood, but that was on her mind. It was possible that she could have been living in the same house when Samuel Baldwin died. Not that anyone in the neighborhood had known Lucy's father then because the house was rental property but certainly the newspaper stories would have made note of the place.

Copies of the newspaper stories were likely in August's research files. Lucy had never read them. Somehow in the flurry and shock of the week he died, her mother had managed to shield her from the news and then she and her mother had left for Santa Fe and more or less permanently erased her childhood so Lucy had only the story her mother had constructed when she took on the name Painter and her own scattered memories, pure in detail and precise but disconnected from a narrative.

For days, she had not been able to sleep at night, *at all,* she'd told Reuben, slipping out of bed not to wake Felix, curled next to her. She'd go up to her studio and lie on the floor under the skylight, the moon illuminating her Vermillion drawings drying on the clothesline between the rafters, flapping eerily in the light breeze through the cracked open window.

A soft resolve and she'd put a pillow between her legs, imagining Reuben beside her, his hand lightly on her belly, his warm breath on her neck.

Later, she lay on the floor, her knees up, a light sleepiness coming over her. She was alone with her work and Reuben had vanished. Comforting to be alone, she thought, surrounded by her work as if without it, she was invisible even to herself.

Vermillion, poor Vermillion in the act of becoming, so far from finished, and Fervid P. Drainpipe and Belly and all the others. Her inventions, not separate from her like a child is separate, like Maggie or Felix, but *herself* in fact. Proof of her existence.

It was possible that August had been brain-damaged in the fall and would forget things, even the book he'd been in the process of writing.

Possible also that he'd tell the nurses or one of

the doctors about Samuel Baldwin. Or Zee would make her way into his room in the hospital when he regained consciousness and ask him question after question and August would say what came into his mind about the man whose suicide in Lucy Painter's house had been national news. He might even tell Zee Mallory the truth of why Samuel Baldwin had chosen such a way to die.

Ne dis jamais de notre honte, Lucy's mother had warned her, as if the telling of what had happened to her father was always on the tip of Lucy's tongue. As if the truth were some catastrophe waiting in the wings and only Reuben, to whom she had told the real story, had loved her enough to understand.

Lucy checked the time. 8:45. Felix would go to the Lerners' at nine and soon Maggie would be back from delivering Onion to the Mallorys and ready to go with Maeve to Vivienne's house. She was washing the breakfast dishes, thinking that if she made enough money when she sold *Vermillion*, she'd get a dishwasher and because the water in the spigot was running she didn't hear Lane Sewall come onto the porch, open the front door without knocking, and wander into the kitchen.

"Maeve's mama is here," Felix announced from under the table where he was picking the old chewing gum off the underside, probably stuck there by students long ago at RISD.

"Yuck." Lucy turned around, wiping her wet hands on the painting smock she was wearing. "You'll get some sort of awful sickness, Felix. Wash your hands."

"That *is* disgusting, Felix," Lane said, still in her red robe splashed with white chrysanthemums, tied at the waist, barefoot, her hair falling loose of its high bun. "I can practically see the germs walking over the chewing gum in their military uniforms."

"You can?"

"Hundreds of them with hairy heads and big lips," she said as Felix scrambled out from under the table and hurried over to the sink, pulling up a chair to wash his hands.

"I'm sorry to intrude," Lane said, "but it's so gray out this morning, I couldn't bear to stay in the house."

She sat down at the kitchen table, folding her robe at the split, her long legs crossed at the knee, settling in as if a plan to meet at Lucy's this morning had been prearranged.

"Coffee?" Lucy asked, leaning against the sink hoping her irritation wasn't evident.

"Coffee would be good. You'll tell me if I'm interrupting."

"You're not," Lucy said, and then because her voice in her own ear sounded unconvincing, she added, "I'm free all day."

"Good. I hate Saturdays when Will is at the lab."

229

The lab where Will Sewall was a research psychiatrist with a particular interest in schizophrenia was at the National Institute of Mental Health, and since the Watergate scandal, he had been serving as a special consultant on the president's team of physicians worried about Nixon, who had a history of erratic behavior, and his mental stability.

"Most Saturdays he's at the lab," she said, retying the sash of her robe tight around her waist, which was the wide waist of a thin, leggy woman without hips. She shrugged and then from nowhere, she seemed to pluck words out of the thickness of the day, the heavy weight of thunder clouds bearing down on their morning.

"He's impotent."

Lucy caught her breath. She didn't even know Lane Sewall but nothing in her bearing suggested confession.

"I fell in love with him because he plays the cello."

"I didn't know he played the cello," Lucy said, getting up for cream and sugar, pouring herself a cup of coffee although she had already had too much but her plans for this morning had changed course with Lane's arrival.

"I love the cello," she said. "It's my favorite instrument, although I know so little about music and play nothing myself, but I listen, I listen to everything, especially when I'm working."

Which was not true. She listened to children's stories on tape for Felix.

"Sometime come over and he'll play and you'll think he's falling in love with you but he isn't." She shrugged. "That's Will."

Rufus came to pick up Felix to play at his house and then Maggie crashed through the hall, calling to Lucy that she was late, late, late because she'd been at Zee's and saved Onion from being smashed by a car and now she had to hurry to meet Maeve in front of her house to go to Vivienne's.

"Okay?"

Lane requested more coffee. No cream this time.

"Is Maggie's father married?"

She had a way of speaking, slow and a little slurred, as if she had been drinking, which she had not.

"Your children's father," Lane said, something in her voice that Lucy couldn't identify thinned to a silk thread of sound. "Never mind," she went on, waving her hands as if to swat away what she had just said, rearranging her legs so the one crossed over the knee swung back and forth, hitting the table leg with a thump. "It's not my business anyway but I'm impressed at your confidence. Just you and your children as if you'd decided in favor of immaculate conception and miraculously it has worked."

231

"Well . . ." Lucy got up to get blueberries from the fridge.

"That was meant to be a compliment, you know."

The gray light of the morning articulated the shape of Lane's face, her soft features, pretty but not beautiful, her cheeks flushed and damp.

"I have muffins," Lucy said, setting muffins and butter and jam on the table.

"Muffins," Lane said. "Lovely."

She leaned towards Lucy, her elbows on the table, her chin supported by her fists. "I actually came over for a reason beyond company on this depressing day," she began. "I suppose I wanted to tell you myself before it became a matter of neighborhood conversation, as things do in Witchita Hills, even though I love it here better than anyplace I've ever lived and Zee is my closest friend. Are you getting to know her?"

She took a muffin, breaking it into small pieces, brushing the pieces across the butter, dipping them in jam, and eating so slowly Lucy thought she would jump out of her skin.

"I'm getting to know her a little," Lucy said nervously.

"Zee's my best friend. But chatty. You can tell that about her. She holds the neighborhood in her hand."

"I know she's in charge."

"Yes, in charge. That's Zee. In charge of us all,

even our children, and I wanted to tell you how much I like Maggie and glad I am that she and Maeve are getting to be good friends and they are, you know. I even think they lie upstairs on Maeve's bed and study Will's copy of *The Joy of Sex*."

She laughed, an awkward, artificial laugh, on the edge of crying.

"Sex and joy," she said. "The concept is lost on me."

Lucy's legs were beginning to shake and she twisted them around each other, pressed her knees together, her arms wrapped tight around her chest.

"I thought you should know from me and not from Zee because she doesn't have girls. You know all she ever wanted was a girl—and you and I do have girls and our girls are so close. It's lovely, isn't it?"

"It is lovely."

Lucy got up, opened the fridge to pour herself a glass of milk.

"I have been diagnosed with breast cancer," Lane said, "and that's why I've left graduate school and why I'm at home but you mustn't tell Maggie because Will and I are *not* telling our children. You understand?"

"I'm so sorry," Lucy said, her face burning, too easily upset by personal information. "I am so very sorry."

"Never mind. I'll either die or not," she said. "*Don't tell the children*. That's our philosophy. Will's and mine."

"Of course."

"You don't tell your children everything, do you?" Lane asked. "Zee insists she does but I don't believe her for a second."

"I suppose I don't."

"I didn't think you'd be that kind of mother. How could you—too much has happened to you they couldn't possibly understand." She started to stand and then leaned back against the chair. "I'm reading *Fear of Flying*. Have you read it?"

"I don't read very much fiction," Lucy said.

"But you write."

"I think in pictures," Lucy said.

"Interesting," Lane said. "Well, everyone seems to be reading *Fear of Flying* so I thought I should."

She got up then, slowly, pressing her temples, the color drained from her face, and for a moment Lucy was afraid she was going to throw up, the way she leaned forward towards the floor, this almost-stranger, about to be sick on Lucy's new linoleum.

"Are you all right?"

"I've such a headache," Lane said. "I have them and they come over me like lava."

Lucy followed her to the door but at the door Lane stopped. She leaned against the wall as if for support and Lucy could tell she wanted more from her, some connection or revelation, and she was just about to say something vaguely insincere like *Thank you for stopping by* when Lane took her by the wrist.

"If Maeve knew I had breast cancer, it would kill her," she said with surprising force. "I can tell you disapprove."

"But I don't," Lucy said, quickly. "I don't at all. I don't tell my children everything either." She took a breath. "I couldn't."

Lane gathered her robe around her, wrapping the skirt across her legs.

"I should confess that I lied to you," she said, taking on a child's voice, a little lisp over the *s*'s. "Will actually isn't impotent at all. I don't know why I said that. I really don't. But of course there's a reason. Always a reason, I'm told in my psychology classes. Will's concerned I'm *losing it,* whatever that means." She started down the steps. "Still raining, isn't it?" She turned and gave a little wave. "Thank you for the coffee. I imagine you made the blueberry muffins yourself."

Lucy watched her make her way down the front steps in the warm rain, holding the railing, moving slowly as if it might hurt to walk, and when she had crossed the street without looking back, walked up her front steps, Lucy went into the house.

Exhausted, she sank into the new couch in the living room and watched the rain pelting on the roofs of the houses.

Reuben would most likely not be at the office since it was a Saturday, but she called him anyway. She wanted to tell him about Lane Sewall, who was certainly losing it, breast cancer aside.

Lane is not telling her children. Is that lying or shielding them from the truth? Or were those the same thing? She would ask him.

AUGUST'S HOUSE WAS smaller than hers and well-kept, the kitchen spotless, not even the residual smell of food. Maybe he didn't cook for himself. Only for Lucy. She had never seen him cook from the window in her kitchen or the one in her bedroom where she occasionally watched him. Maybe he had a cleaning lady who kept a key and did not even know that he was critically injured in the hospital. No one in the neighborhood was privy to August's personal life, and so no one would know whether or not he had a housekeeper unless they had seen her go in the front door.

She went to the study first, which was on the second floor, assuming that was the most likely place to find the manuscript, and it was tidy as if no one had worked there for months, as if it were a study out of a decorator's magazine arranged to be photographed. Stacks of books were on his desk, a picture of August as a child with a couple who must have been his parents, the mother holding a small boy, probably Gabriel. A small Buddha in stone, legs crossed. *A Buddha?* A single candlestick with a terra-cotta candle, the room painted pale green, deepening the terra-cotta. Maybe August was in love with colors too. There were dead tulips in a celadon vase on the desk, faded red and drooping.

She searched the drawers, the closet in which manuscripts and books were stored, some paintings, photographs in frames, one of which must have been his wife. Anna. His sheepskins, also framed from Kenyon College in Ohio, his Ph.D. from Yale. Boxes marked *Childhood: India 1933–1948; Marriage: 1960–1971. Anna Russ: 1936–1971.*

She took the box marked *Marriage* off the shelf and opened it. Through the window in the study overlooking the backyard, she could see Mrs. Greene kneeling in her garden, in a yellow slicker clearing out the winter as Lucy imagined she might be. Any moment now, she would stand up, glance at August's house, and perhaps with her sharp nose for change might even guess that someone was there.

The box was full of loose photographs. There were many of a tall, slender, fair-haired woman, not pretty but pleasing, eyes set wide.

Conventional. Lucy assumed the photograph was Anna.

There were two rooms upstairs, August's bedroom and the study. The bed was made, the spread pulled tight, nothing on the tops of dressers or tables, not even photographs. The room was painted mustard yellow, an oil painting over the bed which showed a farmhouse with a blue door, half obscured in high grasses, and a single sheep in the foreground.

It was as if he planned to vacate the morning of his fall and didn't wish for anyone to find a mess.

There was another bedroom used for storage with four large steamer trunks and boxes and boxes of books marked BOOKS TO SELL. Paintings lined up against the wall. Downstairs in the dining room lay open books. File cards were in a case on the table, a book about seventies architecture opened and marked with notes in the margin in nearly invisible pencil, a typewriter with paper on which he was typing. In the middle of writing that morning, he must have decided to clean the gutters and gone to the side of the house facing Lucy where he kept his extension ladder and lifted it so it reached just under the eaves. Or maybe he was thinking about Lucy, about coffee and a hot muffin and what he would read to her from his manuscript after the gutters were cleared.

Nothing in the dining room either. Just the work he was doing; no sign of the manuscript.

SHE CHECKED THE time. An hour and thirty-two minutes since she'd entered the back door. Any moment now, Josie would bring Felix home so she had to hurry, out the back, checking first to see if Mrs. Greene was still working in her garden, which she was not. A quick dash across the yard into her own backyard and up the steps, through her door just as the phone stopped ringing.

"Lucy," the answering machine had recorded, "If you get this, call me at the office ASAP."

Thirteen

NO ONE WAS in the booths of Café Stella at four in the afternoon on the last Monday of April— only the waitress, Brigitte, sitting at the bar smoking Salem menthols, her back to Lucy and Reuben, who sat across from one another in the last and darkest booth next to the stage where that night the Blue Horns were doing a Joni Mitchell concert.

Lucy's hands were closed in Reuben's larger ones, his leg under the table between her legs.

They were quiet, Lucy at a loss for words.

That morning at the International Inn on Scott Circle, Room 603—*international* chosen because the hotel would be full of strangers, they had been together on the clock. Two hours until Felix got out of preschool, Maggie's teacher's conference at one-thirty, then Maggie to Maeve's after school and Felix with a babysitter Lucy had gotten at American University.

Four to six to talk about *important things* at Café Stella, and then Reuben would take the seven-thirty shuttle back to New York.

He had come to Washington at the last minute to have lunch with John Dean, the White House counsel who had agreed to cooperate with the Watergate investigators without resigning his post at the White House. *Betraying the president to save his own skin,* Reuben had said when he called Lucy on Saturday morning to say *Yes, yes, yes!* He was finally coming to Washington first thing Monday morning.

Someday, perhaps even soon, John Dean would have a book to write about his role in Watergate, which was why Reuben had been sent to Washington.

There were things she needed to say to Reuben but Lucy was afraid to talk.

HE LOOKED OLDER and thinner. Naked, his hipbones had protruded like pointed trowels in the flesh of her stomach that morning. His hair was fading, not gray exactly but the way she supposed dark red hair turned gray by paling to a kind of soft pink, and he seemed somehow frail and girlish to her.

"Two months is a very long time," she said.

"Pneumonia was terrible for us but it's over and we'll work on a better plan to be together."

"It's only . . ." She stopped.

"So tell me . . ." He leaned over and kissed her lips.

"I'm afraid to tell you the truth," she said.

"Is it anything I don't already know?" he asked. "That we haven't already talked about."

"We have talked about everything," she said. "Again and again the same things but never with answers to the questions."

In the dim light of Stella's Café, his eyes were dark green, not hazel, the pupils dilated, darting in spite of his effort to hold his attention on her.

Brigitte had gotten up from the bar and ambled over to their booth.

"Something to drink?"

"We're still fine," Reuben said with some irritation.

"Order *something* or I have to ask you to leave." She shrugged. "Policy."

"No one's here so we're not exactly keeping people from ordering," Reuben said.

"We're not a bus stop."

"Then two hot chocolates with whipped cream."

"No hot chocolate on the chalkboard menu,

right? Only coffee, tea, soft drinks, and alcohol," she said, and went through the swinging doors to the kitchen, coming back with beers.

"I'll leave you alone now."

Reuben released Lucy's hands and lit a cigarette.

"So tell me the questions to which we haven't found answers."

Sometimes she hated the way he spoke to her, lifting his brows, a pained expression in his eyes suggesting she took all the patience he could muster.

"We haven't found the answers to how we will deal with our children now that they're older and we're living three hundred miles apart."

"Week by week, month by month, the way we have always dealt with these children unless there is a crisis."

"There is a crisis," Lucy said.

"Okay," he said quietly, and she could feel him cooling to the conversation, even as his hand lay heavily on her arm. "What crisis?"

Nothing would come of this. She knew that. Reuben would say he was doing the best he could to "fix" the situation and Lucy would retreat to her promises of self-reliance and independence and personal integrity made before she understood what it meant to raise two children alone. And that would be followed by the small argument about Felix—*Maggie, yes,* Reuben would say. *I thought when Maggie was*

242

born that we would be together for good, and then Nell came and it was impossible. I couldn't leave. Not then.

But Felix had been Lucy's choice. Somehow that decision had become the end of the story, Reuben's trump card, his winning hand.

"I have told you about Zee, who lives across the street," Lucy began.

"A lot."

"Well Maggie is sort of in love with her and maybe that's natural because she's eleven and Zee is seductive."

"Do you mean sexually?"

"No, but she's very taken with Maggie. She swoops her up and makes off with her."

Lucy slipped her legs under her, her arms tight across her chest.

"Maggie is turning into a liar," she said.

Reuben rubbed his hands together, his elbows on the table, his body forward so he could speak quietly.

"Lucy." He left her name in the air.

"I want to be exact, Reuben. I don't want anything to go wrong in this talk."

"You have always been leery of women," he said. "This Zee is no surprise."

The room was damp and chilly but Lucy was perspiring, beads of sweat gathered on her forehead. She pressed her hand against a pulse beating in her temple.

It was an old conversation she'd had with Reuben many times.

"I'm leery of people, Reuben. Not women."

"I don't know this woman who is after Maggie but I think you have to be careful when it comes to—"

"I am careful," Lucy said, getting up, heading across the café to the restroom to wash the flush from her face, the perspiration from her forehead.

In the mirror over the sink she looked at herself. Her skin was blotched, red, and puffy under her eyes. She sat down on the toilet and held her face in her hands. Maybe she would stay there until the bar filled and Reuben left for his flight to New York.

She wondered did she love him or was this stew of emotions that felt like love really fear that he would leave?

There are no happy endings, he had told her once. *The end is the end.*

Was this the end? she wondered. Had he had enough of the arguments between them, Lucy's longing and what he called his *responsibilities*. Was this life they'd woven together unraveling and she had failed to notice, the way she often failed to notice the reality of things, and had time run out, leaving her no chance to rewind back to the place where this day began.

"Lucy." Reuben banged on the door to the ladies' room. "Are you okay?"

She checked the splotches on her face, ran her fingers through her hair, unlocked the door, and stepped into the smell of beer and cigarettes.

"Let's get out of here." He took her hand, his finger rubbing softly on her palm.

He drew her into a courtyard along the street, leaned up against a building pulling her towards him, his hand on her back, his tongue wandering softly in her mouth.

"Remember that piece of land I told you about in Nova Scotia?"

"I thought it was Maine."

"Then Maine," he said, taking her hand walking south. "I wanted to build something for us on the tip of that point."

They came to the bottom of Georgetown on M Street at Wisconsin Avenue.

It was near six by the clock on the National Bank building and Reuben checked his watch.

"Ten minutes," he said. "Can you keep a secret about today?"

"About business?" she said. "No, I don't want to talk about business." She dropped his hand. "Actually I don't want to talk."

She wanted to walk along Wisconsin Avenue pretending nothing at all, swinging arms and kissing.

The day was quickly fading to a wet dusk, the streetlights flickered on, and ahead on Wisconsin

Avenue, a taxi was turning towards the curb to pick up Reuben.

"Before you leave . . ." She wasn't even sure what she wanted to say.

"I love you, Lucy Painter," he said, tilting her face towards him. "You are the love of my life."

He scrambled into the taxi, leaned forward to direct the driver, and as the cab pulled away from the curb, he blew her a kiss.

She could see him in the shadow of the cab's backseat and he was waving.

WHEN GABRIEL RUSS rang the doorbell, Maggie was sitting in the kitchen watching the clock. Her mother was somewhere, not at home yet and late. The babysitter had taken Felix to the library and Maggie had burned the chocolate chip cookies and burned her own tongue tasting them.

Gabriel walked straight into the front hall carrying a paper bag.

"Hello, Maggie, but I call you Margaret," he said. "I have a present for your mother from my brother."

He handed the bag from Leed's Market to Maggie.

"Last week on Thursday when I saw him, my brother, Augustus, at the hospital eating oatmeal for breakfast and a banana, he told me to get this present from the top of his desk in the study and to bring it to him at the hospital. And today, he gave it back to me and asked me to bring it over to Lucy Painter because that was exactly what he was planning to do on the morning that he and the ladder fell into the street. So here it is," Gabriel said. "Happy Birthday."

"Do you know what it is?" Maggie asked.

"It's a present and presents are surprises so how would I know what it is since it's a surprise."

"Well, thank you," Maggie said, taking the Leed's Market bag.

"Thank *you,* Margaret. I call you Margaret because Maggie is a nickname and I have a disagreement with nicknames and that is why I am called Gabriel which is my real name instead of Gaby which would be my nickname if I liked nicknames. That's all for now," he said, and waved heading down the steps.

Maggie opened the bag, took out a manila folder with BOOK marked in red and secured with rubber bands. Paper-clipped to the folder was a note to her mother: *Dear Lucy: Check Chapter 9 pages 135–200. SAMUEL BALDWIN. Love, August.*

Something about the note captured Maggie's attention. A message specifically intended for her mother. A thing of importance.

Any moment, her mother would be home.

Maggie crumpled the note and tossed it in the trash, rifled through the manuscript and took out

Section 9, pages 135–200, and slipped them between the pages of her social studies text. She put the rubber bands around the manila folder and pushed it under the new couch in the living room. Upstairs, she stuffed the social studies text into her crowded bookcase with her other books.

Later, she thought with some excitement, she would read the *important* pages.

Just the act of hiding the manuscript under the couch where her mother might find it felt to her like freedom.

IT WAS ALMOST seven when Lucy arrived home and parked the van. Reuben would be on the plane to New York, back at home by the time she took Maggie and Felix out to dinner at the Pizza Palace in Chevy Chase. Nell would greet him at the front door, kiss his cheeks with her tiny bow lips—*You'll never guess what happened today,* she'd say in her high-pitched voice. He'd pour himself a beer and sit down at the kitchen table while Elaine made dinner, telling *her* the business secret that Lucy had no interest in hearing. *What a great trip to Washington,* he'd say. *So much accomplished.*

Maybe they'd kiss when he walked in the apartment, his lips still sweet with Lucy's body.

Maggie was slouched on the couch, *To Kill a Mockingbird* face down on her stomach. Her eyes were closed.

"The babysitter took Felix to the playground and then the library," Maggie said. "She's a moron."

"Oh?"

"He was playing out front and she was sitting on the steps making out with her boyfriend. Felix could've been run over while they kissed."

Lucy's chest tightened. She walked into the kitchen, turning on the light. The gas was on, the teapot almost empty of water.

"I told the babysitter I'd be here by seven at the latest. When did she leave?"

"Hours ago," Maggie said. "I don't even remember."

"Well get your coat and I'm driving to the library to find Felix and then we'll get pizza at the Palace."

"I don't like the Pizza Palace pizzas."

"You don't have to eat them," Lucy said, shutting the car door, turning on the engine.

Maggie sat in the front seat, her feet on the dashboard.

"I called Uncle Reuben today because I haven't talked to him since Friday," she said.

"You called the office?"

"His secretary said he had gone to Washington for a meeting and wasn't coming back to the office and then I wondered how come he doesn't see us while he's here and I thought maybe the meeting he was having was with you."

Lucy hesitated.

"He came for business but I had a drink with him."

"And did he say anything about us?"

"Of course he did. He sent you kisses and hugs and said next time he *would* see you and it's taken him so long to get over pneumonia and he does look terribly thin and wan."

"He's dropped us."

Lucy pulled up to the library just as the babysitter was walking out the door with Felix.

"Sorry about that. I know I'm late to bring him home," the babysitter said, taking the money Lucy gave her, counting it, sticking it in her pocket. "Usually I get five dollars an hour."

"I paid you three," Lucy said. "I understand your boyfriend was at the house while you were working."

She picked up Felix, carrying him down the steps, into the backseat.

"Why did you pay her when she wasn't supposed to have her boyfriend there?" Maggie asked, reaching back to give Felix a pat.

"I paid her less and told her the reason for that was her boyfriend."

"She also smoked, didn't she, Felix?"

"Cigarettes," Felix said.

They drove around Chevy Chase Circle into Maryland and pulled up to the Pizza Palace.

"Zee says it's perfectly fine with her if we go

over to the Mallorys' when you're busy so you don't have to pay for a babysitter."

"It's not perfectly fine with me," Lucy said.

They ordered pepperoni and grape soda and sat in a booth, Maggie next to Felix, who was drawing pictures of robots. The restaurant was new with white tile walls and a black tile floor, the pizza baking in a wood oven behind the counter. The booths full of families, mothers and fathers and children sitting at Formica tables with large pizzas in front of them, pulling off triangles of tomato and cheese, stuffing them in their mouths so their mouths were too full and the tomato dripped out of the corner of their lips and the mothers were shouting at the children to do this or not do that and the fathers were unhappy.

"You were right, Maggie, " Lucy said, getting up from the table, leaving a twenty-dollar bill although it was much too much for the service and the cost of the pizza and sodas. "This Pizza Palace is terrible."

"Can we get ice cream?" Felix asked.

"Of course," Lucy said, nuzzling her face in Felix's neck, hurrying out of the restaurant before one of the unhappy fathers took out his anger on her family for no reason at all except that Lucy was alone with her children, no father evident, no father necessary. "We'll get a double-decker chocolate chip ice cream cone with jimmies."

Summer 1973

Fourteen

LUCY DISCOVERED AUGUST Russ's manuscript in late June under the new couch in her living room. Her bare foot intersected with the folder while she was scrubbing the yellow material of the couch's slipcover to get rid of the ketchup stain from Felix's hot dog the day before.

It was midday, a Tuesday, and alone in the house, she had just finished working on an illustration for Vermillion. A new Vermillion, one which had unfolded after August's fall, after Reuben's drive-by visit to Washington, sometime in the middle of the illustrations she was doing for the old Vermillion, the story developed.

On her hands and knees, she lifted the couch skirt and there was August's manuscript secured in a rubber band—578 pages, he had informed her the last morning he visited.

Lucy made hot tea even though the day was already too hot, adding extra honey and milk. She took a handful of oatmeal cookies and sat down at the kitchen table. Going page by page, not reading exactly but skimming, and that might take hours. She checked the clock. Near eleven. Felix finished play school at two. Maggie wouldn't be home until five so that gave her time.

Would the obituary be included or were the

articles she knew had been written about her father quoted in full? Was Lucy's name mentioned? Lucy Baldwin, age twelve.

The skin on her hands was active, wet with perspiration.

How often had her mother said to her, speaking mainly in French when they were living in Santa Fe, *Samuel Baldwin destroyed our lives.* Or had her mother *ever* said that? Did Lucy simply intuit what had never been said although she had heard it as spoken?

Car-o-leen Bald-ween, she had called herself before Lucy's father died.

Later Painter, *Peinture.*

"In painting, there is sometimes a new picture painted over an old one," her mother had told Lucy one night at dinner in their garden in Santa Fe, "so you cannot even see the first painting unless you have a sense it's there. So we, Lucy, you, and I, are now the second painting and the first painting is obscured."

Her mother had come from France in 1936 to study architecture in Chicago, living in the same building in Lincoln Park as her father, who was practicing law. They met in the elevator, she on her way to classes and he off to meet with the mayor on city business. She had helped him with his tie.

Caroline Framboise was her name. *Car-o-leen,* he called her. He liked having a French wife. It must have seemed exotic to him, a suggestion of his virility and worldliness because she was French and wore black dresses skirting her calves and perfume. No lipstick or color on her high cheekbones. Only mascara.

He was an American of conventional demeanor, though more complicated than he was willing to reveal.

Caroline Framboise was a distant, preoccupied, nervous woman with a strong sense of either decorum or morality—Lucy was never quite sure of the origin of her mother's opinions—older than her father. The life they lived in Chicago and later in Washington, D.C., was almost Victorian in its convention and reserve, less artificial in Lucy's memory than a true reflection of who they were.

About her mother Lucy had felt a vigilant concern, an occasional rush of affection but seldom love.

When she got older, Lucy assumed that what had seemed arrogant in Caroline Framboise was actually a mask for shyness or alienation from her complicated husband and his country. But such recognition came too late.

It was her father whom Lucy loved and he loved her with constancy and joy and a sense of humor entirely absent in Caroleen Strawberry, as they sometimes referred to her in private.

She turned the first page of the manuscript to

the dedication—*TK*. A kind of ease settling over her. Summer. A light breeze, too warm but soft, coming through the open windows next to the kitchen table.

Witchita Avenue had been quiet that summer during the day. Maggie was at drama camp in the morning and then she walked with Maeve to the village of Chevy Chase, D.C., and the two of them scooped ice cream with Vivienne, whose father owned the shop. Zee was in her television room with Robin Robinson and maybe Lane watching the Senate Watergate hearings which played in the kitchens and living rooms of families all over town. In May, Miles Robinson had been appointed to the office of special prosecutor investigating Watergate and the neighbors appropriated his role at the center of current history to their own lives. Lane Sewall had completed radiation treatments for breast cancer and seemed to be the only one among them in psychotherapy which conversations she reported to each of her friends separately—*Keep it a secret,* she would say to each one. Gabriel spent his days at the hospital sitting in the waiting room watching soap operas, as he liked to do since he had been advised that visiting with August was counterproductive to his brother's recovery. August was expected to recover, not fully perhaps, but miraculous, as Zee liked to say.

Most early mornings Lucy went to the hospital, brief visits since Felix came with her and sat with Gabriel in the waiting room.

Potluck suppers at the Mallorys' were weighted with talk of politics and in the evening the mothers sat barefoot, in sundresses with their cold wine, and if Lucy Painter was *not* present, they talked about her.

Maggie had left early that morning, heading down Witchita Avenue in the direction of camp with no intention of going. She turned left at the bottom of the hill, walked past the Aikens' garden on the corner of Connecticut and Witchita and left again up the hill, passing through the backyards of the neighbors until she got to the Mallorys' where Blue was lying in the blistering heat, his dripping wet tongue hanging out of his mouth. The umbrella table was turned over on its side, the open umbrella broken in two.

In the front, Zee was waiting for the bus to pick up the twins for St. Alban's Day Camp. Maggie could see her through the window—a lavender sundress, strapless with a full skirt and bare feet, her thick blond hair piled on top of her head, her hands cupping the faces of Luke and Daniel, kissing them goodbye, waving as the bus took off up the hill to pick up Sara Robinson.

At night, sleepless, Maggie thought about Zee. About her perfect hands, with two gold rings, one with a pinprick red stone in the center which she wore on the little finger of her left hand. No wedding band. The way her fingernails were kept short, unpolished with perfect half-moons at the cuticle. Maggie would lie on her side, her head on an old flat pillow, her own hands circling her face imagining the hands against her skin were Zee's. It was delicious and unbearable, nothing Maggie had ever known, the way this woman, this mother, had seeped into her consciousness. She would fall asleep with Zee's head on her pillow.

And if she didn't fall asleep, couldn't fall asleep for the tremulous excitement in her blood, she would imagine her bedroom, in the room next to Zee's, between the boys, listening to her breathing in the next room. In her daydream, Adam was always away, always on a business trip. Just Zee in the king-size bed breathing the quiet shush of bird's breath.

Maggie loved the way Zee's toes were long but straight across, evenly lined up, the way her skirts fell just below the knee and her back was small, narrow but very straight.

Zee turned towards the house, blew a kiss through the window to Maggie and opened the back door for her to come in.

"Hello, my astonishing Maggie," she said. "Such a morning I've had. Gabriel couldn't find his trousers and came across the street in his boxers on backwards with the place for his penis to stick through in the back, thinking he might have left the trousers at my house and the doctors called from the hospital to see if I could keep him from coming so often and I said I'd try but it was difficult. And then I put him in a taxi and here you are just in time for us to have a day together if you aren't going to camp."

"I'm not going to camp." Maggie slipped into a chair in the kitchen, looking across the street at her own house. "Do you think my mother can see me here?"

She had dropped *mama* for *mother*. A chilly sound, *mother,* which seemed just right.

"I don't," Zee said, hurrying around the kitchen cleaning up breakfast dishes. "The morning sun is coming straight through the front windows and it's just too bright for her to see across the street."

"I'm hating camp so I wanted to come over today," Maggie said. "I hope you don't mind."

"I love it," Zee said. "You know I love it."

She put her hands together, resting them against her lips.

Sometimes when Maggie and Maeve sat up against the bed, giggling over the pictures in *The Joy of Sex*, Maeve would lean across Maggie and kiss her lips.

"Not hard," Maggie would say. "Just brush them very lightly. Like this."

261

And Maeve would. Softly like the bristles of a makeup brush across Maggie's full lips.

"I haven't told my mother that I'm not going to camp today. Do you mind calling camp?" Maggie shifted in her chair, kicked off her sandals.

"Just this once, Maggie," Zee said.

"I won't ask you again," Maggie said. "But I'm sort of upset and my mother never understands."

Zee picked up a peach from the bowl on the table.

"Want one?" she asked.

"No thanks," Maggie said, digging in her shorts pocket for the number of the drama camp.

"Here goes." Zee dialed the number, a conspiratorial smile at Maggie as she told the director Maggie had the flu and wouldn't be at camp.

She poured them both a glass of lemonade.

"So tell me what's the matter."

"Everything," Maggie said. "Let's go someplace and talk."

"It's hot," Zee said, "but we can go to the Potomac and walk along the bike path. No one is likely to be there in the middle of the day."

They got into Zee's van.

Maggie slipped down in the back while they drove past her house just in case her mother was looking out the window.

"So I saw August last night," Zee said. "He's

lovely and looks well. His color is good although he has one sleepy eye and his speech is fuzzy."

"That's what my mother told me."

"They're keeping the visits very brief but I'll take you as soon as they let me know." She turned onto Arizona Avenue from Nebraska, heading to Thompson's boathouse. "You and your mother had gotten close to August after you moved here, isn't that right?"

"Not me. My mother did. He came over to read his book to her."

"He did? "

"She said he needed someone to listen, I think, because his wife died and he had no good friends."

"He had us, the group in his neighborhood."

"He's weird. Weird people like my mother."

Zee drove into the boathouse parking lot, coming to a stop, pulled up the brake, turned off the engine.

Her arms were strong with long, stringlike muscles and tan. Maggie hadn't noticed that before.

"Shall we rent a canoe?" Zee asked.

"No," Maggie said, slipping down from the van. "Let's just walk."

Zee took her hand.

Maggie didn't know where to begin. Lately she had been thinking without regret that she hated her mother. Hate was not a word she had been allowed to use at home but she didn't know another to describe what it was like with Lucy. She couldn't stand to watch her pad around in her sloppy shirts, her messy curls, or drink her tea with little slurps, or click her teeth against her spoon when she was eating, especially ice cream. It wasn't anything in particular that Lucy had done. Just *being* was enough. In the same room, in the same house, with the same repeated conversations. Even her mother's quiet breaths as she lay in sleep next to Felix curled like a cat under her arm irritated Maggie.

"I have no father," she said. "You know that."

"You do have a father," Zee said. "You just don't know who he is, isn't that right?"

"If I don't know who he is, then he doesn't exist," Maggie said.

"That's not exactly true. He exists but not to you."

"Then maybe it's true to say that I'm *embarrassed* not to know who my father is."

"Why would you be embarrassed?"

"In New York, everyone knew I didn't have a father from the beginning so that's who I was. Just Maggie with a mother and no father and Uncle Reuben, who was my mother's best friend. And here I'm just a girl called Maggie who arrived in Witchita Hills without a father."

Zee was a fast walker. Everything about Zee was quick, Maggie thought, the way she moved, the speedy way she spoke in a low, musical voice, the way her hands moved like birds flapping into flight.

Her mother was almost sleepy in her movements, careful in the way she spoke, lost in her own slow-moving, meandering imagined world. She even seemed bewildered by the layout of her daily life, as if she didn't know which way to go—to the kitchen, start dinner, upstairs to the studio, to the dining room, out back to clear out the garden. Everything delayed.

It drove Maggie crazy.

"You should ask your mother about your father. You're almost twelve. It's probably reasonable that you should know something," Zee said, wiping her damp hands on her skirt.

"I did ask my mother."

"And what did she tell you?"

Maggie hesitated.

"Never mind," Zee said quickly, swinging Maggie's arm way up in the air as if to punctuate the conversation. "Everyone has a reason to keep silent about things."

"Do you?"

"Of course."

"I want to know things," Maggie said. "I want to know everything. Our family has too many secrets. You asked what my mom told me about my father? She said my father lives in New York City and that he's married."

265

"Well . . ." Zee stepped aside, taking Maggie with her to make room for a group of cyclists coming down the shaded path in their direction.

"Married!" Maggie said, leaning against the trunk of a large oak. "And I wondered how come this father of mine isn't married to my mother but I didn't ask that."

"Maybe," Zee hesitated, clearing her throat, "he was already married to someone else."

"You mean before."

"Before you were born."

The cyclists had passed them and Maggie moved ahead, walking in front of Zee. *Before* had not occurred to Maggie. She assumed he hadn't *wanted* to marry Lucy, that she wasn't good enough for him, and nor was the baby Maggie good enough.

Would it be better for him to have been married when he met Lucy or not? Maggie wasn't clear about what she wanted of this father, but the thought of him married ruined her hope that he'd eventually materialize for her.

With Lucy, he had only had sex, nothing like love or marriage or forever between them. And just sex was *dirty,* Maeve had told her.

"I'm reading *The Joy of Sex*, I guess you know that book." Maggie leaned into Zee's shoulder. "It's interesting."

"Very interesting," Zee said.

"Maeve and I talk about positions."

"I haven't looked at the book so I don't know about positions exactly."

"You're *married!*" Maggie laughed.

"You would be surprised how little some married people know," Zee said.

"I thought you knew everything. That's how you seem."

They crossed the bridge over the creek and circled back to the boathouse along the railroad tracks no longer in use.

"My mother . . ." Maggie began, stopping short of finishing.

She was going to say Lucy Painter knows very little. She doesn't even live in a world of real people, just her creepy invented animals, her colors which are like living people to her, her crazy little stories that Maggie used to love and now she hated.

"I don't think I should talk about my mother with you," she said quietly.

"Probably not," Zee agreed.

"The trouble is that it's too easy to tell you the things I've never told anyone and you act as if what I say is perfectly normal. Even about sex and my mother and being married and all the time I've been thinking how different I'm getting to be from how I used to be. I don't even know what to wear in the morning."

Maggie opened the front door of the van and climbed up in the passenger seat.

"I think I love you," she said.

The heat of late morning and mossy dampness, heavy with the smell of mulberries, filled the inside of the van's cab like smoke. Maggie leaned back in her seat, glancing at Zee's profile as she arranged the rearview mirror.

"I hope you don't mind that I've told you that," Maggie said.

"I am so happy that you told me that," Zee said.

She turned on the engine, reached across and took Maggie's hand.

"I love you too," she said. "Sometimes I even pretend that you are the daughter I never had."

LATER, UPSTAIRS IN her own house before the twins came home from camp, Zee locked the door to her bedroom, lay down on the end of the bed, putting a pillow over her eyes to keep out the afternoon sun. Gabriel might be coming back from the hospital at any moment and stop by to see her. Or Lane arriving home from her appointment with the oncologist would want to talk.

Zee needed time to think.

Driving home, Maggie had asked about guilt.

"Guilt is a complicated word and I don't have an answer for you," Zee said.

Guilt was Adam's word. He applied it as a definition for his life—his time in Viet Nam, fighting the war when he should have been a conscientious objector but didn't have the courage—the way he felt surviving the war when so many of the men he knew or didn't know had died—the haunting looks on the faces of the Vietnamese children, his parents slipping into old age, his children. *Waste.* Especially waste. What had been wasted in the war, in his law practice which kept him from being with his sons, in his marriage which had splintered after the accident.

The waste that came of their dishonesty.

"What's the matter with you for chrissake, Zelda?" he'd ask. "Why don't you feel anything at all?"

"What is—is," she'd reply, steadily. "I go from there."

"And where is there?" he'd ask, the repeated melody of an old conversation.

So far Zee had managed her life by plugging into electrical currents—all lights burning in her house, all things to all people. But something was happening as if she could not move fast enough to outrun herself any longer, as if for years she had counted on the long shadow repeated in front of her and that was beginning to disappear.

She must do something. *Doing* was the solution.

Robin was at home watching Miles on television when Zee called.

"The group hasn't seen August for days," Zee said. "I thought we'd go tonight."

"But I thought we were supposed to come one at a time so he's not overwhelmed," Robin said.

"I saw him this morning and he seemed okay. Much better. I could tell by his eyes."

"Will Gabriel be there?"

"Tell Josie that I promise he won't," Zee said

"You'll ask Lucy to come too, right? I saw her today at the grocery," Robin said.

"Gabriel tells me she goes early in the morning almost every day. Alone, of course. You know Lucy!"

"Just ask, that's all," Robin said.

Zee sat up on the end of the bed holding the telephone in her lap, her legs folded under her.

Was Robin suggesting that Zee didn't like Lucy? She *did* like her but it was complicated. Just that week on the Mallorys' front porch talking in the summer twilight, Josie and Lane and even Victoria were discussing Lucy Painter. Not unkindly exactly, but critically.

Remote, they had called Lucy. *Concealed. Distrustful.*

Had *careless* been the word Zee used about Lucy as a mother? Two children without a father? Who exactly was Lucy Painter, and how could you trust a woman like that?

She dialed Lane, who was in her study looking up *manic depression.*

"Listen to this," Lane said, describing the manic phase of bipolar disorder from a book in Will's study.

"Definitely not me," she said. "At least not the manic part."

"The manic part is me," Zee laughed.

"So I'll be there at seven-thirty," Lane said. "And the oncologist said so far so good."

Josie's secretary took the message.

"No need for Josie to call me back," Zee said. "Just be here at seven-thirty if she can."

She didn't call Lucy.

After all, what could Zee do about Maggie's crush? Just a girl's crush on an older woman, an almost twelve-year-old girl, ripe for crushes and low-level anger at her mother. Not Zee's responsibility.

By the time the twins came home, Zee was feeling herself again. She changed to a short blue skirt, shorter than she usually wore, checking in the mirror to see if her calves were too thin. A white T and sandals, bronze blush. She took her hair out of combs, letting it fall to her shoulders.

Luke came home from camp with a bloody nose, blood dribbling off his chin onto his T-shirt.

"Luke's fault," Daniel said, crossing the hallway where Zee sat on the steps with Luke, pinching the bridge of his nose to stop the bleeding. "He started a fight with Alex on the bus and Alex just hit him back."

On his way to the kitchen, Daniel kicked Blue as he headed through the hall, not hard, but the dog made a little yelp.

"Do not kick an animal, Daniel," Zee said. "Ever."

"Do not kick an animal, Daniel," Daniel replied. "Ever."

"I didn't hit Alex first," Luke said, following his mother into the bathroom where she washed his face, stuffed his nostril with toilet paper to stop the bleeding. "Daniel hit him first but Alex is afraid of Daniel so he hit me instead."

"I'm so sorry, Lukie," she said, kissing the top of his head. A troubled boy, Daniel, his father's son. "Your brother can be mean."

"Like Dad."

"Not like your dad," Zee said. "Sometimes brothers can just be mean, but he'll outgrow it."

"I wish he weren't my brother," Luke said, a catch in his voice.

"But he is and you love him."

Zee sat on the closed toilet seat, taking Luke in her lap.

"I don't, Mama. I don't love him," he said. "I love you best and then Dad and last Daniel. I wish I had a sister."

The weekend in April when Adam came home from Cavendish, he had been particularly depressed. He'd pulled up in the car late on Sunday afternoon, left his luggage in the trunk, come in the house and collapsed in front of the television screen.

"I'm not going to Cavendish again without you," he told her. "Miranda is *our* problem. Not mine."

Zee said nothing.

Nothing to say, she thought, broiling lamb chops for dinner, the boys' favorite.

He slept alone on the couch that night, something he'd never done by choice, the television on mute casting its eerie light across his body and Zee crouched on the stairs watched him sleep.

ROBIN ARRIVED AT the Mallorys' early, sitting in a rocking chair on the porch with a glass of wine while Zee put the twins to bed.

"Is everyone coming?" she asked when Zee came outside to join her.

"I think they are," Zee said, on the edge of temper and for no reason that she could name.

"Before they come, I wanted to ask you about abortion."

"Have I had one?" Zee asked. "No. I haven't."

"*Would* you have one?"

"I don't know," Zee said. "I knew women who did before *Roe v. Wade*—and even one who died from an abortion when I was at Michigan—but since it was legalized this year, no one has brought up the subject."

Zee had her tubes tied when the twins were born, but now, had she the choice, she knew she wouldn't have an abortion. She would never say that, certainly not to Robin, who had told them that she couldn't handle another child beyond Sara.

"I didn't have my tubes tied because Miles was dead set against it."

"It was a loss when I had it done," Zee said. "I didn't think it would be but sometimes . . . you know."

This talk of abortion irritated her.

Across the street, Lucy was passing her dining room window carrying Felix on the way to the kitchen, Maggie sitting on the railing of the porch staring into space.

"I've just been wondering now that an abortion is possible, whether we will. Any of us good friends," Robin was saying.

"Are you pregnant, Robby?" Zee asked.

"No, no. I have a friend . . ." she began. "Actually I don't know anyone. I've just wondered what I would do if it happened. We're not very careful, Miles and I, especially lately since the hearings began and he comes home so late and needs to blow off steam. He hates the look of himself on television." She poured herself more wine. "Half a glass," she said aloud. "Did you ask Lucy to come tonight?"

"I called and she wasn't home," Zee said, waving to Josie walking up the street.

There was no way for anyone to know she hadn't called Lucy unless Lucy said she hadn't received a call, but the subject wasn't likely to come up.

"Is anyone up to date on the Louds?" Josie asked, heading up the steps, taking crackers from the tray of wine and cheese. "Or don't you watch *American Family*. I'm getting a little sick of it."

"I've watched most episodes," Robin said. "Last night Miles said that he thought it was telling to watch a real family like the Louds dissolving on television in front of our eyes and a real president on television doing the same thing."

"You think Nixon is done?" Josie asked.

"Miles says he is. I'm not supposed to say this but there are tapes that the president crazily recorded implicating himself. So yes. He's probably done."

"Cancer-free!" Lane called, walking gingerly up the steps. "So far."

She sat down on the arm of the rocker.

"Robby. You look so pale."

"I'm spending the summer watching my husband on television so of course I'm pale." She got up. "I'm also feeling a little drunk and I've got to pee so don't go without me."

"Is Lucy coming?" Lane asked.

"She has a message from me," Zee said.

"On the subject of Lucy," Josie said, "I saw Mrs. Greene tonight when I came home and she called me over and asked me how well I knew Lucy Painter."

"How come?"

"She didn't say how come. Only that divorce was becoming epidemic in the country. She'd read it in the *New York Times* and wasn't Lucy divorced."

"And you said no?" Zee asked.

"Of course, and she said it was unfortunate for an educated white woman with advantages to have children out of wedlock when the pill is available and that she had lived in the neighborhood for thirty years and Lucy's house had always drawn peculiar people like her."

"Time to vamoose, Mrs. Greene," Zee said, passing the cheese and crackers. "She's been here longer by double than anyone I know in the neighborhood."

"You know the trouble with Witchita Hills." Lane took out a cigarette, stretched her legs, crossing them at the ankle. "We make up a story about ourselves to live in this outpost of Washington, D.C., so our lives have an acceptable order. But our lives don't, which is why we won't tell the truth. Not the real, unacceptable truth."

"Give me an example," Josie asked.

"If Will were having an affair, I wouldn't tell

you." Lane stood up, stretching. "Or if there was a chance you already knew, I'd say *oh yes—of course. We have an open marriage.*"

"That's probably what I'd do," Robin said.

"Is it? But we're very close friends," Josie said. "What do you think, Zee?"

"I think it's time to go," Zee said hurriedly. "Get in the van and we'll head to the hospital."

She climbed into the driver's seat and turned on the engine. She wasn't feeling well at all. As if the heat of the day were crowding her, but it was evening and not that hot and she was suffocating.

LUCY HAD SKIMMED most of August's manuscript by the time she picked up Felix at play school, and then there was lunch and laundry and grocery shopping to do, a call to Reuben, and one particular illustration for Vermillion. She was working on mixing the iridescent bronze shimmering on her hummingbird's wing, holding up the pallette to the light—and then she painted Felix's toenails bronze while he sat on the edge of her drafting table listening to *The Hungry Caterpillar* again and again on tape.

She made waffles for dinner with sausage but Maggie wouldn't eat. All afternoon since she got back from the ice cream shop, she had sat on the front porch staring into the middle distance, barely moving.

"I'm not hungry," she said. "I'll sit at the table but I won't eat."

"That's fine," Lucy said.

"Don't you like waffles?" Felix asked.

"Not enough to eat them."

"Don't you like to eat?"

"No, Felix, I don't."

"Then you'll die, I think," he said.

"Probably, I will." She opened a copy of *People* she bought at the drugstsore, agitating for a response but Lucy said nothing.

"Mama," Felix said, "Maggie says—"

"She will eat when she's hungry, darling, and whatever else she might do, she is not going to die."

"Did you see the group on Zee's porch tonight?" Maggie looked up from the magazine.

"I did."

"Do you know what they're doing?" Maggie asked.

"They often have a glass of wine at night after dinner."

"How come you don't go?"

"You know I go, Maggie. Just not that often."

"Well they left to go to the hospital to see how August is and I guess they didn't invite you."

"I don't think a hospital visit is by invitation," Lucy said. "Besides, I have already seen August today."

"Well, big deal." Maggie sat in petulant silence concentrating on her magazine.

After dinner, she went back to the porch, sitting on the railing as she had been, her legs extended, and when Lucy went out with the trash, her eyes were closed.

She was not expecting Gabriel. Since he'd moved next door from Zee's house, he liked to sit in August's study and watch television until it went off the screen. But after Felix went to bed, she heard him downstairs calling to her.

"Hello, Lucy Painter, the painter," he said, coming through the front door, stopping at the picture of Reuben beside the door.

"I know that person," he said. "He is on television. What's his name?"

"His name is Reuben Frank."

"I think he's on *Days of Our Lives*."

"Quite possibly," Lucy said.

"I have come with a mission. Mission means church in California English, but I have not come about church. I have come because my brother, Augustus Russ, called August for short, asked me if you would read the book he is writing about shame on you. Do you know that book?"

"I do," Lucy said. "Before he fell he often came over in the morning to talk to me about it. He needed a listener."

"Yes, he needs a listener to listen to him

because his wife Anna is dead and so she can't listen any longer. You know that."

"I do."

"So I came home tonight and unlocked the front door and turned on the television and opened a can of beets for dinner and then I suddenly remembered I was supposed to ask you about shame on you and so here I am just as I promised my brother Augustus called August who has a very bad memory since he cracked his head open."

Lucy was grateful for once that his sentences were so endlessly long she had time to think of a response.

"As soon as August is out of the hospital and well enough, we will talk about the book," she said, heading to the kitchen to turn out the lights. "Just not now."

Gabriel followed her.

"Maybe you'd like some ice tea or ice cream."

"I would like some tea ice cream with chocolate sauce," he said, sitting down, his small hands folded on the table, while she scooped chocolate mint in a bowl and boiled water for tea.

It was almost midnight by the time Gabriel left and Lucy was wide awake. She checked on Felix stretched out on her side of the bed and went quietly upstairs to her studio. *Biography of the Outsider in America* was facedown in the drawer where she had hidden it covered by her art smock.

She was a slow reader and it was after 2 a.m. when she finished Chapter 8, a chapter entitled "The Splendid Deception" about the careful concealment of President Roosevelt's paralysis. Page 135 and so far no reference to Samuel Baldwin. She turned the page to Chapter 10, page 201. *Althea Enright: Daughter of a Nazi Collaborator.*

There was no chapter 9. She flipped quickly through the remaining pages. Pages 136 through 200 were missing. Ten stories of the shame of outsiders and she had read them all but the last two chapters so the missing pages must be the story of Samuel Baldwin.

She put the manuscript back in the drawer face down, covered it with her smock, turned out the light and went downstairs to her bedroom, pushing Felix aside so there was room for her to slip into bed.

Fifteen

LATE IN THE afternoon on the Friday after the Fourth of July, August arrived home by ambulance to a small crowd gathered with balloons and champagne standing in the street in front of his house. The usual collection on Witchita Avenue, including Mrs. Greene and the elderly man who lived with his daughter on the other side of Lucy and the speech therapist who had been working with August in the hospital. Gabriel was standing on the sidewalk in a business suit and tie with Victoria's mother visiting from Indianapolis. Victoria, whose business card read *Jill of all Trades*, had been hired for the short term as a part-time caregiver and was dressed in a facsimile of a nurse's uniform—tight white Capri pants, a white T, and ballet slippers—appearing at all of her pickup jobs dressed for the occasion.

When the decision was made to release August from the rehabilitation hospital, Gabriel discovered his calling.

I will take care of my brother, Augustus, for the rest of his natural born life, he announced to the women of Witchita Hills.

"Natural-born?" Josie asked. "Could someone explain?"

He stood as if at attention, his short arms pressed to his side while the stretcher bearing August was carried inside.

August, propped up with pillows, smiled wanly, raising his fingers in a wave.

"That's it for cleaning the gutters," he said to no one in particular, and Josie remarked later that his eye-hand coordination was *off.*

He was thinner than he had been, his hair long and scruffy, his eyes opaque as if he had developed cataracts. He had grown a beard speckled beige.

When the ambulance arrived, Lucy was upstairs in her studio with Felix, working on Vermillion. Violet, a broad-tailed hummingbird with a full wingspread of iridescent green and bronze was spilling over the end of the page as if the page could not contain the spread of her wings, which covered the lifeless body of Vermillion. All that was visible of Vermillion was his tail wrapped around a large branch.

Lucy heard the commotion on Witchita Avenue. The ambulance with August was arriving and she was just on her way downstairs when the doorbell rang and through the glass she saw Miles Robinson.

"Miles Robinson," Felix announced.

It was not the first time Miles had arrived unexpectedly in the last few weeks.

"I didn't see you in the crowd so I came up to check if you were here," Miles said. "Maggie's down there with Zee."

"Where's Sara?" Felix asked.

"Visiting her grandparents in Chicago with her mother," Miles said, walking with Lucy down the front steps.

Zee was standing with Maggie just apart from the group, thinking how August's accident had fallen from her mind lately. How everything but Maggie had fallen from her mind.

One week she was arranging a vigil so he'd never be alone, arranging dinners at the intensive care unit with her friends, waiting for the doctors, keeping the neighborhood updated on his latest prognosis, bringing Gabriel into the circle of her own family.

And then she wasn't. She simply lost interest. Not only in August, who just weeks before had gotten her through lonely nights when she was lying sleepless next to Adam. She had also lost interest in her dear, dear friends, her *chicks,* who had depended on her above all others. She still served coffee and muffins or donuts and fruit out of her kitchen every morning but sometimes she forgot to go out on her own front porch for wine. There they'd be chattering without her while she lay on her bed, the twins asleep, Adam watching television downstairs, and Zee checking for the lights in Maggie's bedroom to go out.

"How bad does he really seem?" Josie asked Zee.

"Zee says he's still disoriented and his speech is soupy," Lane said.

"He's hard to understand, is what I said." Zee wrapped her arms around Maggie's shoulders.

"Can we go in his house?" Lane asked. "I've never been inside."

"Bad idea," Josie said.

"We could bring him a glass of champagne," Lane said. "What do you think, Zee?"

But Zee was watching Miles Robinson, home early from the Watergate hearings, walking towards the group bending down to talk to Lucy full of animation.

And the sight of them together, of Miles' obvious pleasure in being with Lucy, sent Zee's mind spinning.

Victoria was hurrying down the steps, her frizzy topknot the size of a yellow tennis ball bouncing to and fro.

"Oh my god, did you see Gabriel?" She was shaking her head. "If I were August, I'd remain in a coma indefinitely."

"Do you think he'll ever be able to get back to his ordinary life?" Josie asked.

"He's going to be fine," Victoria said. "That's what the doctors assume. More or less normal."

"Did you hear that the book August has been writing turned up at Lucy's house?" Lane asked. "Maggie told Maeve that Lucy had discovered it under the couch when she was cleaning the slipcover."

"I heard that," Josie said. "True, isn't it, Maggie?"

"It's true." Maggie shrugged. "Weird!"

"Did you read it, Lucy?" Lane asked as Lucy joined the group.

"I skimmed it," Lucy said. "I knew about the book but I have no idea at all how it might have gotten under my couch."

"HAVE YOU EVER seen this?" Lucy had asked Maggie.

"Did you ask Felix?" Maggie said.

"He's three," Lucy had said. "Of course I didn't ask him, but someone took the manuscript from August's house and put it in ours."

"That someone was not me," Maggie said.

"It's a manuscript about 250 pages long and it's missing some pages."

LUCY SEARCHED MAGGIE'S room for the missing pages, searched the house, the laundry room, the basement, even under the seats of her VW van. But the pages didn't turn up.

"I don't know what to think," she told Reuben.

"We know she's been looking for answers ever since she was little," he said.

"Lately she's been lying," Lucy said.

"Let's say it was Maggie and she did take the missing pages and she does read the manuscript. Not very likely for a girl her age, a boring manuscript of however many pages it happens to be," Reuben said, "and she does find out about your father. What likelihood is that?"

"If she reads the pages and they are about my father, she won't know who it is. Right? Only that we happen to live in the house where a man died. And he had the name Samuel. After all,

August has no idea that I'm associated with the man in his book."

"Maggie has a grandfather with a terrible secret, so she thinks, and he's dead and his name is Sam."

"That's too much of a leap for Maggie."

"August could even have discovered that this dead Samuel had a daughter named Lucy?"

"Why are you doing this to me, Reuben?"

"Because I think you should tell her the truth. I think you should tell everyone who matters to you the truth."

"I'm not ready," she said.

"You'll wait so long, it will be too late."

"Whatever that means."

And Lucy let that problem sink into the quicksand of her daily life.

In time, she would ask August when he was well enough to concentrate. Meanwhile, *Maggie and Zee* were the subjects on her mind. At night, she would lie in bed too stiff with tension to sleep.

"Are you staying at Zee's for hot dogs?" Miles asked Lucy.

"I need to take Felix home and cook dinner for us."

"Do you mind if I follow you?"

"That would be nice," Lucy said, taking Felix's hand up the many steps to her house. She was hesitant with Miles, perplexed.

It wasn't the first time he had come to her house alone without Robin—a distant, self-contained man more likely to be in his own house working into the night than to visit one of the neighbors.

In late June on a rainy night, he had walked up the hill from the bus and stopped to help Lucy take groceries into the house.

"What a warm cozy house," he said as he left, which had seemed out a character for a man like Miles to notice.

Later in the summer at a Mallory potluck, he carried Felix home after he had fallen down the back steps and hit his head. He stayed with Lucy, sitting on the arm of the couch while she cleaned out the cut and settled Felix in a blanket with warm chocolate milk.

"You know how to watch for concussions so call us if he seems worse," Miles said, touching her shoulder as he left.

She wouldn't have even noticed that his hand had glanced her shoulder if he were a different man and not so awkward—long-legged, slender, almost arthritic in the stiffness of his movements so just his hand on her shoulder called attention to itself, as if he'd thought about it first, dared himself, and then didn't quite have the courage to follow through.

Now he sat at the kitchen table with the glass of wine that he'd brought from Zee's, took off the navy blazer he was still wearing, and rolled up the sleeves of his shirt.

"An unbearably hot summer to be spending in front of television cameras and lights," he said.

"It is hot," Lucy said. "I've never been on a television set so I didn't know it was so hot."

"It's the lights," he said.

The shadows under his eyes were nearly black, his eyes damp with weariness, his hand holding the wineglass trembled.

"Exhaustion," he said when he caught Lucy watching.

Something about him disrobing in her kitchen, his jacket off, his sleeves rolled up, his thick gray hair plastered to his head with perspiration surprised Lucy and moved her.

He was a quiet presence in the room, his chair tilted back on two legs, looking out towards the garden, dusk lifting over the horizon.

"The investigation is costly," he said finally. "Taking down a president like this."

"You're taking him down?"

"Nixon did it to himself of course. Everyone involved did, but it's the darkness about it all. I feel the need for something innocent in my life when I come from work at night."

"Sara?"

"She's too grown up and already at odds with us."

"I know," Lucy said. "Felix is my something innocent."

Felix had come in the kitchen with his Legos and poured them out on the kitchen floor.

"I'm building a cave right now," he said.

"For you?"

"For my sloth."

Miles sat down on the floor in his polished black shoes and trousers, gathering a pile of Lego pieces in his clean, clean hands.

"Vermillion is the name of my sloth and he has three toes," Felix said.

"Vermillion is the hero of the children's book I'm doing," Lucy said.

"Then he certainly needs a cave." Miles was on his hands and knees. "You tell me what to do."

"You make the cave so it's perfect with only blue and white Legos, no red or yellow, and it has to be big enough for Vermillion to fit."

"How big is Vermillion?"

"Big," Felix said. "He is a boy sloth and boy sloths are big and he hangs by his tail from a tree branch and he's dead, right, Mama?"

Miles looked up at Lucy.

"In a children's book?"

"Not really dead. Just full of sorrow," Lucy said. "It ends happily for Vermillion."

She felt a surprising rush of happiness and relief with this man on the floor playing with her

290

son, this make-believe husband opening a window on an ordinary domestic life.

She set the table and snapped the beans, sliced tomatoes, put tuna under the broiler, and when dinner was ready, she went to the door to call Maggie, who was lying on her back with Maeve on the Mallorys' front porch.

"I have plenty of tuna if you'd like to stay," she said.

"I can't. I have work but there is something I'd like to ask you when you have time," Miles said. "Not now during dinner with the kids."

"You can come later after they're in bed. I'll be working tonight too."

Lucy could see Maggie head across the street and up the steps, banging through the screen door.

"Or tomorrow."

"I will come tonight," he said.

"Hello, Miles and Mother," Maggie said, walking right by Miles on his way out of the door and straight up the steps to her room.

"Aren't you going to have dinner?" Lucy asked.

"I had dinner with the other families in the neighborhood. Hot dogs. Delicious so I'm not hungry."

THERE HAD BEEN a report of rain. Zee set up a table on the porch, brought baked beans and sauerkraut and a macaroni pasta to the table, lemonade and wine, double chocolate brownies and two gallons of Bryers vanilla. Plates and silver rolled in cloth napkins, wineglasses so the children could pretend they were drinking wine instead of lemonade.

In the front yard Adam was grilling hot dogs.

Tipsy—Zee had noticed.

She put a hot dog in a bun, slathered it with mustard and onions.

"Eat this," she whispered, handing him a plate. "You're drunk."

"Absolutely on target, Zelda," he said. "Thank you for the news flash."

Maggie followed her into the kitchen.

"Can I help?" she asked.

"You already helped me get ready for the party." She kissed Maggie's curly head. "Last-minute parties like this are so great but I wish your mother could have stayed longer tonight."

Maggie shrugged.

"She's weird."

"Maybe she already had a plan with Miles who I notice is over at your house now." Zee took out a punch bowl and poured cranberry juice and ginger ale, emptied two trays of ice. "She might have asked him for dinner since he's probably lonely. Robin is at Lake Michigan with Sara and her parents."

She handed Maggie the punch bowl.

"Miles Robinson is having dinner at my house?" She balanced the punch bowl against her bony hip. "Creepy. He's not the type."

"For dinner?" Zee asked.

Maggie laughed. "For dinner at *my* house."

It was drizzling and the children had gathered on the huge front porch with their hot dogs and drinks. Maggie plopped down beside Maeve.

"Miles Robinson is at my house for dinner," she said.

"Bor-ing," Maeve said. "He's the most boring man I've ever met but he is sort of handsome, don't you think? I mean if you like older men, he's better than the other fathers, especially Adam with his crinkly red face."

"Except for Miles' chin," Maggie said. "So pointy."

"I like pointy," Maeve said. "But I bet he's too freaked out about women to do any of the positions like 69 in *The Joy of Sex*."

And Maggie giggled although she was uncomfortable with the thought of Miles Robinson at her house mixed up in a conversation about *The Joy of Sex*.

"Maybe Miles has a crush on your mother," Maeve said.

"I don't think so," Maggie said. "He's not the type to have crushes and my mother doesn't have boyfriends."

"Never?"

"Never."

"Well she had you and Felix so she must have had a boyfriend for a while."

"Maybe, but he didn't want to marry her so I guess it wasn't much of a crush," Maggie said, and just saying out loud what was in her mind made her suddenly feel sick.

"She's pretty, Maggie. Even my old-fashioned stuffy dad has crushes, like he has a little one on your mother. He says *That Lucy is crazy cute*."

"Disgusting."

"That's what my mom says," Maeve said. "*Dis-gust-ing* like she's jealous, which she probably is."

Zee sat down between Lane and Josie on the top step of the porch, their husbands gathered around the grill with Adam.

"Have you noticed Miles Robinson lately?" she asked.

"He's tense," Lane said. "But he always seems tense and now that he's doing the Watergate thing, he has a reason to be."

"I don't mean Watergate," Zee said. "It's just odd but this is the third time I've seen him go over to Lucy's house without Robin."

"I haven't seen him there before, but he's there now," Josie said. "I watched him walk up the steps behind her."

"I didn't know they were friends," Lane said. "It doesn't make sense that they would be, but who knows with Lucy." She draped her arm around Zee's shoulder. "He's so uncomfortable with women it's like talking to a plate glass window."

"Well, Lucy is imaginative and arty," Zee said breezily. "Maybe she brings him out of his shell."

"What are you *thinking*, Zee?" Josie asked.

"Nothing, just noting that it's unusual. *Zip, zip*." She pretended to zip up her lips. "Maybe Lucy has a way about her that makes a man like Miles comfortable."

"I do know one thing," Lane said. "He wants another child."

"I know that too," Zee said. "And Robin is done with babies."

"That isn't exactly answering your question about what he's doing at Lucy's house," Josie said.

"I don't have a question." Zee hopped up, collecting plates. "Just a quick observation. Nothing worth noting."

In the kitchen, she stood at the sink looking out at the backyard where the beds of flowers were in full and spectacular bloom before the heavy heat of summer sucked the life out of them. She loved this moment of June in Washington, the purple lilacs spraying their perfume as far as the open kitchen window.

"Losing your grip, Zelda?" Adam asked,

coming up behind her, his hands in the sink, washing off the grease.

"My grip?"

"Never mind," he said wiping his hands on his shorts. "I just came in to get another beer."

"What do you mean, Adam?"

"Just an observation," he said. "I've known you for a very long time."

In the coming dusk, the shadows of evening falling across the kitchen window, Zee could make out her reflection and what she saw was her face as a young woman. Still vibrant, even beautiful. She wanted to believe that.

What she'd said about Miles and Lucy Painter was deliberate. Planting seeds of trouble as she had done since high school for no reason, and in the case of Miles Robinson without evidence except the unlikeliness of his pursuit of any woman. Nothing about Lucy except what Zee wanted people to think for her own purposes.

And what were her purposes?

The ends do not justify the means, her mother used to tell her father about nearly everything. When Zee finally understood what her mother had been saying, she disagreed. Otherwise she would still be in Revere, Michigan, married to a local boy, always pregnant, working half-time at her mother's jewelry store.

She had never longed for anything in quite the visceral way she longed for Maggie Painter, this replication of her hopes and dreams, this child of her heart. She was willing to do anything.

"Zee." Maggie burst into the kitchen. "*Why* is Miles Robinson at my house?"

"Probably visiting, don't you think?"

"Lane and Josie were outside talking about it as if there were something *wrong* in his being there."

"Oh no, Maggie. Nothing wrong about it at all. I'm sure they didn't mean what you might be thinking."

She ran her hand across Maggie's cheek, casually.

"I'm thinking nothing," Maggie said coldly, and she headed out the front door, across the street and up the front steps to her house.

Zee's heart sank.

"What did you say to Maggie?" she asked Lane as she came into the kitchen with a stack of plates.

"I'm afraid Josie and I took your observation too far, Zee, and Maggie overheard us suggesting that something was happening between Miles and Lucy."

"I meant absolutely nothing by it."

"I'm sorry. I'm so sorry but it did honestly sound as if you were implying—"

"I was *not*."

In a heat of anger, Zee took the keys to the van from the kitchen drawer, got in and backed out of the driveway.

"Is something the matter?" Josie called.

"Nothing," Zee called through the open window. "Make yourselves at home."

She drove out of Witchita Hills, across Connecticut Avenue, and parked in the shadows across from Lafayette School.

Adam was right. Something was certainly the matter with her. If she lost Maggie, she wanted to die. That was how she felt.

MAGGIE SLAMMED HER bedroom door and sat down at the end of her bed with the light off. The party at the Mallorys' seemed to be winding down. Josie was walking across the yard with Rufus, and Zee was backing out of the driveway, heading towards Connecticut Avenue.

She pulled her knees up under her chin and burrowed her face in the space between them.

Just half an hour ago, she had loved Zelda Mallory beyond all measure and hated her mother. Now she hated her mother *and* Zelda Mallory. She felt terrible about her feelings and not terrible. She wanted to move away from Lucy's house, far, far away, and she wanted to move into the Mallorys' house across the street.

It was too much. The frustration and sadness, the carefully constructed entrapments that adults design to capture children, the sense of failure that had accompanied every moment of her life since she was born without a father.

Maggie got out of bed, remembering the pages she had pulled out of August's manuscript. The lights were out in her room but the streetlights outside her window illuminated the bookcase, and kneeling beside it, she took out the social studies book.

In the long summer afternoons sitting in Zee's kitchen while she cooked dinner, she had almost forgotten about the pages she had hidden in her textbook.

LUCY SAW MILES in the light from the street-lamp, walking down Witchita from his house, in shorts and a T-shirt. He stopped on the sidewalk in front of the Sewalls' where Will Sewall was wrestling with the beagle trying to put his leash on. And they spoke, Will's hand on Miles' shoulder.

She was in her studio. Felix was sleeping, Maggie's door locked, her light on, and Lucy was standing by the window.

A restlessness about the evening as if the heat itself were impatient.

Dying had been on Lucy's mind, not in an actual sense and she wasn't fearful about it. Just a sense she had of something happening. Once on a walk in Santa Fe, she had found a snakeskin on the path behind her house—not a large snake and the skin itself was dull in color and brittle. But she wondered about the color of the snake which had emerged from that reptilian refuse. Was it more brilliant than the one he'd left behind, more intricate in design?

Miles was knocking at the front door. She had watched him walk up the street, knowing he was coming to see her but not rushing to answer the door.

"Miles Robinson is here, Mother," Maggie called from behind her closed bedroom door. "You might want to answer the door."

"I didn't know if you'd be coming back," Lucy said, opening the front door.

"Apparently I left my wallet on your kitchen table."

"I must not have seen it."

"I was distracted when I left but I'm sure it's here."

And there it was when Lucy turned on the light in the kitchen, as if he'd left it intentionally on the seat where he had been sitting.

"Maybe I'll stay for a few minutes, if that's okay," he said, sitting down at the table.

"I'd like that." Lucy slipped into a chair across from him.

"You probably think it's odd, my dropping by when I'm not a casual person . . ."

"It's perfectly fine," Lucy said. "August used to drop by—just come right in without asking. I liked that."

"August always struck me as a recluse. I hardly

know him except that the women are nuts about him, and for no reason that I can see." He shrugged, reaching over for a plum in the bowl of fruit on the kitchen table.

"Mind?" he asked.

"It's surprising to me how little we know about one another," he went on. "Even living in the same house day and night as I do with Robin. Like August. Who could imagine?"

"He wanted me to listen to his book."

"Instead of reading it."

"I think he wanted to hear it in his own voice," Lucy said, conscious that Maggie had opened her bedroom door, that she might be headed downstairs. And then what? Maggie was not in the humor for visitors.

"Well, I suppose I am asking you to listen too." Miles stood, tossed the plum pit in the trash, and leaned against the cabinets.

A shiver went through Lucy, a flutter of butterflies in her stomach.

"If Maggie comes downstairs in a bad humor, I'm going to have to ask you to leave," she said.

"Of course."

They stopped talking to listen, Lucy walking to the bottom of the stairs.

"Maggie?"

"I just called Uncle Reuben from your studio phone," she said.

Lucy stiffened.

"And what did he say?"

"I wanted him to know that Mr. Robinson was here, in case he was interested. *No problem,* is what he said."

Lucy heard her bare feet slap across the wooden floor in the hall, her bedroom door slam and click.

"Whew!" she said, sitting down.

"Who is Uncle Reuben?"

"My editor," she said. "I doubt Maggie really called him, but if she did, I'm sure his wife was furious to hear from her at almost midnight."

"Young girls are complicated."

"I don't know what Maggie was trying to provoke," Lucy said. "But provoke is what she does."

"Sara too and Maeve Sewall. I was just talking to Will. You probably know he's been appointed a psychiatric advisor to the White House because of the concern about Nixon's mental health."

"I heard that, actually from Maggie, so it must have come from Maeve."

"Will said it's tricky how much the tension of Watergate is contributing to the president's erratic behavior, but Nixon was problematic before."

"Is Nixon what you wanted to talk to me about?" she asked, concerned that any moment Maggie would come downstairs. "I hardly ever listen to the news and we don't have a television. I'm afraid I have nothing to say about Watergate."

"Good," he said. "Because I've come about myself."

She folded her arms on the table, her eye on the clock above the stove.

"I wonder if you've heard anything about Robin from the other women?"

"What might I have heard?" Lucy shrugged. "I'm not very close to these women, certainly not a confidante."

"I know that but I thought some gossip might have come your way."

"Only from Maggie and nothing about Robin."

"Then I'll tell you what I think has happened and I'm asking *you* because that group seems to operate as a team under Zee's direction and I don't want to make a federal case of this," he said. "And somehow I trust you, maybe because you're an outsider in this knitting circle of Witchita Hills."

Leaning across the table, his hands folded tight together, he told Lucy what he had come to ask her about.

He had wanted another baby for a long time but Robin thought another child would be too much for her. And then, sometime in late October, she agreed but she didn't get pregnant. He asked if she'd be willing to see a fertility doctor and she

303

said *yes* in a year if nothing happened. By March, two months into this year, Miles *knew* she was pregnant, a little mound above the pubic bone, her breasts—*well, you know what happens.* By June, she still hadn't mentioned the pregnancy and finally just before the Fourth of July, he asked her and she replied, *No,* sadly. *She wasn't pregnant.*

"I knew she was lying."

"What do you mean?"

"I'm quite sure she had an abortion," he said.

"I'm not up to date on things like this and I don't have a talky relationship with other women."

"I feel the need to find out the truth."

"You're a lawyer."

He shrugged. "I'm a husband. Wouldn't you want to *know* in my place?"

"I really don't know what I think," Lucy said. "There are *always* secrets between people. Necessary secrets and lies."

She stood up, pulled the chair away from the table.

"I don't understand what you mean by *necessary.* But I'm part of an investigation of a public lie and possibly the victim of a private one." There was a tremor in his voice, a high tenor voice. "A lie can be dangerous between people."

And then without warning, nothing in the air

to alert Lucy, he got up from his chair, took hold of Lucy's waist, and pulled her towards him, his hand on the side of her face, tilting her chin.

And he kissed her, his lips soft, his tongue along the inside of her cheek, not a long kiss but urgent.

"Thank you, Lucy," he said, and put his wallet in the pocket of his shorts. "Thank you for listening."

She turned off the kitchen light and stood in the darkness, watching as he opened the door and walked onto the porch without looking back.

Somewhere in the neighborhood, a person looking casually out the window would see Miles Robinson leaving her house, would check the time—11:15, and make assumptions.

How had that happened? she asked herself.

Maggie's light still shone under the door, a tape of the Beatles playing but not loud, and Lucy could hear the rustling of papers.

Overcome with weariness, she kicked off her shoes and climbed fully dressed into the bed next to Felix, rolling him on his side, Miles' kiss still alive in her mouth.

MAGGIE PROPPED UP her pillows, turned on the light next to her bed, and opened the pages of August's manuscript.

Chapter 9:
SAMUEL BALDWIN:
AGAINST THE GRAIN

On the 21st of June, 1951, Samuel Baldwin, special assistant to President Truman, was found hanged in the basement of an investment property he owned with his wife on Witchita Avenue in the Witchita Hills section of northwest Washington, D.C. On the previous Thursday evening, Mr. Baldwin was arrested in the men's room of the YMCA by an off-duty policeman. He was in the act of sexual intercourse with a former military officer in the United States Army, an act which is still as I am writing this, in the spring of 1973, considered illegal under the Constitution of the United States.

On Sunday morning following the event, Mr. Baldwin called President Truman to offer his resignation. He was aware that news of the incident and his arrest would appear in detail the following morning in newspapers all over the country.

At the time of his death, he had been a senior advisor to the president appointed following the bombings of Hiroshima and Nagasaki by American military. According to the obituaries, he was an esteemed lawyer in Chicago with an impeccable professional record known for his gentle manner, dry wit, and integrity. He leaves his wife and twelve-year-old daughter, who live in the Capitol Hill section of Washington, D.C.

Maggie put down the pages.

That a man had committed suicide in a house on Witchita Avenue after he was arrested for having sexual intercourse with another man was of particular interest to Maggie. She was not interested in the man himself but she would like to know the house in which it had happened. Sexual intercourse between men intrigued her. She couldn't imagine the particulars.

The story lingered in her mind and she couldn't sleep. Or else she couldn't sleep because of Zee and Miles Robinson. She turned out the light and lay against her pillow staring into the darkness. The last time she remembered looking at the alarm clock beside her bed, it was 3 a.m.

Sixteen

LUCY WOKE UP in darkness at the other end of the bed, tangled in her sheets, her legs locked together, her thoughts bustling around the highways of her brain. It had been days since she had spoken to Reuben, at least since he'd gone to Cape Cod with Elaine and Nell on vacation. *Communication will be minimal,* he'd said. They were traveling with other couples, a house party, and Lucy had braced for that separation. But something was different which she couldn't name. It didn't have to do with Reuben, predictable Reuben, but with her.

Mostly these mornings she woke up thinking about Miles Robinson. Not with longing. What had happened between them had nothing to do with love or even desire. Miles was like Fervid P. Drainpipe, a sweet, formal man without the language for connection, lost in his work for lack of knowing how to live in the world. He had kissed Lucy because he didn't know another way to thank her for listening to him or because he was thinking of kissing her and surprised himself by doing it or because he was lonely at home.

But for Lucy, Miles' kiss had been a promissory note.

Lying on his back, on his pillow at the right end of the bed, Felix was looking at her.

"How come you're sleeping at the other end of the bed, Mama?" he was asking when they heard a terrifying scream and leapt from the bed, rushing to Maggie's room.

Maggie woke up in the dark to a commotion of voices in the front yard of the Sewalls' house.

"I have to leave *now!*" Will Sewall shouted at Maeve leaning out of the open window of her bedroom.

"Something awful has happened," Maeve shouted.

Maggie sat on her bed peering through the white ruffled curtains in her window overlooking Witchita Avenue.

It was more night than dawn but she could make out the figure of Will crossing the front lawn and opening the door of his red convertible. He backed out of the driveway and headed in the direction of Connecticut Avenue.

Maeve ducked out of the window and turned on the overhead light so she was visible from the street.

Standing perfectly still in the middle of her bedroom, she shattered the morning silence with a high-pitched scream which trailed off to the wail of an injured animal.

In a breath, Lucy was in Maggie's room, Felix behind her.

"What was that?"

"Maeve," Maggie said.

"What happened?"

"I don't know," Maggie said. "She just screamed."

Lucy crawled onto Maggie's bed and looked out the window, holding back the curtains.

"Will left in his car and Maeve asked him not to go and Will drove on anyway and then she turned on the light in her bedroom and screamed."

They sat on the side of Maggie's bed and watched the Sewalls' house, watched Lane come into the bedroom in her robe and Maeve throw herself facedown on the bed and Lane sit beside her.

Teddy came into the room in his pajama bottoms and leaned against the wall.

"It doesn't look like a catastrophe," Lucy said.

Maggie got out of bed and put on shorts and a T-shirt.

"I'm going over to see what happened."

"Not yet," Lucy said. "It's five in the morning and everyone seems to be okay."

Maggie opened the drawer of her bureau and took out a stack of T-shirts and shorts and long pants, arranging them in piles on the bed. She went into her closet and took two sweaters and a sweatshirt off the shelf, her slicker off the hanger, the only dress she owned, and folded them on the bed.

"What's going on?" Lucy asked quietly.

"Why are you still dressed in the same clothes you had on last night?"

"You didn't answer my question," Lucy said.

MAGGIE WAS BURNING. Her cheeks were hot.

"Are you still in your clothes from yesterday because you're having an affair with Miles Robinson?" she asked, pleased with the casual sound of her own voice.

Lucy picked up Felix and took him to his own room, taking clothes out of his drawers.

"You get dressed, darling, and then I'll make muffins and you have a playdate this morning. With Andrew from preschool."

"Well?" Maggie asked, leaning against the door to Felix's room, following her mother into her own room.

"Not in front of Felix," Lucy said evenly. "You wouldn't be asking me that question about Miles, to which the answer is *no,* if you believed it was true."

"Last night the mothers at Zee's potluck suggested that it *was* true," Maggie said. "Even Zee."

Maggie had slung the straps of her blue duffel bag over her shoulder.

"Things aren't working out between us," she said.

"It's not a question of whether things are working out between us," Lucy said without breath. "I am your mother and you are my daughter . . ."

"I'm going over to Maeve's," Maggie said, articulating as if Lucy were hard of hearing. "That's what I'm doing now."

Lucy didn't try to stop her. She couldn't stop her. She wasn't at all sure what she *could* do with Maggie. There was no map. The rules for raising children had gone out with her parents'

311

generation of daughters who had lived as Lucy had, in patient silence, acting by standards which had lasted generations, waiting to grow up to make their decisions, following the patterns of their own lives.

THE FRONT DOOR shut and she watched Maggie hop down the steps, run across the street and up the few steps leading to the Sewalls' front porch and knock.

Lucy was making coffee and blueberry muffins when Maggie came back to the house.

"Did you know Lane Sewall had one breast off because of cancer?"

"I knew that she had cancer," Lucy said.

"Well they chopped off her breast. How come you didn't tell me?"

"Because the Sewalls decided to keep it to themselves for the time being."

"And why would they decide to do that?"

"I don't know, Maggie. People sometimes decide on the better of two bads and I suppose they thought in Maeve's case it was better for her not to know."

"It's too late!" Maggie said, heading upstairs. "She knows. Will Sewall got a call at five in the morning to go to the White House because President Nixon is sicko and the telephone woke Maeve up and she walked into her parents' bedroom and there was her mother, who she'd

312

been told was sick with exhaustion, and instead she was sitting on the side of the bed with her robe open and one breast gone."

She ran upstairs, closed her bedroom door, locked it, and sat at the head of her bed considering the selection of clothes she had organized. It wasn't even seven o'clock.

THE DAY WAS going to be unbearably hot, the kind of swampy Washington heat that lingers deep in the body, and Lucy was conscious that she had been sitting in her kitchen, her feet on the table, her eyes half closed. Maggie was still upstairs behind locked doors.

Sometime during Lucy's sleepy reverie, Maggie came downstairs, sat at the kitchen table, and folded her arms.

"What exactly is an affair?"

Lucy was slow to respond.

"I mean is it just sleeping with someone?"

"An affair is when two people have a relationship," Lucy said, at a loss for the precise language to use, uncertain where these questions were going.

When Maggie was small, Lucy had read somewhere, maybe Dr. Spock, that you answer a child's question honestly and without elaboration. But that suggestion didn't work well for Lucy since there was so much she didn't *want* her children to know.

313

"With sex?" Maggie asked. "A relationship with sex?"

"You can have an affair of the heart," Lucy said. "Without sex like the one I have with August."

"Or Uncle Reuben," Maggie said matter-of-factly. "But with my father, you had sex."

"Well . . ." Lucy's heart was in her throat. "Yes, with your father. Of course."

"And he was married then."

"He was married when I met him," Lucy said.

"So you had a *real* affair because he was married, right? And he wouldn't get unmarried and that's what an affair is. You have to be married."

"No, not necessarily," Lucy began.

But Maggie was done with her investigation. She hurried upstairs and closed her door. Lucy could hear the old lock click shut.

LUCY HAD NEVER undressed with a man until Reuben.

With Reuben, she had shed her clothes, the careful layering of skin that had accompanied her attenuated life for as long as she could remember. They had made love the night she'd gone to New York with her illustrations for *Belly Over the Banana Field*. He signed a contract for her book, took her out to lunch at a small, dark café, freezing outside, a relentless wind, the promise of an ice storm.

"We can stay here all night," he said.

And they did. Upstairs in one of the rooms the café rented out for overnight guests, making love on a noisy iron bed. Reuben had undressed her, kissed her lips, soft wet kisses on her neck and forehead, his fingers lacing through her hair, his lips on her belly.

"I was a virgin," she said, lying in his arms looking out the tiny window at the weather.

"Yes, you were," he said.

They had the weekend together before his wife returned from Connecticut and they spent the whole of it inside, above the café, coming down occasionally for a cup of coffee or soup or toast. A glass of wine.

"I have never felt this way in my whole life since my father died," she'd said. "Completely safe."

"I am not your father," Reuben said.

"I don't want you to be," Lucy said. "It's just delicious to feel safe even though I'm not."

"And I am married."

She laughed.

"Probably I would prefer that you were not married," she said.

"So would I."

But in all the years that she had been with Reuben, more alone than actually with him, no one else had kissed her until last night.

This morning her body tingled with a kind of

mindless, languid expectancy as if she had dreamed the kiss, and so she was astonished when the reality of Miles Robinson passed her dining room window. She waited for the doorbell but almost immediately he went by the window again, going in the other direction.

The note he'd left had been stuck in the crack of the door sealed in a business envelope with *Lucy Painter* typed on the outside.

Dear Lucy,

Thank you for your wise counsel last night. It has been very helpful to me in coming to a decision professionally among other considerations.

Yours sincerely, Miles

Lucy read the note, folded it and put it in the pocket of her jeans. *Among other considerations?* Whatever he had meant was too strange to decipher.

"Maggie," she called upstairs, thinking to check on her but already she was late to pick up Felix from his playdate and so she headed out the front door.

"I'll be back in about fifteen minutes," she called. "We need milk and cereal. Do you want anything else?"

Maggie didn't answer. Lucy checked her window as she passed the house and could make

316

out her shadow through the curtains moving back and forth.

When she returned with milk and cereal, M&M's for Maggie, Felix slung over her shoulder fast asleep, Maggie had gone.

Her bed was made, the clothes she'd been arranging on her bed that morning gone, the duffel and yellow slicker and her dotted Swiss sundress gone. Her toothbrush and toothpaste kept in a mug in the bathroom gone.

Lucy lay Felix carefully on top of her bed, pulled the door to, kicked off her sandals and tiptoed downstairs, standing at the front door, looking out.

The boys in the neighborhood were playing street hockey. Adam Mallory was standing on his front porch with a bottle of beer leaning against a pillar, Will Sewall's convertible back in the driveway and Josie was on her bike heading towards Connecticut Avenue. The sun was too low and bright to see through the front door of the Mallorys' house but Lucy imagined that Maggie was inside.

When they left New York City, Maggie had stopped holding Lucy's hand, the way they used to do wandering through the Village together, swinging their arms in a high arc. She was embarrassed by her mother's public affection, she'd said.

"I *wish* you'd be friends with the other mothers

in the neighborhood," Maggie had said recently. "You only have August and we've already been here for six months."

"I'm busy with you and Felix and my work," Lucy said casually.

If they wanted her to join them, they could insist she come for coffee in the morning or wine at night, was what Lucy said to Reuben.

"I bet they've asked you one way or another," he'd said.

"They're very different women from me."

"We're all pretty much alike, as you know since you write books about the way people are."

"I write books about animals," Lucy said.

"Well . . ." he began, and she hung up the phone.

She went upstairs where Felix was sleeping and lay down on the floor listening to his quiet breathing.

Whatever death felt like in its stealthy advance, Lucy was in the process of discovering.

ZEE WASN'T SURPRISED to see Maggie walking up her front steps with a navy blue duffel over her shoulder. Somehow she had expected it intuitively, a kind of inevitability, that one day this month or next, in the fall, in the winter, Maggie would be *hers,* lodged in her house, her kitchen, her daughter by proxy, sleeping in the guest room next door to her boys on the second floor, across the hall from her.

"This is crazy," Adam had said under his breath while Maggie was upstairs unpacking her things in the bureau of the blue and white guest room facing the back of the house. "This child has a mother and you're not it."

"Temporary, Adam. She's almost a teenager, hating her mother at the moment and then she won't hate her. I was like that," Zee said, making sandwiches for lunch. "We're a bridge—from here to there and Maggie is walking on the bridge."

"I'm *not* worried about Maggie, who will survive without you," Adam said, taking a beer out of the fridge. "I'm worried about you, my wife, the mother of my three children."

Zee turned quickly, the breath gone out of her, and walked out the back door, down the alley, leaning against the O'Donnells' back fence. Sobs lodged somewhere in her belly rising in her throat and she could not stop the plaintive cry of grief, a sound she had never heard uttered from her own mouth.

She had two living children. Twin boys. Miranda was dead.

Mrs. O'Donnell had heard her, must have heard her since she'd opened the back door and Zee crouched on the ground, her face in her arms, muffling the sound of weeping.

Minutes passed before Mrs. O'Donnell went back in her house and closed the door—before Zee stood, rubbing her cheeks pink, deep breaths from the stomach, what she'd learned in childbirth. She shook loose her hair.

"Don't ever say that again," she told Adam as she went back into the house.

It was time for Adam to move out, take a room in the lawyers' club downtown, meals served, a bar, time for them to live in separate places before their marriage actually burned to the ground. There was too much sadness between them.

She would discuss it tonight after supper, after the children were in bed, when she was confident she could speak to him reasonably. She'd make a trade. If he'd go now and stay away until the beginning of September when school started again, giving her time with Maggie, time to settle down, then she would go to Vermont with him right after Labor Day.

When she came back, Adam was sitting at the picnic table with the boys eating sandwiches.

"Hey Mom," Daniel said, "how come Maggie Painter is moving into our house?"

"Daniel doesn't like her," Luke said.

Zee slid into the end of the bench, taking a sandwich from the tray.

"I invited her," she said. "She's been having a hard time with her mother."

"She can't come in our room," Daniel said.

"I doubt she wants to," Zee said. "All I ask is that you're civil to her. Complain to me if you have to, but quietly."

"I can't be civil," Daniel said.

"What does *civil* mean?" Luke asked.

"Civil is going to be a problem for me," Adam said.

"Then make some other plans," Zee said.

"We could go on a camping trip," Daniel said.

"Rufus is going to Assateague with his father," Luke said. "We could go there."

"What about that, Adam? We don't have any plans until we go to Michigan for Labor Day," Zee said. "Maybe this weekend in Assateague? The boys could bring friends."

"Great, Dad. Let's do that, just us guys and Mom can stay home with diddly-squat."

"Let me tell you boys something about diddly-squat. I like Maggie and I like her mother, which is where she ought to be living, but I don't want to hear anything bad about either one of them from anyone at this table." Adam got up and looked directly at Zee. "Got it?"

THAT NIGHT, ADAM moved into the study.

"I'll take the boys to Assateague this weekend because they want to go and we need a break."

Zee held her breath, trying to focus on Adam's face but her eyes kept wandering.

321

"All right," she said, unwilling to fall into an argument. "That's a plan."

"You have to understand that this is a compromise so you can have the weekend with Maggie, but when I get back, Maggie goes home to her own family and we, you and me, address the truth about ours."

"That's fine," Zee said. "No worries."

The end of the weekend was a long time away and for the moment, she would buy what time she could in small pieces.

LUCY WAS IN her studio drawing with Felix when Victoria came rushing upstairs in her ballet shoes with a message from August.

"Whew," she said, cresting the top step to the studio. "A long way up."

"Mama's drawing a book with me," Felix said without looking up.

"Oh, very nice, Felix. So many books. I've never been here, you know, and I love the wild pictures of that green whatever it is."

She reached up to look at a drawing of Vermillion drying on the clothesline.

"Vermillion the Three-Toed Sloth," Felix said.

"Very fetching, these sloths."

She leaned over the work table to look at the book Felix was making.

"August wants me to ask you if you've had a

chance to read the manuscript Gabriel brought over a couple of weeks ago."

"I know the manuscript is here but I didn't know Gabriel brought it," Lucy said.

"You know Gabriel. I got the whole story from him with the conversation repeated verbatim. Maggie was here—you were someplace—Felix was with a babysitter at the library. He said it was a Happy Birthday present for you and he called Maggie Margaret because he doesn't like nicknames. That sort of Gabriel thing."

"Maggie didn't tell me. I found the manuscript under the couch."

"She probably forgot all about it," Victoria said. "Girls! I love them but they're so undependable. Anyway, I came to tell you that August is ready to talk about the book."

"Tell him of course, I haven't gotten to it yet but I'll read it in the next few days."

So Maggie had been the one to remove the pages and hide the manuscript under the couch. Lucy was not surprised. It was comforting to have proof that at least she knew some of the workings of her daughter's mind.

"Done," Victoria said, heading for the stairs. "I'm amazed at how he's improved, aren't you?"

"When I saw him yesterday, he seemed so much better."

"I can almost understand everything he says

and the docs expect a full recovery," Victoria said, heading down the steps. "Lane told me about Maggie by the way. Bummer!"

IT WAS GETTING dark so the lights in the Mallorys' house would be on and Lucy might be able to see Maggie. The Mallory boys were wrestling on the front porch, the porch light on, the hall light on, the kitchen dark. Somewhere upstairs, Maggie had to be unpacking her duffel.

I can't live with my mother any longer. Was that what Maggie would have said?

Or had Zee lured Maggie in that way she had of occupying someone's mind? A child, even a girl as young as Maggie, would begin to believe that Zee Mallory's thoughts were actually her own.

"ARE WE GOING to eat dinner tonight?" Felix asked quietly, burrowing his face in her long skirt.

"Of course we're going to eat dinner."

"But I'm not hungry because Maggie is gone."

She picked him up, pressing his warm body against her own.

"How did you know Maggie had left? Did she tell you?"

"I just knew."

She scrambled eggs and they sat silent at the table nibbling at toast, Felix glancing over at his mother. Lucy could feel him watching her but she didn't look at him for fear she would weep. And then what? He asked for six stories that night instead of three and she read him all of them even after he had fallen asleep just to hear the comforting sound of her own voice.

Afterwards she went to Maggie's room and sat on her bed in the dark, leaning against the pillow, aligning herself in the center where Maggie usually slept, on her back, her arms stretched above her head, her head facing away from the window. Maggie had a way of sleeping with her eyes slightly open, only the whites showing, and when she was very young, the look of her vanilla eyeballs had sent shivers down Lucy's spine.

She sat up against the headboard and listened for Felix.

The lights were still on at the Mallorys'. Lucy could see the shadow of Zee walking across her bedroom.

If you lose a child, she was thinking, how do you find her in the light of day?

Late, Lucy didn't check the time but it felt very late when she heard a knock on the front door and she went to the head of the stairs where she could see a person through the window at the top of the front door if he was tall enough.

Lane was tall enough and Lucy went downstairs to let her in.

"I'm sorry to come over at this hour but I noticed the light still on in Maggie's room and imagined you in there," Lane said, walking towards the kitchen. "Maeve told me that Maggie *ran away from home*. Her words."

"I suppose that's true."

"To Zee's."

"She hasn't let me know but I assume she's at Zee's."

"She is."

It was midnight by the clock over the stove. Midnight and Reuben hadn't called. Certainly he could have found a telephone on the street and called if Elaine and Nell were in the house all day. He could have found a way on this most terrible day in Lucy's life.

"Something is the matter with Zee," Lane said. "That's really why I've come over to talk to you. You must have noticed."

"I've noticed that she's very nervous."

"She's lost interest in everything, our group of friends, August, her own children. Adam is worried to death. We're all worried."

"I am worried about Maggie," Lucy said evenly.

"Of course. Of course you are. Zee has always had a thing for little girls. Will knows about mental breakdowns of course, since that's his work, and he thinks she is having one."

Lane got up from the table.

"I had no idea it was so late. I seldom sleep."

"Are you suggesting that Maggie is at risk?"

"I'm actually saying nothing except that Zee seems to be falling apart."

Lucy followed Lane to the door.

"Even the day that August arrived and Miles Robinson went to your house for dinner, Zee was sharp-tongued, remember? And she's never been like that. Always lovely to all of us."

Lucy opened the door, turning on the porch light as Lane walked down the front steps.

"Good luck," Lane called, and blew her a kiss.

"Thank you. Thank you for coming over," Lucy said, realizing as she spoke that she had meant it.

The Mallorys' house was dark, a filtered light coming from Zee and Adam's bedroom, otherwise completely dark in the front. She couldn't see the back and she had never been upstairs although people said there were a lot of bedrooms so Maggie must have been sleeping in one of them and then the twins, either together or apart, and Zee. Possible that Adam slept alone.

She would go to the Mallorys' first thing in the morning when things seem more possible than in the dark and Adam Mallory was sober.

Maggie could say *No.* Likely she would and Lucy would throw her daughter over her shoulder, knock Zee Mallory to the floor with the other arm, *Do not ever come near us again*— cross the street, up the steps to the house, and drop Maggie onto the new couch.

This is the house where you live, she would say. *And I am your mother.*

She crawled into bed with Felix, moving as close to him as she could so his breath was synchronized with her breath, the heat of his body warming her skin.

What she felt was homesick.

Felix flung his small, plump arm across her breast.

"Mama?" he asked, lifting his head. "Who is your best friend?"

"You are and Maggie."

"But me and Maggie are children."

"I suppose I like children best then."

"My best friend is Teddy Sewall, but he doesn't like me so much because I'm little."

"Little and amazing." She kissed his hot, damp cheek.

"I know," he said sleepily. "You always tell me I'm amazing."

A full moon flooded the room with the kind of strange incandescent light that agitates the spirit, and as Felix slept, Lucy found her mind a rushing river.

In the house on Capitol Hill where she grew up, *home* was her father's study and she used to sit in a big leather chair, her legs over the arms, a drawing pad on her lap, sketching the girls in her class as animals, not specific animals but invented ones, and while she worked, her father was at his desk, papers piled high, reading or talking on the telephone. From time to time, he blew her a kiss across the room.

"Jump shot to you from me," he'd say, and they'd both laugh although she didn't understand *jump shot* but it didn't matter.

ZEE SAT UP in bed, her arms wrapped around her legs, listening to her house. In the boys' room *silence* so they must have been sleeping. Adam was in the kitchen by the refrigerator, of course, and walking up the steps to the second floor, down the hall to the study. Maggie was lying in bed in the guest room reading, Blue and Onion licking their bellies at the bottom of her bed.

After Adam went to the study, Zee tiptoed down the hall, knocked lightly on Maggie's door, and walked in.

"Hi," she said.

"Hi." Maggie stretched and yawned.

"I'm so happy you're here. Deliriously happy."

"Me too."

She knelt down on the bottom of the bed, her body too warm, her head splintering, not with a headache although it ached but rather with a kind of rawness as if her skin were bark and it was peeling off the trunk. Maybe she had a fever.

"I feel a little peculiar being here when I live there," Maggie said. "That's all."

"You'll get over that. This is just a break,

right?" Zee said, taking Maggie's foot in her hand, rubbing her ankles. "We all need a break from our daily life."

Adam was in their bedroom when she went back, in the dark, the room lit by the moon, sitting on the end of the bed, her nightgown in his hands.

"What are you doing?"

"This was in the bathroom I'm using." He handed it to her. "Zee?"

"Can we *not* talk tonight?"

"I think there's something the matter with you. I'm worried. Not angry, not sarcastic, not any of the things I've been. Just worried."

"I think there's something the matter with both of us, Adam."

"So what are we going to do?" he asked, rubbing his hands.

"Tonight, we're going to bed. Then you'll go to Assateague with the boys and you'll come back and we'll talk. Just like you said."

MAGGIE TURNED OUT the light and lay on her back waiting for sleep. The moon filled her bedroom with shimmering light and she was restless. She had planned to show Zee the pages from August's manuscript to see if she had heard of Samuel Baldwin, who had died on Witchita Avenue. Maybe she had known him.

But the pages were intended for Lucy. It was

possible they might reveal something about her mother that Maggie wouldn't understand because there were secrets that had been kept from her for a reason.

She didn't feel safe at home any longer and she didn't feel safe at the Mallorys' either. Maybe, she was thinking, she would never sleep again.

Seventeen

ZEE WATCHED ADAM load up the van with the backpacks and coolers, his old cooking gear from high school overnights at Lake Michigan, a new four-man tent he'd purchased for the occasion. It was early Friday morning and the women in the neighborhood were gathered on the steps of her porch, Rufus and Daniel playing soccer in the front yard, Victoria skipping down the front steps of August's house. The weekend was promising, sunny with occasional clouds, less heat and humidity than usual in late July.

Across the hall, Maggie was in the bathroom taking a shower.

"What are you going to do when we're gone, Mom?" Luke came in the room to kiss her goodbye.

"I'll go swimming with my friends and maybe go to the movies," she said, giving him a hug.

"You never go swimming," Luke said.

"Maybe I will today. I haven't made a plan yet."

But she did have a plan. She had made it days ago when Adam agreed to take the boys to Assateague.

"Will Maggie be here when we get back?" Luke asked.

"As far as I know."

"Daniel wanted me to find out because he doesn't like her very much."

"I know that."

"Daniel says you like to pretend she's your little girl."

"Well Daniel doesn't know everything, Luke."

She kissed him goodbye and watched as he ran down the front steps and climbed into the backseat of the van with Daniel, dragging poor Blue, who was too feeble for a camping trip with boys.

Adam was on his way upstairs to get his backpack and she braced herself for an interrogation like the ones she had from him every night since Maggie had moved into the guest room. He was worried about her, he said. She was anxious and irritable. He actually missed the things about her that used to drive him crazy.

"I don't want anything to happen, Zee," he'd said.

"Like what?" she asked.

"I don't know. Like something. Lately you've seemed unsteady." His voice drifted off. "Increasingly unsteady."

Adam was right. She knew *something* was the matter with her. She felt untethered, floating in an unfamiliar atmosphere, illness coming on like influenza for weeks. Disconnected images streamed through her mind. Just that morning she woke up with a sense of weight in her right hand as if the hand itself had doubled in size while she slept. Examining it in the morning light—were her eyes open or was this an image in her mind?—the hand was unrecognizable, in the process of changing shape, hardening, becoming what was in fact a block of wood, painted white with the letter *C* on it. An old-fashioned alphabet block. *C* for cat and for carrot and for coal and for coat and for crayon—a yellow tabby cat, an ordinary carrot, a piece of black coal, a red coat, a purple crayon.

She'd shaken it until it began to materialize again as a hand, her own hand with silver bangles and a turquoise ring on the index finger.

A picture settled in her mind. She was in the backyard of their stone and stucco row house in West Philadelphia where Adam was in his last year of law school at the Univeristy of Pennsylvania. Zee was throwing away the toys, the teddy bears and fuzzy rabbits and musical mobiles, even the wooden alphabet blocks which had belonged to Zee when she was a child.

"Your mother called," Adam said. "You were taking a shower. I told her you didn't seem yourself. *Together* was the word I used, but *together* doesn't translate in Revere, Michigan."

"I'll call her back."

The night before her mother, who called regularly now that Adam had told her Zee was coming apart, had remarked that it was troubling for Zee to take in someone else's daughter just because she wasn't speaking to her mother. *Taking advantage,* her mother said. And didn't Zee think it would be a good idea to talk to someone about it.

"Who would you suggest?" Zee had asked.

"Like a church pastor," her mother said. "One of those people who helps you out of trouble."

"A therapist is what you mean."

"One of those, yes," her mother said. "Because you have never spoken to anyone about the accident, even to Adam. That's what he said. He said you won't talk about troubles and these things can grow like cabbage inside you and take up all the room."

"My troubles are fine, Mother, not at all like cabbage, whatever that means."

Adam stood at the door to their bedroom.

"We'll be at the campgrounds and back on Sunday before dinner," he said. "If you need help, any help, call Will Sewall. He's an excellent doctor."

"You've had occasion to prove that?"

"Zee, trust me. I love you. I want this *not* to be happening."

"A double negative?"

"If anything, it's a double positive," he said, and left, pausing beside the van to speak to Josie.

Across the street, Lucy had descended the long length of steps in front of her house and was standing with Felix next to the brick wall, leaning against it, seeming to watch the Mallorys' front porch where Zee's *chicks* had gathered for coffee.

Adam backed the van into the avenue and headed off, waving to the women on the porch.

Maggie was out of the shower and dressed in shorts over a bathing suit, on her way down-stairs. Zee heard her bare feet on the hardwood floor and called her, not wishing to run the risk of running into Lucy especially, or any of the women on her porch.

"Your mother's in front of your house and may be coming over here," Zee said. "I thought you'd want to know."

"With Felix?"

"Yes, Felix is there."

Maggie went into Zee's bedroom, where she was pulling clothes out of the closet stuffing them into her small duffel.

"I'd like to tell Felix goodbye so he'll know I'm not mad at *him* while we're away on this trip."

"Of course, Maggie," Zee said, her voice soft. "But I wonder whether it will make it more difficult for Felix when you go."

"Why would it?"

"I may be completely wrong, but you know children and how they can worry if you tell them you're leaving but not worry if they don't know you've left."

Lucy had called Zee that morning.

"Just checking on Maggie," she'd said.

"She's fine. No problem," Zee said, the tone of her voice disarming. "I'll take good care of her and in no time she'll be ready to go home."

Lucy didn't reply and it sounded as if she had disconnected but Zee couldn't be sure.

"Did you tell my mom we were going to wherever?" Maggie asked.

"Of course."

"And she said okay?"

"She didn't say *okay* but she didn't say no."

Zee had *not* told Lucy and Lucy wouldn't have said okay but she wasn't going to risk delaying their departure while Maggie worried over whether or not to leave.

"Of course, your mother would rather you didn't go," Zee said. "She'd rather you go back home but I told her about our trip and not to worry and she seemed fine with that."

336

Zee had spoken carefully. Some truth but not too much.

"You *do* want to come with me, don't you?" Zee asked with just the right cheerful tone.

Maggie's face was turned towards the stairwell window overlooking the front of the house so she could see Lucy and Felix across the street. He was leaning against Lucy's legs, his small arms folded across his chest. She would write a note to Felix, an *I love you forever* note, quickly out of Zee's sight and ask Maeve to leave it on the front porch.

"I *do* want to come," she said.

"Great!" Zee hurried on, not to leave space for reconsidering. "I thought you did. We're off then in just a few minutes. Are you packed?"

"I'm packed."

"Take a sweater. It'll be cold at night."

"I have one."

"And any of my jewelry you'd like to wear, second drawer on the left in the bathroom."

Zee watched Maggie go back into the guest room and come out with her packed duffel, smiling as she headed into Zee and Adam's bathroom.

"I borrowed your turquoise and yellow beads with a silver cross."

"Perfect on you," Zee said.

Outside in the street, Gabriel Russ had materialized and was talking to Lucy.

• • •

MAGGIE HAD BEEN thinking of Felix, how small and wide-eyed and serious he was, how much he loved her. She could feel the way his brown eyes followed her around the room, melting in dark streams when she came home from school or lay on her mother's bed and read to him.

At night before she went to sleep in the blue guest room at the Mallorys' house, she'd blow him a kiss across the street, projecting his face on her mind's screen, wondering if he could feel her thinking of him.

"So let's bolt out the back door now, darling," Zee said. "I'll feed Onion and grab some fruit for the ride. We're taking Adam's car, which is parked in the alley."

Maggie left by the kitchen door, stuck her duffel in the backseat, and climbed in the car, pulling down the visor over the passenger seat to check her lips, wet with creamy lip gloss from Zee's top drawer.

She looked eighteen, she thought, her hair pulled back into a fuzzy bun, her cheeks flushed with borrowed rouge. Zee was hurrying across the yard, opening the low gate to the alley, her necklaces jangling. From that distance the crow's-feet around her eyes, the parentheses around her lips were camouflaged and Zee looked eighteen too. They were best friends for life.

"We're off," Zee said, hopping into the driver's seat, lifting Maggie's hand and kissing her fingers.

"Off to where?" Maggie asked.

Zee had said nothing specific, only that they were going somewhere. A surprise.

"Oz," Zee said. "I bet you've never been there."

REUBEN HAD CALLED early that morning while Lucy was making breakfast for Felix, incapable of eating herself since Maggie left.

It was the first time she'd spoken to him since he'd left New York for the Cape and she resented him for that. *Hated* him, she decided, and it pleased her, the sound of an unspeakable word caught in the wide net of her mouth.

He had left two messages on her answering machine, feeble messages laced with excuses. *Elaine's parents are here so I haven't been able to break away to call,* he'd said in the first message. *I'll try again tomorrow. Hope things are great.* The second message two days later. *The Brownings from Elaine's office have come with their kids for several days so I'm pretty tied up but tell Maggie and Felix I love them and especially* you *and I think of you every minute of the day.*

"Hello, my heart," he said when she picked up the phone.

339

"Maggie has run away from home." Her voice was flat.

"She has?"

"She crossed the street yesterday and actually *walked* away from home."

"So you know where she is."

"It doesn't make a difference that I know," Lucy said. "She packed her suitcase with her favorite things and left."

There was a long familiar pause while Reuben reassembled.

"A little rebellion isn't life-defining," he said. "You understand that, Lucy."

"Call me when you're back in New York and free to talk," she said.

"On Monday morning I'll be back in the office." He sounded relieved to disconnect.

Lucy sat down with Felix, sharing his blueberry muffin, then cleared the table, rinsed the dishes, wiped blueberry off Felix's mouth, combed her curly hair with her fingers.

It was seven-thirty, a Friday morning about the time the women in the neighborhood met at Zee's for coffee.

"I'm thinking we'll maybe go to the Mallorys' with the other mothers and you can play on the front porch."

"Will there be kids?" Felix asked, dragging his yellow chicken with half a red beak which he had chewed off. "Maybe Teddy."

"Maybe."

"Will Maggie be there?"

"I don't know," Lucy said, standing on the front porch, Felix's small, sure hand in hers, her heart fluttering in her chest. "I hope she will."

The women were gathering on the porch. Lane was already there and so was Josie, dressed in a pants suit for work, Robin Robinson sitting on the top step folded over like a doll, her arms around her knees. Lucy had not seen Miles Robinson for days but she thought about him.

Simply as a kiss. A disassociated kiss.

Victoria, in a leotard and tights for the ballet class she taught at the community center, was on her way down the steps from August's house and waved to Lucy, who leaned as if resting against her brick wall, summoning the courage to cross the street to enemy territory.

She had made a promise when she left New York to extend herself beyond the boundaries of her own house, something she had never felt the need to do in the West Village. There she had her work and her children and Reuben.

Just watching the women spread across the front steps of the Mallorys' filled Lucy with a nostalgia for something she had never had.

"Are we going to Zee's, Mama?" Felix asked.

"I'm thinking about it." Lucy crouched down to his level and pulled up his sagging shorts.

341

"Teddy says that Zee has toys in a box on the front porch."

"You have a lot of toys too, Felix."

"Not in a box on the front porch."

"We can get a box and put it on the front porch."

"Do you know how come Maggie moved across the street to Zee's house?"

He rested between Lucy's knees, leaning against her with his full body weight.

"I think she moved because she's a little mad at me."

Felix folded his arms across his chest, considering.

"Maggie told me she's mad because you tell lies."

Lucy smarted. Of course Maggie would have said something like that to Felix.

"What is lies?" Felix asked.

"Like the story of Pinocchio who tells little lies and his nose grows," Lucy said.

"I don't like Pinocchio very much," Felix said with obvious pleasure in his role as critic. "I love Winnie-the-Pooh and Christopher Robin and they don't tell lies, right?"

"Right."

"So tell me what is lies?"

"If you do something that is not the right thing to do like take a toy away from Teddy Sewall and hide it and when he asks you where the toy is, you say you don't know and that is a lie because you do know."

"Why does Maggie say that you tell lies and so she has to move to Zee's house?"

"I don't tell lies. Maggie isn't exactly right about that. I keep secrets and she wants to know the secrets."

"I want to know them too."

Gabriel Russ was trotting around the path from the back of August's house and down the steps, a little round bun of a man wearing August's Bermuda shorts and a T-shirt with *Save the City* in red letters, much too large for his body, scurrying on his bare feet, plump with squared-off toes.

"Hello, Lucy. You are just the one I am looking for, you and Felix the Great."

"We're going to Zee's house now to play with her toys in a box," Felix said.

"No, no, not at all. Not today," Gabriel said, waving them on to follow him. "My brother August Russ wants you to come over for coffee with us. It's Friday morning and we have chocolate donuts on Friday mornings and very delicious coffee and August Russ is sitting in the kitchen waiting for you."

"Later we'll go to Zee's," Lucy said relieved. "Now we need to be with August for chocolate donuts. I'll be right back."

She crossed the street to the Mallorys' side of

the avenue, walked down the long path, stepping over a basketball, a scooter dropped on its side, a melted ice cream sandwich in a pool of chocolate on the flagstone, knocked on the door, looked through the glass. The house seemed empty. Onion, lying on the Oriental rug in the hall, looked up at her when she knocked but didn't move. The women had dispersed with their coffee cups.

Adam had been gone for more than an hour and Zee with Maggie beside her in the front seat of Adam's Toyota was just turning left on Connecticut Avenue headed to the Beltway.

Lucy walked up the front steps to August's house, catching a glimpse of Felix. She would watch the Mallorys' house all day. They would be back, at least for lunch unless they'd taken a day trip. Certainly by dinner when it started to get dark.

AUGUST WAS SITTING in a wheelchair in the kitchen, the legs of the wheelchair lifted to an angle. His face was ruddy with color and his hair had been cut.

"Hacked off," he said. "Gabriel did it."

Lucy kissed his cheek.

"You look better than you did day before yesterday when I was here."

"I'd be fine if I weren't so weak but my brain seems normal as it ever was, god knows why."

"My brain is not normal but normal is normal, isn't that right?" Gabriel asked. "Which is why I was fired from my job after twenty years putting shiny shoes on men's feet."

Felix scrambled onto the couch in the corner of the kitchen, his feet on the cushions, his head on the arm.

"My sister Maggie lives with Zee Mallory," he said glumly. "I guess you know that."

August poured Lucy a cup of coffee.

"Cream?" he asked. "I don't have milk."

"My sister Maggie lives with Zee Mallory," Felix said again, a chocolate donut in his hand, chocolate on his cheeks and lips. "Did anybody in this room hear me?"

"I did hear you," Gabriel said, sitting down beside him on the couch. "You said *My sister Maggie lives with Zee Mallory*."

"I know that's what I said but nobody was listening."

"Maggie is only visiting Zee. Isn't that right, Felix?" August asked.

Felix shook his head.

"Victoria told me she was having a sleepover for a couple of nights."

"That's right," Lucy said, "but Felix is inconsolable."

"I'm very sad too," Gabriel said. "Inconsolable."

"Why are you sad too?" Felix asked.

"Because your sister Maggie is living with Zee Mallory. Just like you, I am sad too. All day and all night, which is why we're eating a chocolate donut, right?"

"Right," Felix said.

"I especially like a chocolate donut because it makes me happy when I'm sad and now today, this morning sitting here with you, I'm very happy."

"Right," Felix said, putting the donut on his lap, licking the chocolate off his fingers. "You know the reason Maggie is mad?"

"I didn't know she was mad," Gabriel said.

"She is very mad," Felix said, "because Mama tells her lies and lies and lies. That's how Maggie said it to me. Lies and lies and lies."

The kitchen was still, only the sound of the coffeepot making its quiet clicks and the guttural animal sound in Gabriel's throat when he was nervous, Felix smacking his lips, his tongue following the line of chocolate in the corner of his mouth.

Outside in the front of the house, a squeaking of brakes, a horn, and Lucy, her legs folded under her, was frozen in her seat.

She looked over at August, his head, just slightly to the side, his eyes soft, his face in repose, watching her kindly.

"That *is* why Maggie left," Lucy said so quietly she could barely hear her own voice.

• • •

AT LUNCHTIME, GABRIEL made sandwiches—
*Mayo or mustard? Pickles? Tomato and lettuce?
Peppers, red and green.*

"Tomato, lettuce, and peppers," Lucy said to
Gabriel. "Red peppers if you have them."

"Oh no, we don't have peppers, not red, not
green. I'm pretending I'm not here in
Washington, D.C., at August Russ's house but
that I have a job at Jack's Sub Shop in Albany
next to my shoe store where I have been fired
and you have come for lunch at my sub shop."

"No peppers, thank you," Lucy said, wrapping
a light blanket around Felix, who had fallen
asleep with his yellow chicken under his chin.

"That's what they say behind the counter—
they shout out *Peppers, red and green. Tomato
and lettuce. Wheat bread or white.*" Gabriel was
spreading mustard on wheat bread. "Welcome to
my submarine shop in Albany, New York. I am
Jack."

LUCY SETTLED INTO August's kitchen as if they
were a family. No talk of lies or August's
manuscript. Just the mundane daily chatter of
people who belonged to one another.

Felix woke up in time for lunch and later he
stood at the sink helping Gabriel with the dishes
and then they all took a walk, Felix sitting in
August's lap, Gabriel pushing the wheelchair

347

down Witchita to Connecticut Avenue, along the avenue, stopping at the bookstore where August bought Felix *Mr. Popper's Penguins* and two Spider-Man comics, at the toy store where August bought a plastic figure of Spider-Man himself which Felix coveted. They crossed Connecticut, down McKinley, and left on Broad Branch, stopping at the market for penny candy and a coffee, up the hill to Lafayette School, sitting under the trees in the filtered sunlight watching Felix play with two little girls on the jungle gym. It was almost five when they started back home, stopping at the Safeway for groceries.

"Spaghetti for dinner," Gabriel said. "I make my spaghetti with tomato sauce and noodles and meatballs too."

"Which is what we think of when we think about spaghetti," August said.

"Right," Gabriel said. "And I am thinking about spaghetti."

"Spaghetti is delicious," Felix said.

After dinner, after the dishes were done, candles still lit on the kitchen table, a second bottle of wine half gone, Felix sat on the couch looking at Spider-Man comics. Lucy was stretched out, her head back, her feet crossed at the ankles resting on a chair.

It was eight o'clock, a warm summer evening beginning to crawl towards night and she didn't want to go home in the dark, where Maggie's absence spread without mercy through the house.

"You and Felix could stay the night," August said. "I have an extra bedroom and it's getting dark."

She *could* stay, Lucy thought. Here with August and Gabriel, across the street from the Mallorys'. She'd be able to see Maggie if the bedroom August offered was at the front of the house. Or she could stay right where she was in the warmth of the kitchen flickering with candlelight.

"Maybe," she said.

"The bed has clean sheets," August said.

"Clean green sheets with brown ferns on the pillowcases," Gabriel said. "Real cotton. One hundred percent. Not polyester."

But in the end Lucy refused. She needed to be in her double bed with its soft mattress next to Felix, who never slept in his own bed, needed to sit in Maggie's room with her own angled view of the Mallorys' refuge for unhappy children.

Upstairs Gabriel was looking for the carbon copy of August's book.

"I don't know why those pages would be missing from the manuscript," August said when Gabriel returned with the book.

"Strange, yes?"

"So the only part that was missing was the section I wanted you to read in particular about the man who was a special assistant to President Truman in the White House when he died in your house. A midwesterner," he added as if the fact of this geography was an important detail.

She knew this. She had known it from the beginning when August mentioned her father.

"He hanged himself on a Sunday morning in the summer of 1951 after he was discovered in a homosexual act at the downtown YMCA, which is what I describe in the book. Sodomy is what the papers reported."

Her mouth was bone-dry, her lips tightened around her teeth.

"My take is that he must have killed himself because he was a public figure in the White House—not a man who had any past mental problems, no indications of instability as far as I could see—only a peripheral life considered aberrant in our society and he knew that the following morning the newspapers were going to print the story of the incident at the Y."

The air was empty and hot even with a fan blowing her hair off her face but Lucy was clammy.

"I have the articles," he said. "You might like to see them."

"Why are you telling me this?" she asked finally.

"Why did I write about him, you mean?"

"Why did you want *me* to see these pages?"

"I thought you would be interested because someone had died in your house," August said. "That's the sort of thing that would interest me because . . ." He shrugged. "The book is social history and his story reflects the prevalent attitudes towards homosexuality which still exist today. And besides, I admire Samuel Baldwin."

"I am interested," Lucy said, and the words tumbled out before she had a chance to think of what she wanted to say or how to say it, to consider the consequences. "I'm interested in all of it, the book you're writing about shame and homosexuality and secrets and why people cover up secrets with lies. All of that, every bit of it. And I know the man . . ." She took a breath, grabbing it out of the air as if the air in the Russ kitchen might disappear. "Samuel Baldwin was my father."

THE LIGHTS WERE out at the Mallorys' house that night. Lucy had noticed it at dusk after they left August's house, after he had followed her in his wheelchair to the back door, taking a light hold of her wrist—*I am so sorry,* he'd said. *No wonder.*

No wonder? As if August knew her inside out.

IN MAGGIE'S BEDROOM, she sat on the bed, holding back the curtains. They could be at the movies or maybe at the Sewalls' or at the coffeehouse next to the Safeway listening to music. Not something Maggie had ever done before.

Lane answered the phone on the first ring.

"I thought it might be Will," she said.

"I'm sorry," Lucy said. "Just me wondering if Maeve knows where Maggie is tonight. It doesn't look like anyone is home at the Mallorys'."

"Adam took the boys to the beach to camp out. I know that," Lane said. "Maeve?"

She must have put her hand over the receiver because Lucy sitting cross-legged on the bed, her cheeks burning, the phone pressed against her ear, couldn't hear what got said between them.

"Maeve doesn't know but Maggie did ask her to drop a note at your house for Felix and it's in the mailbox." She took a deep breath. "Honestly, Lucy, I don't how you can stand what is going on . . ." her voice trailed off.

"I can't," Lucy said.

MAGGIE BEGAN TO seriously worry when they left the Garden State Parkway in New Jersey for the New York Thruway to Albany. It wasn't the first time she was conscious of trouble. *Someone is following us,* Zee said just past Baltimore on Route 95 checking the rear-vision mirror again and again. Maggie had turned around to look at the boxy red car behind them.

The woman in the red car? she asked.

It's a man and he was right behind me in the Baltimore Tunnel and he's still there.

But the red car with a woman driving pulled over to the right lane as they were talking and that was the last they saw of it.

After they left the Joyce Kilmer rest stop on the New Jersey Turnpike, left it in a hurry without getting the hot dog Zee had promised, Maggie started to make a mental note of *where* they were.

"I didn't have time to wait in line," Zee'd snapped.

Between the rest stop and the exit to the Garden State Parkway, Zee's driving became erratic. Once she slowed down in the left-hand lane so the cars behind her honked. *I hate impatient drivers,* she said, pulling over to the far right lane, hugging the back of the car in front of her, switching to the middle lane and driving what felt to Maggie like too fast.

"I'm sorry about the hot dog," Zee said. "We need to be there by six."

"We need to be where?" Maggie asked, knowing she should have kept silent.

"Where we're going," Zee said.

North in New York State. That's the most Maggie knew and was afraid to ask anything else.

If she leaned back in her seat, pretending to

353

look out the front window, she had a peripheral view of Zee's profile, of her jaw moving as if she were grinding her teeth. Maggie made a note of that too, gathering observations in case she had to tell someone, maybe at a gas station—they would have to stop for gas sometime—her mother would be the one she'd call. Or Uncle Reuben.

Zee was holding the steering wheel in a death grip—those were the words that passed through Maggie's mind—*in a death grip,* so she must have read that line in a book.

When they stopped for gas, if they stopped for gas before they got to *where they were going* as Zee had described it, she would call Lucy or Reuben collect. Explain to Zee that she was going to the restroom, find a pay phone out of sight, call her mother to tell her where they were located, just in case, headed north on Route 87 in New York. Nothing to be exactly alarmed about. She didn't want to *tell* on Zee.

Just beyond the exit to Woodstock, New York, Zee started to pull off her necklaces. Actually tear them off, breaking the chains, beads scattering in her lap, tiny red and blue and green dots, pulling on a heavy silver choker, the blue veins in her neck quivering.

"These things are driving me crazy," she said, brushing the beads off her lap. "They're suffocating."

Maggie fixed her eyes on the road. They had scarely spoken since the Joyce Kilmer rest stop.

"I'm *not* okay if that's what you are wondering," Zee said finally. "And that is what you were wondering, I can tell, looking at me out of the corner of your eyes. I'm sick. I'm sick to death."

The Mallorys had been the ones to give the going-away party for their next-door neighbors in the row house where they lived in West Philadelphia where Adam was in law school at Penn. Every time it was the Mallorys who gave the parties, and they were high-spirited, noisy parties with chips for dinner, wine and beer chilling in an old barrel in the backyard, rock and roll on the stereo. Dancing on the tiny deck. Everyone ate very little and drank too much but they were young and in graduate school without responsibilities beyond themselves, a few married but none with children.

Only Adam and Zee Mallory had a child, who on this summer evening the first of August, 1962, was two days short of her first birthday and walking. She had started walking at nine months old, zipping around the apartment on her plump bare feet, and now at almost one, she spoke in fractured sentences. Give Mama kiss. Say bye bye bye bye to Daddy. More ice cream. Like that.

Amazing, their friends said, and the Mallorys had agreed.

Zee was grilling the hamburgers, the stereo box in the open window, Adam dancing with a woman she didn't know. Two doors down, someone shouted for quiet.

It's after ten. People are sleeping, a man's voice said.

After ten registered with Zee. Late to be serving dinner, too late for Miranda to still be up.

ZEE WAS FEELING peculiar when she pulled into the Joyce Kilmer rest stop. Different from the nightmares and nerves and morning sweats of the last few weeks, the way Adam had been when he came back from Viet Nam. Now it was as if she were dissolving into someone else, as if she knew that the feel of her body, the hum of her brain, the rush of blood through her veins was in the process of disappearing. Soon to be gone, a stranger in her place.

She walked through the glass doors of the rest stop into the wide, gaping space of the cafeteria and shops and restrooms, people watching her as she walked by, a man standing by the ice cream kiosk making assumptions. She could feel his eyes on her back.

She needed to take control. Buy a Pepsi, wash her face with cold water, check the size of her pupils in the mirror of the ladies'. Her mother had told her that Dr. Richards had determined her first cousin June had gone crazy by looking at her pupils with a flashlight. *What did Dr. Richards see in June's pupils?* Zee had asked.

In the cubicle in the ladies', she sat on the toilet seat, put her head in her hands, closed her eyes, pressed her palms hard against her eyeballs to erase the colors flashing across her vision.

"Watch out!" she said aloud, and a voice from somewhere in the ladies' replied, "Watch out?"

Had she actually said *Watch out* or had she heard it from somewhere else the way she had been hearing things, in the last week—a rat-a-tat-tat in her head as if there were nails hammering in her brain and one morning waking, she'd heard "Watch out" called right into her ear. *Watch out,* and she thought it was Adam speaking or one of the boys but the sound had come from inside her head.

She stepped out of the cubicle where a woman putting on her lipstick in the mirror asked, *Was that you who said watch out?*

"No, it wasn't me," Zee said softly, not to call attention although she was urgent to hit the woman right in the lips so her bright red lipstick would smudge like blood across her face.

"You never know," the woman said.

"You never know what?" Zee asked. "Why are you looking at me like that?"

357

"I'm not looking at you. I'm putting on lipstick and looking at myself," the woman said. She had a large nose like a man's and eyes set too close together.

"Don't follow my car or I'll call the police," Zee said, squinting as she passed the mirror.

She walked from the ladies' through the cafeteria quickly before the space expanded beyond her and she couldn't get out. She didn't have time to buy a Pepsi or the hot dog Maggie had requested. The place was too large. She wouldn't be able to get to the car unless she hurried and the woman in the ladies' might already be behind her. She didn't look back, running through the cafeteria, through the glass doors, across the parking lot to the car where Maggie was waiting.

"Are you okay?" Maggie asked when Zee got back in the car.

"I'm fine," Zee said, pulling onto the highway. "But a woman in the ladies' room was watching me. She looked under the cubicle at me while I was peeing and I didn't have time to get a hot dog or a Pepsi because of what was happening to the building. Growing, you know, like cabbage."

She would be fine if she could just get to Vermont—maybe not entirely fine but better than she felt with this dislocation in her brain, the sense she had that her brain itself was moving out of her skull.

She needed to go about this trip in an orderly fashion, *I go about my daily life in an orderly fashion,* her mother would say to her. Route 87 North, two hours to Albany, and then the turnoff for Route 7 in Vermont, two hours from Albany/ Rensselaer through Bennington, Vermont, and east through the Green Mountain National Forest. Four hours plus and she'd be home.

"How are you sick?" Maggie asked.

"I'm not sick. I didn't say I was sick," Zee said. "I said I wanted to kill the woman in the ladies' room."

NELL FRANK ANSWERED the phone when Lucy called Reuben in Cape Cod. Ten at night. He might have gone to bed already but Lucy didn't consider the circumstances of their lives. She knew exactly what she was doing.

"My dad's here but they're having a dinner party," Nell said, a raspy voice, a kind of New Jersey accent. Lucy had never met Nell, never heard her speak. "Who can I say is calling?"

"Lucy Painter."

"Lucy Painter's on the phone, Dad."

Maybe the accent was Brooklyn where Reuben had grown up. He had an accent.

"He can't talk now," Nell said. "He'll call you back."

"I'm sorry," Lucy said evenly with a cool certainty. "I need to speak to him now."

The *now* had a force to it and the girl, Nell, responded.

"She can't wait, she says," Nell called, her hand evidently not covering the receiver.

There was a rustle in the background, the sound of voices, of laughter—high-pitched—that would be Elaine—the shuffle of footsteps, and Reuben.

"Hello?"

"I need for you to come to Washington on Monday, before you go back to work," Lucy said.

"I don't know what you're talking about." His voice took on a favored severity. "Please be clear."

"Together we are telling our children that you are their father," she said. "Is that clear?"

There was silence on the other end of the phone and Lucy imagined him leaning against the wall, his face assuming that expression of pain which concealed irritation that his life had been interrupted at just the wrong moment.

"I can't."

"You can," Lucy said, a force field of energy expanding in her chest, a certainty that Reuben *would* come because she had insisted.

It was simple and clear.

"Why now?" he asked, and replaced the receiver on the cradle.

Lucy barely heard the click.

She went to the kitchen, turned on water for tea. In the window across the yard, she could see August in the kitchen reading his manuscript, Gabriel on the couch, his palms together resting against his lips, his legs drawn up, curled and sleeping like the picture of an elf.

She wouldn't sleep but she went upstairs and climbed into the bed with Felix, watching the shadows of the trees trembling in the light wind as night turned very slowly to dawn.

In daylight on Saturday morning, she would go after Maggie until she found her.

Eighteen

It WAS STILL light when they crossed the town line into Cavendish, an orange sun setting in the west over the hills, a still whiteness about the town as if it had been stopped on the clock midlife, its citizens arrested in time. In the distance, a pale quarter-moon hung like an ornament above the steeple of the Episcopal church, a postcard replica of New England churches—*Here's the church, and here's the steeple / Open the door and see all the people.* A game that Zee used to play with Miranda, lacing her tiny fingers, closing the fists, the thumbs as doors, the forefingers as the steeple, and when the doors open, the fingers *are* the people. *Here's the church . . .* she could hear her own voice loud as bells crashing in her ear.

Zee drove down Main Street and right on Oxford, her heart beating so hard that she thought its shape must be showing through her T-shirt. Any moment now, it would jump out of her chest and land bloody and beating on her lap.

Straight on Main past the church, right on Oxford.

Zee had needed to know the facts about Cavendish, committed them to memory when first the village came into her life: a town probably named for William Cavendish, the fourth Duke of Devonshire, the land was granted by authority of the British government in the 1700s. In 1781, Salmon Dutton came to the new town of Cavendish from Massachusetts and his home in the lower Black River Valley had been preserved as the Shelburne Museum. A tourist attraction. He had given the money to build the Cavendish Academy half a mile from the frame white Victorian located behind a stand of pine trees, at the end of an unpaved road, where the sign *The Children's Home* was small and only visible once you got to the building itself. Cavendish: census 1,470 and falling. Somehow in Zee's mind, the fewer people settling in Cavendish, the safer it was for children.

Maggie said nothing as they crossed the town line, although it was clear they had arrived *where they were going.*

"We're here," Zee said, and her voice had

taken on an icy calm. "Pretty, isn't it, Miranda?"

It was the second time since they crossed the line from New York State into Vermont that Zee had called Maggie *Miranda*.

"Yes, very," Maggie said.

They had not stopped for gas since New Jersey so she had no opportunity to contact her mother. She would wait until they were *someplace* and had to stop or the car ran out of gas, as it had done once with her mother in the winter and they'd had to walk in the freezing cold to a filling station for help, Felix screaming all the way.

Maggie had a picture of where they were, had followed the routes carefully, making a note of the geography, and figured that if anything happened—whatever *that* might be—she could run.

"I'll tell you everything I know about Cavendish," Zee said calmly, repeating all the minor facts she had committed to memory. "The Children's Home is a beautiful old house with a lot of land for running around and sheep—there are sheep too, *little innocent lambs of God who on their woolly coat / so bravely bore the punishment of each wee wicked goat*. Something like that. You'll like it here."

It was further down Oxford Street than Zee had remembered and since there was no sign, difficult to find a road at dusk. Zee strained her eyes and then by some miracle, she thought, there was the line of pine trees and the narrow road on the right that led uphill to the Children's Home where Miranda would live until she was no longer a child. Zee turned right, up the hill, and pulled to a stop in a parking space next to the home, which was only the size of an ordinary middle-class home high on a hill so the lights of the town were visible.

Zelda!

Zee turned from the grill, left the hamburgers to burn, following the sound of alarm in Adam's voice. She pressed forward, catching sight of the top of Adam's head above the party crowd. He was no longer dancing but calling Zee's name again and again. The crowd was too dense for her to see what was happening but people were turning their heads, turning towards Adam, pressing forward. Someone screamed Watch out! Zee pushed through and people spread, parting to make a path so she finally had a view of her husband in his new silver blue shirt bent over the barrel of ice, the wine and beer almost gone. His arms were submerged in melted ice, and before she reached him, her knees gave and she fell to the ground and couldn't watch him lift Miranda over his shoulder, slapping her on her back crying HELP in a voice so plaintive it would never leave.

• • •

THE LIGHTS HAD gone on the front porch of the Children's Home and someone—it appeared to be a woman in jeans and a baseball cap—had opened the door.

Zee turned off the engine and watched the woman walking down the steps towards the car with suspicion.

"I have never seen this woman before in my life," she said, opening the car door, stepping out. "I won't let anything happen to you," she said to Maggie. "I promise. Don't worry. You're not in any danger."

She shut the door.

"Hi," the woman in the baseball cap said. "Can I help you?"

"Who are you?" Zee asked.

"I'm Laura," she said, more of a girl than a woman, a splash of freckles across her face, an easy smile. "I'm on night duty here."

"Night duty? I thought there were doctors."

"There is a doctor in town and a nurse on duty and the rest of us like me on night duty."

"I need to see a doctor."

"I don't think it's possible," the girl, Laura, said. "Maybe you can wait and I'll get someone."

"No, no. I'm here for a reason and I need to check your credentials before I tell you the reason."

"My credentials?" the girl asked. "I don't understand."

"Get the nurse. Get someone who speaks English."

The girl hurried across the grass, up the steps, through the door, and almost immediately she was returning with another woman, tall, reedy, in hiking boots and overalls. Short curly gray hair. Something familiar about the woman, Zee thought.

"Mrs. Mallory?" the woman said. "Hello. How nice to see you. We didn't know you were coming."

"You don't know me," Zee said. "I've never seen you before in my life."

"We have met each other. I'm the nurse Angela Brice and you are Miranda's mother. I haven't seen you in a couple of years."

"Miranda is in the car," Zee said, air caught in her throat. "There. Look in the car. She's perfectly fine. Nothing the matter with her. Open the car door and look."

It was dusk, a soft, cool evening in Vermont with starlight but in the distance. She opened the door.

"Hi," Maggie said. "I'm Maggie."

"Hello, Maggie," the nurse said. "I'm Angela, the nurse at the Home." She leaned in the car and spoke quietly. "Is Mrs. Mallory all right?"

"I think she's not so well today," Maggie said, starting to get out of the car.

But her legs were too heavy. She wanted to sleep, in the car in the dark with the door closed and the windows shut and the nurse guarding her so nothing could happen.

Zee took hold of the girl, Laura, holding the collar of her red flannel shirt.

"It wasn't my fault," Zee said in her face. "I suppose everyone has told you it was my fault but they are wrong."

LUCY WAS SITTING on the front porch when Adam arrived home from the beach with the twins. She had been there since dawn, Felix still sleeping, the front door opened so she could hear him if he called. August had said she should call the police if Zee didn't come back with Maggie by morning, and she had called them early before dawn, sitting in the kitchen with the officers, telling them what she knew, that Maggie had left with Zee, that she had left a note for Felix, that they were driving Adam Mallory's car—Lane gave her the information about the car—a blue Toyota Camry two-door D.C. plates. Zee had *not* asked permission to take Maggie away and her daughter was a minor, only eleven. The police took down the information and stood up to leave.

"Not necessarily a crisis," the one officer said to Lucy as he left, but kindly.

She hurried down the front steps and crossed

the street where Adam was unpacking the camping gear.

"Do you know where Zee is?" she asked.

"Sleeping, I assume."

"She's gone. She left with Maggie yesterday after you did," Lucy said. "She *took* Maggie."

Adam opened the side door of the van and let the rumpled, sleepy boys out with Blue, who ambled after them, and put his backpack strap over his shoulder.

"Want to come in?" he asked.

"I will," she said, following him into his house. "But Felix's still sleeping."

"We couldn't sleep in Assateague," Adam said. "There were enough mosquitoes to kill an army so we got up, packed our gear, and came home." He unlocked the front door. "I'll check Zee. She hasn't been well."

"What does that mean?" Lucy asked, going up the stairs behind him.

"Zee's been off her game but she'd never hurt a flea if that's what you're wondering," he said.

Zee's bedroom door was open, the bed made, clothes strewn across the floor as if she'd dropped them on her way out.

Adam checked the answering machine but there were no calls. No note left in an obvious place.

"You've got to help me, Adam," Lucy said.

"I'll get the boys in their beds and then I'll call around."

He walked back downstairs with Lucy.

"I'll get back to you once I know."

FELIX WAS STILL sleeping at seven when the day was fully light, warm, not hot with a breeze from the south. Lucy stayed on the porch, sitting on the top step, needing to be outside in case there was news which she might miss. Nothing seemed to be happening at the Mallorys'. The boys had probably fallen into bed but Lucy hoped that Adam would be over to tell her as soon as he knew something.

By seven-thirty, the neighborhood was up, Miles Robinson walking to the bus, working on a Saturday. He waved, walked on, but something must have occurred to him because he turned back, came halfway up the steps.

"I'm sorry, Lucy. Robin has kept me up on what's happening."

He was an awkward man and she was grateful that he took notice of her alone on the steps and bothered to speak to her this morning.

Lane, in her robe, waved as she came out to get the paper.

"Any word?"

"Not yet," Lucy said.

Josie called across the street to ask if Felix wanted to go to a puppet show with Rufus at ten.

"Not today," Lucy said. "I need him with me."

She made scrambled eggs and toast and juice

which Felix ate sitting on the front step of the porch next to her, his body pressed up next to hers. She brought her coffee.

"Is Maggie coming home yet?" he asked.

"Not yet," Lucy said, reaching in the pocket of her jeans for the note Maggie had written to Felix. "She sent you a note and Maeve put it in our mailbox. Do you want me to read it to you?"

He nodded.

"*Dear Felix, my brother,* is how it begins. *I will love you forever.*"

"I *know* that," Felix said matter-of-factly.

"Well that's what she writes in her letter to you."

He took the note written on lined school paper and looked at it.

"Is *forever* today?" he asked.

"And tomorrow and the next day and the next and the next."

He crumpled the paper and put it down between them.

"Can I watch TV?" he asked.

"We don't have a TV," Lucy said.

"I know that, of course."

He finished his eggs and took the plate back to the kitchen.

"Can I watch TV at Maeve and Teddy's house?"

Lucy hesitated.

"I would like you to stay here with me, Felix."

He was pensive, resting his elbows on his knees, leaning his chin on his fists.

"Sometimes eggs taste yucky," he said. "Like these eggs were a little yucky."

Down the street, Robin Robinson was walking their new Lab puppy and waved and kept on walking up the street, stopping at Lucy's, coming up the steps.

"Maybe I'll play war on the kitchen floor because we don't have a playroom like the Mallorys do." He got up. "Some of my soldiers are going to be dead in the war and I'll need new ones."

"Later," Lucy said. "This afternoon. We'll check the toy store."

Robin sat down on the step, lifting the wiggly puppy into her lap.

"Lane called me last night," she said. "Have you heard anything from Zee?"

Lucy shook her head.

"Nothing so far. Adam didn't even know she had left," Lucy said. "He thought she was home."

"I'm so sorry," Robin said. "It's awful. I don't know what else to say." She put her hand lightly on Lucy's knee. "Something is the matter with Zee, whom I love. Suddenly, just this summer, it's happened. Or maybe since August fell."

That's how the women spoke of Zee, as if to tell any actual truth about her was a betrayal.

"I don't know Zee that well," Lucy said.

"Children love her."

Lucy expected Robin to leave then, everything said that could have been said between them, a pleasantry, a note of sympathy. But she didn't leave and for a while she didn't speak, both of them looking out on the avenue as if there were some expectation.

It was Robin who interrupted the silence.

"Maybe you've heard that I had an abortion."

Lucy sat very still, her stomach tight.

"Miles told you."

"Not exactly," Lucy said.

"He told me that he had."

"He told me that he *thought* you had."

Robin leaned against Lucy, holding the railing to pull herself up.

"He told me he kissed you but don't worry. It was Miles, not you. I've been so cold with him— but last night thinking about Maggie and about you, I simply wept myself to sleep. I wanted you to know that."

And she walked down the steps, the puppy under her arm, hurrying up Witchita to her house without looking back.

It was almost eight, a bright, unforgiving sun moving overhead, already hot when Adam banged through his screen door and dashed down the front steps. He had showered and changed clothes as if it were a workday.

372

"Zee's in the hospital," he said. "But Maggie's fine. She should be calling you."

"Was there an accident?"

"No accident. Zee is ill," he said. "She was taken to a hospital there."

"Where is *there?*"

"Cavendish, Vermont. A friend that Zee knows in Cavendish has taken Maggie in. They arrived last night."

He was standing halfway up the steps, his hands in his pockets, his hair rumpled, too long, his eyes flat as if they had died early before his body gave out.

"I drink too much," he said. "I need to stop."

And he left, hurrying down the steps, across the street, and into his own house.

MAGGIE DIDN'T CALL.

Lucy sat on the floor playing on the enemy side of Felix's war game, watching the clock almost by the minute, waiting for the phone to ring.

"You're not good at being the enemy, Mama," Felix said.

"I'm sorry, Felix. I don't like to be the enemy."

8:25. She would wait until 8:30 and then go over to the Mallorys'. She hadn't even asked where in Vermont Zee was taken to the hospital.

Onion was sitting on the front porch biting her nails, the front door shut and locked when Lucy tried it. Blue splayed on the rug in the hall didn't even lift his head. She knocked again but no one answered.

She would go home and call the Mallorys first and if Adam didn't answer she'd call the police again. She had the description of Adam's Toyota, D.C. license. An all-state alarm. That should be possible.

Across the street, Mrs. Greene was standing on the sidewalk in her straw gardening hat with her clippers addressing the azaleas in the front yard of her house.

"The Mallorys aren't at home," she called. "Adam left a few minutes ago with the boys in a Diamond taxi." She pushed the brim of her gardening hat off her face, wiped the perspiration from her brow. "I don't know why he called Diamond, do you? Yellow Cab is so much better."

Lucy's stomach fell. She took Felix in her arms and walked without breath the distance between the Mallorys' front yard and her front steps. Passing her VW van, she might not have noticed the note on the windshield if Felix hadn't called it to her attention.

"We got another letter from Maggie," he said. "On our van."

From Adam Mallory printed in pencil on the back of a laundry slip:

The Children's Home. Cavendish Vermont. Adam

• • •

MAGGIE STAYED IN the passenger seat of Adam Mallory's blue Toyota facing forward as the ambulance pulled up without its sirens and stopped behind the car. Zee, agitated, her arms flailing, was sitting on the ground with Angela, the nurse, and Laura, the girl on night duty, and an older man in blue jeans and a dress shirt, the sleeves rolled up. Perhaps he was a doctor. Maggie hadn't seen him arrive.

She watched them put Zee on the stretcher with straps around her chest and legs, the nurse, Angela, holding her hand, her face close to Zee's, and Zee struggling to get free.

Then Angela was leaning in the car, her breath on Maggie, the cinnamon scent of Dentine chewing gum.

"What an awful trip for you," Angela said.

"Not great," Maggie said.

"You should get out of the car and come in. There's food in the fridge, I can make you an omelet. I doubt you've even had dinner."

Maggie climbed out of the car.

"Do you have luggage?" Angela asked.

"Just a backpack."

Maggie followed Angela across the lawn. The girl, Laura, put her hand under Maggie's arm, lifting as if she were too weak to stand, and then they were at the house and Angela opened the door, flooding the porch with light.

"I'm Angela," the nurse said, pouring Maggie a glass of lemonade, taking chocolate chip cookies out of the cupboards. "And this is Laura."

Laura sat down at the table next to her.

"I'm Maggie Painter," Maggie said, helping herself to a handful of cookies. "We didn't stop on the highway to eat."

Angela put Maggie in a bedroom at the head of the stairs on the second floor with a single bed and a dresser and a rocking chair, a small rag rug on the floor, a cheap reproduction of a Mary Cassatt painting with a fleshy red-cheeked mother, a powder-puff baby on her lap—two windows overlooking the back of the house from which Maggie could see the slender silver moon curled in a perfect *C,* a splattering of stars.

"Does your mother know where you are?" Angela asked, standing at the doorway to Maggie's room.

"She knows I'm with Zee," Maggie said.

"You've met Miranda?"

"I haven't met her," Maggie said.

She wasn't sure about Miranda—who she was or what her relationship was to the Mallorys. But she was beginning to understand that there had been a story and any truth about Miranda would not surprise her.

"It's her birthday tomorrow. That's probably why you and Mrs. Mallory came to Cavendish," Angela said brightly. "She's going to be twelve."

"We did come for her birthday," Maggie said, deciding it was wise to seem completely informed.

"Well, you'll get to meet her in the morning."

The sheets were crisp, a cotton blanket on the bed, a flat pillow, too flat. She climbed under the sheet fully dressed, listening to the noises in the house like mewing, as if the house had kittens stuffed in the corners of it.

She propped up her thin pillow, folding it in half. She needed to stay awake all night and in the morning, early before anyone was up, before she *had* to meet Miranda, she'd find a telephone and call a taxicab and go to a bus station or a train station and home.

She lay in bed wide awake and watched the night go on and on. At one point, the necklaces she'd taken from Zee's drawer became so much the focus of her attention that she took them off, got out of bed, opened the dresser, and put them in the empty drawer, climbing back under the sheets. It was too cold, she thought, and took the sweater Zee had suggested she bring from her backpack.

As the night wore on, she found herself thinking about her house in Witchita Hills, about her room and her mother's room and how the sun came into the kitchen in the morning, turning the old table yellow, how Lucy looked in her jeans and paint shirt, her back to the kitchen table, scrambling eggs. She could imagine the smell of sugar cookies baking in the oven in their old apartment in New York, greeting her when she opened the door coming from school.

Everyone she knew in New York City loved Lucy. Maggie had been proud of that.

She'd have to call Rebecca Malone as soon as she got back home. She hadn't talked to her since she'd left New York although for a while, they had written letters back and forth about this and that. But nothing all summer, nothing since Maggie had fallen in love with Zee Mallory.

She wanted to start over from the beginning before things began to change. A revision was what Maggie was after. She'd begin when she was eight years old and completely happy, on the day that Felix came home from the hospital and Reuben was there with carrot soup and hot bread which he had made himself and flowers for Lucy and balloons and a locket for Maggie, which she had lost the next day at school but never told Reuben.

She watched the sky brighten, fading black to charcoal gray, to light gray, and then she must have fallen asleep. When she opened her eyes, the room was light, the sun exploding through the window, laughter from somewhere on the floor below. She jumped out of bed, made the bed tight at the corners as if she had never slept there, zipped her backpack, and went downstairs.

378

The mewing had stopped but somewhere she heard voices.

The downstairs of the house was spare with couches and children's toys in the living room and dining room and a large kitchen with a table in the middle, a telephone by the stove.

"Hello, Maggie."

Laura was making oatmeal.

"The children left early this morning for an excursion to the playground but they'll be back soon."

"What about Zee?" Maggie asked. "Where did they take her?"

"They took her to the hospital in town but it's a very small hospital so they are moving her to a different one in Hanover, New Hampshire, not far from here, but the facilities in Hanover can take care of her illness."

"What is her illness?" Maggie asked.

"She had a kind of breakdown according to Angela," Laura, the girl, said without hesitation, giggles spilling out of her mouth. "I'm so sorry," she said quickly. "It's not funny but sometimes I laugh when I'm nervous and last night made me nervous. Besides, I'm from New England and we tell the truth here."

"Will she be okay?" Maggie asked quietly.

"Nobody has told me anything except your mother called—I almost forgot—and she said she's coming to get you."

"Coming to get me?"

"She'll be here by lunchtime because she's flying to Lebanon, New Hampshire, which is pretty close to here and then she's renting a car and picking you up and then she's driving back to Lebanon and you're taking an airplane home." She poured the runny oatmeal she had been making into a bowl. "I'm pretty good at information. Brown sugar in your oatmeal? Milk?"

"Brown sugar is fine," Maggie said. She was upset that Lucy was coming—coming even before she had a chance to think about what had happened with Zee.

She hated oatmeal.

"Did you hear the commotion last night?" Laura asked, plopping down across from Maggie.

"I heard what sounded like kittens."

"That was Miranda and she was making her little kitten cries. So adorable. I'm sure Mrs. Mallory told you that she doesn't speak."

"Yes, she told me," Maggie said, hoping that the flatness of her response would silence the girl, Laura. She didn't want to talk about Miranda, and she didn't want to see her.

Miranda, who mewed but could not speak, was the name Zee had called Maggie, as if in Zee Mallory's mind she had slowly merged with this child, Miranda.

Laura put bread in the toaster.

"Mrs. Mallory didn't let us know she was coming so it was a complete surprise," Laura said. "Mr. Mallory comes. Twice a year at least. But not Mrs. Mallory. Are you their niece?"

"No, their friend," Maggie said. "Good friend. We live across the street."

Maggie got up and rinsed out her bowl in the sink.

"What did my mother say when she called?"

"The telephone rang and I answered and she said this is Lucy and I understand that my daughter might have arrived at your place with Zelda Mallory and I said *yes and she's still sleeping* and your mother said that she, your mother, would be arriving in Lebanon on the eleven o'clock plane and all the rest I told you about, including renting a car. I agreed that it was about a forty-five-minute drive and I would tell you the details."

"Did she say anything about my little brother, Felix?"

"She did, and asked me to tell you that Felix would be staying with someone named August while your mother is coming to Vermont to pick you up and also that you will be home in Washington, D.C., in time for dinner."

"Why didn't you wake me up so I could talk to her?"

"Because she didn't ask me to wake you up. She said she was in a hurry to make the plane."

381

The front door opened.

"Lucky you," Laura said. "They're back from the playground so you'll have a chance to meet Miranda."

THE PLANE TO Lebanon was a prop and almost empty. Lucy sat in the window seat. A young man was directly across the aisle in jeans, a baseball cap reversed, a broken arm in a sling. Seventeen people on the plane in all.

The cab had been late and as she hurried down the front steps when it arrived, Will Sewall was bounding down his steps, running across the street waving an envelope.

"Where are you going?" he asked.

"To Vermont by plane to pick up Maggie," she said. "You know about what's happened from Adam, don't you?"

"He told me about the car ride with Maggie and that Zee is in the hospital. He wanted you to see this before you arrive at the Children's Home." He gave her the envelope. "Their daughter—they have a daughter—lives in the home."

Lucy didn't open the envelope until the plane was headed north and west, flying overland, no water visible, which unaccountably seemed safer to her if the plane were to go down.

Inside the envelope was a newspaper clipping from the Metro page of the *Philadelphia Inquirer*, August 3, 1963.

TODDLER ALMOST DROWNS

The twelve-month-old child of a third-year law student at the University of Pennsylvania and his wife accidentally fell into a tub of melted ice during a party at her parents' apartment on Spruce Street in West Philadelphia last night. She was taken to the University of Pennsylvania Hospital listed in critical condition. Police have cited the parents with negligence.

MAGGIE SAT IN the front seat of the rental car, her legs crossed, her arms folded tight over her chest, looking out the window as the trees whipped by.

Lucy talked.

From the moment she picked Maggie up in the driveway of the Children's Home, claimed her, gripped her daughter's shoulders, kissed the top of her head, thanked the nurse for taking care of her, the girl, Laura, who said how excited she was to meet Lucy because she'd read her books when she was little—seen the child Miranda from a distance carried by a small man with a red beard—*she doesn't walk or talk*—Laura said—*but she's very happy here.*

From the moment she had reached across Maggie sitting in the front seat and pushed down the lock on the passenger side, Lucy talked.

The plane was empty—only a young man with

a broken arm, a student at Dartmouth College who had to do summer school because he flunked physics—got up from his seat and sat down next to mine—Lucy said. I brought a sandwich for you, peanut butter and honey even though I know it isn't your favorite but I was afraid to bring tunafish that the mayonnaise would spoil and of course it isn't even hot in Vermont so it wouldn't have spoiled.

Maggie put her feet up on the dashboard, put the peanut butter and honey sandwich in the glove compartment, and closed her eyes.

I have told you that I was twelve when my father died.

Lucy had decided on the drive from Lebanon to Cavendish that she would tell Maggie about her father. That she would begin there.

Do you want me to tell you about that? About his dying?

Sure, Maggie said, her eyes still closed.

It was June 1951, a Saturday, and my father was painting the house he rented as an income property and maybe someday he planned to live in it or not. Although he probably would have gone back to Chicago which was his home if he hadn't died but he did die and I was the one who discovered him in the basement of that house where we now live.

She glanced at Maggie, who gave no evidence of a reaction.

My mother and I had been shopping for sleepaway camp clothes for me but we didn't call it sleep away then—you either went to camp or stayed at home and if you went to camp you slept there without your parents which is what I did starting at nine years old. But that day, my mother decided that we should stop at the rental house to remind my father that he had to be home early for dinner with friends and so she parked behind his car and asked me to go into the house to remind him about a dinner party but I knew that my father did not ever forget his obligations and I should have known that it wasn't a good idea for me to go into the house because something could have happened in there.

Maggie was looking at her.

I checked for my father in every room of the house and finally I went to the basement and he was there and he had died.

Lucy was lost. There was a turn to Lebanon she had missed, maybe a few miles earlier, and she made a left into a driveway on the two-lane road and set off in the opposite direction.

"I know about your father," Maggie said finally, looking out the window. "He killed himself because he was important in the government and he was caught having sex with a man."

Lucy held her breath.

"I read about it in August's book."

Lucy was driving too fast. She checked the

speedometer. It was essential that she keep her wits about her.

"Did you know it was your grandfather when you read the pages in August's book?"

"No," Maggie said. "Just now I knew when you told me about your father dying. I put it together."

Lucy adjusted herself in the seat, checked the rearview mirror, a truck behind her too close the way trucks tend to be impatient on country roads. She slowed way down just in case a deer or rabbit or raccoon happened to cross the road and she would need to stop quickly and the truck could smash into the back of her small rental.

"I am sorry for keeping secrets or telling lies or however these stories might seem to you," she said. "I should always have told you the truth and did not."

Maggie didn't move, her head turned slightly towards the passing road, a surprising calm about her body.

At the small airport, Lucy turned in the car and they had to run to catch the plane, which was crowded, all the seats full, Maggie in the second-row aisle seat, Lucy in the back. Weather coming in, the stewardess said. The pilot wanted to take off while he could get out.

When they landed in Washington, Maggie waited at her seat, getting in line behind her mother to deplane.

"We'll take a cab," Lucy said leading the way to *Taxis*, settling into a yellow cab. *Witchita Hills at the north end of Connecticut Avenue,* she said, and gave him the address.

Their shoulders touched and Lucy ached to take Maggie's hand but she didn't. The driver swung around the circles, over Memorial Bridge coming up on the back of the Lincoln Memorial and onto Rock Creek Parkway.

"Your name was Lucy Baldwin, right?" Maggie asked finally.

"It was."

"So I would be Maggie Baldwin if you had done everything the same and had me with the man I don't know who is my father."

"I suppose that's right if that's the way things had gone."

"I like the name Painter better."

It was coming on dusk and the parkway was crowded, a warm but not too hot Saturday in Washington, cyclists on the path that ran along the creek, the creek dried out with summer, the trees a thick umbrella over the road, a melody of cicadas through the open window, warm wind on their faces.

Nineteen

REUBEN FRANK WAS coming on the Sunday night of Labor Day weekend. When he called her the morning in late July after he returned to his office from the Cape to say he had to wait until Labor Day weekend, Lucy was confident that he *would* come.

She had left him no choice.

That first night after a late dinner Maggie went upstairs to her room, put on her nightgown, and climbed into bed.

"Could you leave my door open," she asked, "and the light on in the hall?"

On Sunday, she had stayed in bed all day. Lucy brought her trays of food to share with Felix, who off and on through the day climbed into bed with her.

"If you'd like to talk . . ." Lucy said on Sunday night.

"I wouldn't," Maggie said.

She was simply quiet and still, propped up against the headboard, her arms dropped to her side staring out the window. Occasionally Felix climbed into her bed, leaned against the headboard.

"Do you still like Zee even though she kidnapped you?" he asked her.

"She didn't kidnap me, Felix."

"Well that's what Teddy said because that's what his mother, Lane, said to him."

"I wanted to go with Zee to Vermont."

Lane had called to say that the Mallory family would not be back to Washington until Zee was released from the hospital in Hanover. The boys would go to public school in town for a couple of months and Adam had taken a leave of absence from his job. The plan was they'd all return in late autumn.

"They're calling it a nervous breakdown," Lane said, "but Will says there's no such thing. What she had was a psychotic breakdown, he says, but what's the difference."

Later she called to ask if Maggie had said anything about what happened on the trip.

"Nothing," Lucy said. "She seems exhausted."

"I'm sure she was terrified."

"Were you frightened?" Lucy asked Maggie on her second day back.

"I don't know," Maggie said.

Sunday it rained, a thin, warm rain that by night had gotten prickly cold on the skin, continuing into a dark gray Monday morning when Reuben called from New York as planned.

MAGGIE SIMPLY STOPPED. She didn't think about Zee Mallory or what had gone on in the car between Washington and Cavendish or why she had wanted to leave home in the first place. She didn't read or talk or see her friends, not even Maeve, except occasionally she talked to Felix when he crawled into bed and wrapped his body around her.

She didn't feel anything. That was the worst of it. Nothing at all.

She wanted something to hurt, to cause her physical pain.

Then gradually through the month of August, the compulsion to sit on her bed in her room and stare out the window drifted away and what remained was absence.

ON THE SUNDAY before Labor Day, Lucy picked Reuben up at Union Station. Driving down Massachusetts Avenue, the windows down, hot wind whipping her hair, warming her cheeks. She felt a new self emerging. She was settled and at ease, springs of energy lifting her out of her seat, into the air, and airborne she had a sense of flying. She had finished *Vermillion the Three-Toed Sloth* the night before, washed her hair, and climbed into bed late after midnight, falling immediately to sleep.

Reuben had taken the noon train to Washington and was standing on the curb in front of the station wearing khakis and a dress shirt with the sleeves rolled up, strap sandals, his hair thinning. He had lost more weight and was pencil-thin and pale. He didn't kiss her when he climbed into the car. She didn't expect it.

"I've got to be back in New York tomorrow afternoon," he said.

"That's fine," Lucy said.

He put his feet up on the dashboard of her old VW van and lit a cigarette, holding the hand with the cigarette out the window.

"So do you have a plan for this?"

"I see a plan in my mind."

"Describe it to me."

She took a deep breath.

"We go home. I have told Maggie and Felix that you're coming to visit and that you'll only be able to stay for a short time."

"And what do you have in mind for that short time?"

"You talk to them this afternoon, just ordinary *what's going on in your life* kind of talk, go somewhere while I'm cooking, and then we eat dinner and then we go, maybe to my studio or the living room. We could even talk at dinner."

"You *know* I think this is a terrible idea," he said, a catch in his voice. "The wrong idea. The wrong plan."

"We have no choice."

"How much are you telling them?"

"The simple truth. Who you are and who I am."

"And all about your father?"

"Maggie already knows about my father and Felix is too young."

"And this makes sense, Lucy?"

She turned into the Safeway and pulled up to a parking spot.

"I was going to get fish but maybe I'll get a steak because you've lost so much weight you look bloodless." She turned off the engine. "Steak and corn and salad and chocolate sundaes. Okay?"

When she came back to the car, Reuben had closed his eyes, his head back, his arm slung across his brow.

"I don't think I can do this," he said.

"You can, Reuben."

"So . . ." Reuben said, flicking the cigarette into the street, closing the car window to keep out the noise of traffic. "How exactly do we begin?"

"With the story of what happened."

"Something like *Remember Uncle Reuben?*" he said, his tone raw and caustic. *"Well good old Uncle Reuben is kaput."*

"No jokes," Lucy said.

"I don't feel exactly jokey, Lucy."

"Did you tell Elaine?"

"I didn't happen to mention it to her," he said. "I certainly can't imagine *that* conversation."

"I'll go first then. I'll say what happened to *me,*" Lucy said. "I'll tell them I met you when I was very young and I fell in love with you but you were already married and I got pregnant and then I got pregnant again and you couldn't get unmarried but I still was in love with you. And so we concealed the fact that you are their father in order to protect people's feelings like Elaine's and Nell's. We were wrong to do that and now we can't pretend any longer."

"It won't make a bit of sense to Felix," Reuben said, his voice heavy with weariness.

"Don't you think children take in only what they can understand?"

"I don't."

"At least he'll understand that you are his father and now he has one."

Lucy stopped at the curb in front of her house. Maggie and Felix were sitting halfway down the front steps, side by side, Felix waving and waving.

"There they are, so happy to see you. At least Felix is."

Reuben opened the car door.

Lucy unpacked the groceries, shucked the corn, poured a glass of wine for herself, a beer for Reuben. They sat around the kitchen while Lucy cooked. A normal afternoon as if Reuben had been away on a trip and just returned after a long time.

After dinner, they took a walk, Reuben and Maggie and Felix, while Lucy did the dishes. It was still early, not even dusk, the smoke and smell of barbecue from the neighborhood circling up into the trees, the air soft on the skin.

"When we get back," Reuben said to Lucy as they left. "Okay?"

"What happens when we get back?" Felix asked.

"Ice cream sundaes," Lucy said.

THEY ENDED UP on the third floor in Lucy's studio, Reuben bending over the *Vermillion* drawings spread out on the table.

"This is not what I thought it would be, Lucy," he said at the first illustration of Vermillion hanging by his tail from a tree, face out, his large round eyes blank, his mouth parted just slightly, a stillness about him.

"Vermillion is dead," Felix said. "But don't worry because Violet is going to make him alive if you keep reading."

"Reading?" Reuben asked. "But there are no words to read in this book, isn't that right, Lucy?"

"No words," she said.

Maggie had turned around and was leaning against the window.

"Are we really up here to talk about Mama's book?" Maggie asked. "It's like a tornado is about to happen in this room and we're having a conversation about a dead sloth."

"No. We're here to talk to you," Lucy said. "Reuben and I want to talk to you together."

"I don't think I want to talk," Maggie said.

"I'll talk." Felix slid down from the stool.

"We'll talk first," Lucy said, and she started to tell them the story that she'd planned when Reuben interrupted.

"What I have to say is for you, Maggie, less for Felix because it will be hard for him to understand at three years old, but I think you will."

He slid down to the floor, his back against the table, Felix on Lucy's lap, Lucy's blood beating in her temples.

"I was wondering if you have ever felt nothing at all, as if the engine inside of you fell silent and you were a vacant house of a body with nothing going on?"

"Maybe," Maggie shrugged.

"That is how I feel when I leave you kids or I think about you or I remember you when you were born because I was there when you were born, or . . ." He leaned his forehead against his closed fist.

"I'll talk," Lucy said, not trusting Reuben to tell the right story, and she started again.

"I want to say it, Lucy," Reuben said. "I want to be the one to say it."

The studio was silent. Felix shut his eyes tight, pressed his face into Lucy's shoulder.

Reuben got up, pacing. He pressed his shoulder against the wall of the studio, standing across the room from them.

"You have wanted to know who your father is. I know *you* have, Maggie," he began.

"I almost never think about it," Maggie said.

"Well, I am him," Reuben said, his voice cracking. "I am your father. That is who I am."

He was standing at the top of the stairs and Lucy thought for a moment that he might bolt just then but he didn't. He didn't move or take his eyes off Maggie.

"So, I guess we finished the talk, Uncle Reuben," Maggie said, walking from the window across the room, passing Reuben at a purposeful distance, heading towards the stairs.

Halfway down the steps, she looked back at Reuben, her head cocked, a wry smile.

"That must be why I have red hair."

And she turned quickly, hurrying down, jumping the last two steps.

Lucy put the pages of *Vermillion* on a shelf and started towards the stairs.

"So?" Reuben shook his head.

She turned out the light and followed him downstairs, through the closet into her room and out, past Maggie's room, where she was drawing Felix a story.

"What next?"

"I don't know," Lucy said.

"I'm headed back to the hotel and home tomorrow early."

"Do you want a ride to the hotel?"

"I'll walk," Reuben said. "A long walk isn't the worst thing after this day."

In the hall, he stopped at the photograph of him on the Brooklyn Bridge hanging next to the front door with new glass.

"I *am* a lot thinner than I was in this picture," he said, touching the bottom of the frame to level it against the wall. He opened the front door.

"Goodbye, Reuben," she called from the step where she was sitting.

"Bye, Lucy," he said. "Goodbye."

Fall 1973

Twenty

MAGGIE SAT ON the side of her bed in the dark—late November, the Sunday after Thanksgiving, a black, starless evening, the weight of water in the air.

Outside her window, the Mallorys were arriving from Vermont.

Their friends, gathering on the Painters' porch that afternoon, speaking in whispers about Zee, expected them sometime after six.

"As if we don't know what's happened," Maeve said, straddling the porch railing with Maggie. "My father says that we'll find Zee quite *altered*—whatever altered means."

Maggie had felt ill all day. Not as if she were actually coming down with something, but a familiar creeping malaise, a hollow feeling in her stomach. She didn't like to talk about Zee. She didn't even want to think about her. But Maeve insisted on Zee Mallory as the subject of conversation as if she were a stranger in a mystery story of what ifs. *What if she won't talk. What if she brings the child Miranda home to live with them. What if she's gone completely crazy and runs around her front yard with nothing on.*

Maggie wouldn't engage.

Leaning against the posts next to the porch

railing where Maggie was sitting, Lane and Josie badgered Will Sewall for information.

"She should be fine eventually," Will said, "but she is fragile now."

Just after six, Zee's old van pulled up in front of the house and Adam got out of the driver's side door, crossed the lawn, hurried up the steps to the front porch, into the house, and turned on the lights room by room so the place that had been the center of life in the neighborhood was lit up like Christmas, all yellow lightbulbs smiling on the Mallorys' arrival.

Just the sight of it lit up made Maggie teary.

Night after night for months, she had watched the Mallorys' big house, which had since summer been completely dark after the sun went down, a blank on the landscape of the neighborhood even in the flickering streetlight.

Once the lights were on, the boys jumped out of the car and fell onto the street, tumbling into the house like puppies as they raced room to room.

Adam came back out, followed by an ambling Blue, and opened the van doors, calling for the boys to help, which Luke did, and the two of them carried luggage into the house and up the stairs.

In the passenger seat, Maggie could make out the shadow of Zee. She seemed small and still sitting in her corner of the car, her head tilted against the window, no gesture to suggest that she would get out and follow her family into the house.

Just beyond the car, Blue wagged his long tail, barking at her.

Adam came out then, in shirtsleeves without his jacket, opened the passenger side door, reached in, and Zee stepped outside but Maggie couldn't see her until they moved beyond the van and were visible in the streetlight, walking slowly, Zee holding his hand.

She had never seen them hold hands, never seen a gesture of affection between them.

On Thanksgiving afternoon, Maeve had come over with her father's copy of *The Joy of Sex*, hoping to restore the intimacy of their old friendship, which had been secured in the spring and summer by hours lying on the floor on their stomachs, imagining their future lives with some mixture of delight and disgust.

Maggie shook her head.

"I can't," she said, unequal to *The Joy of Sex*. "Maybe after Christmas."

As if Christmas would mark a magical line between then and now. Now she had a father who lived in New York with his wife, Elaine. Which was no different than her life had been before Reuben Frank was her father except the knowing, the fact of it.

The lives of men and women seemed too

complicated to Maggie, too sad and dangerous to be contained in a picture book about the joy of sex.

Downstairs, August and Lucy were talking. August had come for dinner and stayed, as he often did lately. Gabriel too, but he was in her mother's room reading to Felix—*Winnie-the-Pooh* again. He had decided to write a book about a boy called Gabriel and his bear.

MAGGIE HEARD HER mother call out to someone knocking at the front door.

She didn't sit up or look out to see who it might be, except to hope that it wasn't Adam Mallory. Or Zee. Especially Zee.

Someday she would tell Maeve about her Uncle Reuben. Not yet. She didn't want to tell the story her mother had told her about falling in love with Reuben even though he was married. Not because of the story, which she would have liked if she had read it in a book. But this wasn't a book and somehow the story as her mother told it did not make sense. Reuben was still Uncle Reuben to her, an uncle by choice. Perhaps he would grow into her father but for the time being she wasn't even certain that she wanted him to, although she sometimes caught herself looking in the mirror over the sink in the bathroom searching her face in the glass for his reflection.

• • •

ZEE SAT UP in bed while Adam unpacked, Daniel on the telephone calling his friends, Luke sprawled across the bottom of their bed.

"What does Miranda look like?" Luke asked. "Like us?"

"Like your mom," Adam said. "You'll meet her. We'll go up as a family to Cavendish a couple of times a year."

"She has a pretty face and lots of hair," Zee said. "She smiles at us when we say her name but she can't talk."

"Or walk?"

"Or walk."

He rolled over on his back.

"Will I go back to Lafayette tomorrow?"

"Back to your same class," Adam said. "They'll be very glad to see you guys."

"I know. They probably missed us especially because we are the only twins."

Blue had wandered into the bedroom with his old purple elephant which he offered to Zee, dropping it beside her hand, and lay down on the rug rolling over on his back.

"Maggie doesn't live here anymore, does she?"

"She lives with her own family," Zee said.

"Good," Luke said. "Daniel will be happy about that."

"Adam?" Zee asked after the boys had gotten

405

in their pajamas and gone to bed. "Have you spoken to Lucy?"

"I've spoken to everybody."

"And everybody knows about Miranda?"

"They do."

He took off her sweater and turtleneck, slipped off the corduroy trousers she was wearing, tossing them on a chair. She had no underwear. Out of the suitcase he took a one-piece pair of long johns bright red with buttons, the kind a child wears, which he'd gotten for her to wear in Vermont's cold autumn, and climbed into bed next to her.

"Can we sleep with the light on?"

"Of course," he said.

She had been out of the hospital in Hanover for three weeks, staying in the small rental apartment Adam had taken on the Dartmouth campus close to the boys' elementary school. It was necessary that she see Miranda before she left to go home—the doctors at the hospital insisted, using that word *necessary*. Days and weeks went by of reading and walking and sleeping, visits to the psychiatrist, afternoons with the boys. But she wasn't ready.

And then she was.

Miranda was excited to see them. She didn't know who they were except that they had come to see her.

"I don't remember this from the last time. I remember that she knew us."

"This is normal for Miranda," Angela said. "Isn't it, Mr. Mallory?"

She climbed in Zee's lap, nuzzled her head in her mother's neck, squirmy, her arms flailing as if they were semidetached, her knees pressed in Zee's belly.

And then her small fist suddenly flew up in the air, sharp on Zee's cheekbone.

Zee uttered a little cry but she didn't let go, holding Miranda's body tight, pressed against her.

"Good," Angela said. "She needs to be enclosed."

"Was that unusual?" Adam asked.

"The striking out? That happens," Angela said. "And then she settles down. It's reflexive, I believe, and perfectly normal."

In the car after they had left to pick up the boys in Hanover for dinner, to pack to go home to Washington, Zee drew up her knees, resting her chin on them, watching the darkness settle on the farms as they drove east to New Hampshire.

"Did you hear how many times Angela said *normal?*"

"I did," Adam said.

"Such a strange concept, don't you think?" Zee asked. "Normal."

"I never thought about it."

"I was glad Miranda hit me," she said, and laughed, maybe for the first time in months, her hand resting on the seat between them. "It seemed a normal thing for her to do."

• • •

THE LIGHT BESIDE Zee's bed shone on her hands, which were purple, and she held them up out of the direct light to see if they with everything else had changed, if they had turned into her mother's blue-veined hands, but hers were purple only in the light and at an angle, which was reassuring as if intimations of her former self, from long ago when she and Adam were first married, were beginning to surface.

"Adam?"

"Yes?"

"I'm glad to be home."

LUCY WAS MAKING *Boeuf à la Bourguignonne* with stewing beef, bacon, carrots, onions, garlic, thyme, and bay leaves from Julia Child's *Mastering the Art of French Cooking.*

"My mother was French," she was saying to August. "I told you that. 'Caroleen Baldween,' she called herself before my father died." She wiped her wet hands on her jeans. "She was a wonderful cook."

She dropped the small white onions in boiling water, picked up the pot after a minute and poured it through a colander in the sink, turning cold water on the onions to stop them from cooking. She had never cooked with recipes but this was different.

This was a party.

The kitchen counter full of groceries, beef and greens for salad, small red potatoes which she would sauté the next day, crusty baguettes. Roses. She didn't even like roses—but these were soft yellow, the buds just opening, and they seemed the right choice gathered in small bunches around the house, spots of butter yellow in November.

"I've never given an actual party before," she said, cutting the skin off the onions. "People have come by and we've had tea or hot chocolate, and once or twice in New York I made spaghetti and meatballs for the mothers and girls in Maggie's class. But never a party."

On the stove cider was simmering in cinnamon and cloves, filling the house with the smell of winter.

"Tomorrow, maybe you'll show me how to build a fire," she said to August, who was walking now, almost his old self. "I've never even tried our fireplace."

"In Philadelphia, we had a wonderful old apartment near Penn with a fireplace, and before she got sick Anna loved to give parties and cook steaks on a grill over the burning wood."

"Is that why you moved to Washington, because Anna got sick?"

"We moved after she was diagnosed because her parents lived here," August said, sitting on the rocking chair in front of the window, his feet up, the dummy for *Vermillion the Three-Toed Sloth* open on his lap. "Before she was diagnosed, we had decided to separate, but I came with her to Washington because she was sick and didn't want to live in her parents' house."

"You never told me that," Lucy said. "Actually I've told you everything about me and you've told me almost nothing."

"That's true. I have told no one except Gabriel, who forgets."

She looked up and August was watching what must have been the light from a television in the house behind hers, pensive as if he were considering, in the slow process of deciding what to say.

"We were separating because I had failed to make tenure," he went on speaking into the space around them. "And I'd been fired."

"Aren't they the same thing?"

"I was fired for an affair with a student. They were perfectly correct to fire me."

He put Lucy's book on the table, folded his arms across his chest.

"I had a relationship with a freshman student and she informed the administration and that was that. So Anna and I were separating."

Lucy put the onions aside, slipping into a chair across from him.

"I see," she said.

August lit a cigarette, leaning back in the rocker.

Lucy sat very still, her chin in her hands, looking into the darkness just beyond him.

"You're not upset?" he asked.

"Surprised. I guess that's what I am," she said. "Besides, I thought you were falling in love with me."

"I am," August said.

Someone was coming up the front steps.

"Adam," August said.

Through the window Lucy could see the top of Adam Mallory's head.

He came in the house without a coat although it was cold, standing in the kitchen, his arms wrapped around himself, a shadow of a beard, his eyes bleary, an awkwardness to his large body as if he were not able to find a comfortable way to stand.

"It's been a long trip," he said, "but we're home."

"I'm so glad. Would you like a cider?" Lucy asked. "I also have beer."

"Neither," Adam said.

"You know I'm giving a homecoming party tomorrow for you."

"Will Sewall told me. That's lovely of you, Lucy." Adam leaned against the refrigerator as if he were too tired to stand without support. "That's why I came over. I know it will be easier for Zee not to have to explain to people she has known for so long who didn't know there was Miranda."

"Of course."

Lucy wanted to say more, to add something as the room strained with silence, but nothing sufficient to the occasion came to mind.

Adam reached into his back pocket, took out his wallet, brown leather with a single fold, opening it to a small square photograph of a young girl, the size of school pictures.

"She was eleven the day Zee drove with Maggie to Vermont," he said.

Lucy took the picture but it was difficult to make out Miranda's features. In the photograph she looked more like a child than a girl, with black hair in a pixie cut and large, round eyes.

"Her eyes are deep blue," Adam said, and he turned to leave, stopping at the kitchen door.

"Lucy?" He mopped his brow with the sleeve of his shirt. "I'm sorry for the trouble we have caused you. I don't know what else to say."

Lucy got up to see him to the door but he moved quickly ahead, hurrying down the steps, and she watched him cross the street, almost running into the house, the lights off on the first floor. And then she saw him dash by the window in the upstairs hall, heading into his bedroom.

"Oh my," she said, going back into the kitchen.

August was putting out his cigarette.

The air moved with the expectation of a kind of intimacy, too much for Lucy back at the sink, cutting the skin off the onions, slicing them on a wooden cutting board.

"What did you put in the sauce for this bourguignonne?" August asked.

"Bacon and beef stock and tomato paste."

"Red wine?" he asked.

"It's in the recipe," she said, washing the carrots. "Lots of red wine!"

AFTER MIDNIGHT, LUCY lay next to Felix, her head still spinning, her stomach full of butterflies.

The lights went on in the second floor of August's house and from her bedroom window she could see him coming to the top of the steps, his face against the glass, a wave to her, a kiss on the windowpane, and then he walked out of view.

Down the hall, Maggie was still awake.

"Mama?" she called. "Are you sleeping?"

"Not yet," Lucy said.

"Can I sleep with you?" she asked, already her bare feet slapping the hardwood floor.

"I would love that," Lucy said.

Maggie crawled in beside her mother, her head on the same pillow.

Outside the wind was picking up, the gentle cracking of branches, the swish of autumn leaves against the windowpane.

Lucy lay on her back watching the lights from

the cars on Witchita Avenue race across the ceiling, down the wall, a sense she had of expanding life and promise, a certainty about herself as if she were actually capable of growing beyond the old twig bed, beyond the bedroom in the house above the basement where her father had died and into the world.

Wide awake—Maggie's hand loosely in hers, Felix's breath warm and damp on her neck—Lucy was imagining tomorrow.

The butter yellow roses in short fat vases, a fire in the fireplace burning orange when people started to arrive, the buffet table set with votives, wine and cider on a chest in the hall beneath the photograph of Reuben Frank, *Boeuf à la Bourguignonne* bubbling on the stove, the lights dim, Sinatra playing in the living room, the front door flung open to welcome the families of Witchita Hills, her neighbors, her friends, her dear friends.

And they would embrace her as they filed into the house and filled the rooms with laughter.

Acknowledgments

To my family: Po Bich Elizabeth Rusty
Caleb Jessica Kate Aaron
Wide Umbrellas

To Jeff Connie Porter Carol Dolores Frank Glo

And always to Timothy

With gratitude to Jill Bialosky, Alison Liss,
and the team at W. W. Norton

And Gail Hochman

*Witchita Hills exists in spirit but not in fact

Center Point Large Print
600 Brooks Road / PO Box 1
Thorndike ME 04986-0001 USA

(207) 568-3717

US & Canada:
1 800 929-9108
www.centerpointlargeprint.com